W9-AOL-831

QS.49¢X

Adam R Brown
12/20/16

ISOLATED SPLENDOR

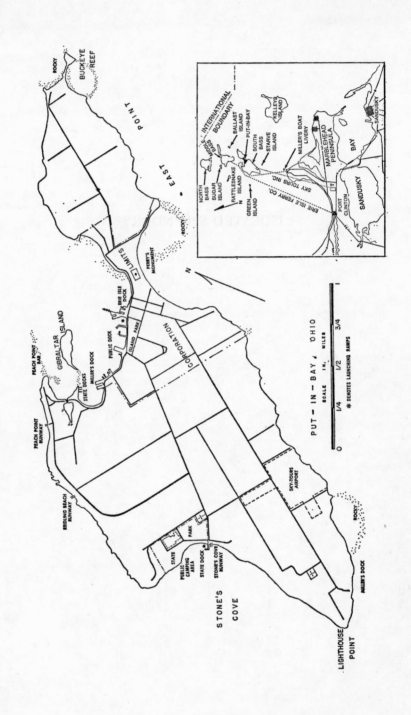

PUT — IN — BAY, OHIO

SCALE IN. MILES

0   1/4   1/2   3/4

* DENOTES LAUNCHING RAMPS

Isolated Splendor:

Put-in-Bay and South Bass Island

By

Robert J. Dodge

AN EXPOSITION-LOCHINVAR BOOK

Exposition Press   Hicksville, New York

FIRST EDITION

© 1975 by Robert J. Dodge

© under the Universal Copyright and Berne Conventions

All rights reserved, including the right of reproduction in whole or in part, in any form or by any means, electronic or mechanical, including photocopying, recording, or by any information storage and retrieval system, without permission in writing from the Publisher. Inquiries should be addressed to Exposition Press, Inc., 900 South Oyster Bay Road, Hicksville, N.Y. 11801

ISBN 0-682-48233-1

Printed in the United States of America

Contents

Preface

Books have been written about Put-in-Bay and South Bass Island before. Lydia J. Ryall [Theresa Thorndale] wrote one of the first, *Sketches and Stories of the Lake Erie Islands*, in 1898, and rewrote it in 1913. Charles E. Frohman wrote one of the latest books, *Put-in-Bay—Its History*, in 1971. In between those two authors, Thomas H. and Marina H. Langlois wrote *South Bass Island and Islanders* in 1948.

This dissertation discusses Put-in-Bay in more detail than did either Frohman or the Langlois. Ryall devotes much of her two books to Put-in-Bay but also writes about Middle and North Bass, Kelleys Island, Pelee Island, and Catawba. Some of her material is fictional and not historical.

I want to thank my many island friends for providing me with material—books, pamphlets, programs, and documents—and to submitting to interviews. With their help much previously unpublished material has been discovered.

The staffs of libraries and governmental agencies were most helpful in my research into island history. A word of thanks goes to: The Ida Rupp Library, Port Clinton; The Library Association of Sandusky; Toledo Public Library; Hayes Memorial, Fremont; Ohio Historical Society; Northwest & Great Lakes Research Center, Bowling Green State University; Recorder's Office, Ottawa County Courthouse; Perry's Victory and International Peace Memorial, Put-in-Bay Village and Township Trustees; and Put-in-Bay School.

Introduction

Located in the shallow western end of Lake Erie is a group of twenty or more islands. One of these, Put-in-Bay or South Bass, served as a base of operations for Oliver Hazard Perry. It was from the harbor called Put-in-Bay that Perry sailed to defeat the British fleet under Robert H. Barclay during the War of 1812. The American victory in the Battle of Lake Erie gave the country and the United States Navy a memorable slogan of positive accomplishment, "We have met the enemy and they are ours . . ." Today there stands at Put-in-Bay a beautiful Greek Doric column, the Perry's Victory and International Peace Memorial. This 352-foot granite shaft commemorates not only a naval battle but a peace which has lasted for more than 150 years. The 3,987-mile boundary between the United States and Canada is the longest unguarded international frontier in the world.

The brigs, ships, and sloops with their long guns and carronades are gone. Their place has been taken by yachts and sailboats. Many captains of these pleasure craft plot a course for Put-in-Bay seeking relaxation from the tensions of the city. Others—yachtless landlubbers—board the ferryboats or airplanes for their trip to an island in Ohio's Lake Erie vacationland. Urban and rural tourists have been coming to Put-in-Bay for over one hundred years. From the top of the Perry Memorial the visitor can observe the site of the Battle of Lake Erie. He can also probe the depths of the caves, bicycle around the island, or sip locally produced wine or grape juice.

The community of Put-in-Bay numbers only 350. It is not urban nor is it rural. Perhaps it could be called a "suburb" of Cleveland—sixty-five miles away—of Toledo—forty miles—or of Detroit—sixty miles. The life-style of the year-round islander or the summer cottage owner is not much different from that of his big-city cousin. The automobile, airplane, radio, and television have come to South Bass. Yet the island resident is still at the mercy of the elements of nature. A fierce storm may make Lake Erie impassable for boats of any size. Fog, high wind, or snow may ground the airplane for a few hours or even a whole day.

Ferryboat and airplane schedules tie most residents to the island. They cannot, with minor exceptions, leave Put-in-Bay earlier than 7:00 A.M. nor return later than 8:00 P.M. Unlike their mainland cousins, they cannot leave or return home in the wee, small hours of the night. Very few islanders own their own boat.

The chief livelihood of the island is the resort business. The season begins in April after the ferries start running. At first there is a trickle of spring fishermen and a number of mainland cottage owners coming to Put-in-Bay to put their island homes in operating condition after the winter lull. Visitation in June begins slowly; the peak tourist months are July and August. After Labor Day the ferryboats and airplanes operate on a reduced schedule. Fall hunters and fishermen come when the weekends are pleasant. The ferries stop commuting by early December leaving the planes—a reliable old Ford trimotor or a modern Cessna—as the only link with the rest of the world. Put-in-Bay is left to the local residents and a few hardy cottagers who fly each weekend to the island from their homes on the mainland.

There can be a spurt of activity in the winter. Ice fishing sometimes draws hundreds to the island each weekend. The season usually begins shortly after New Year's and lasts until early March. A warm winter can mean open water and no ice fishing. Or the ice can last for only a weekend or two during a series of cold and warm spells.

For sixty years the grape growing and wine industry flourished on the Lake Erie islands. Now there is only one winery on South Bass and the acreage in grapes is greatly reduced. Commercial fishing experienced a profitable period in the late nineteenth and early twentieth centuries; today not one trap-net or gill-net boat is based at Put-in-Bay. Charter boat fishing also enjoyed considerable success; today no charter skipper calls Put-in-Bay his home port.

The island now depends on the tourist for its economic existence. Steamboats once brought thousands of people to Put-in-Bay for the day, week, or the entire summer. The season during this era lasted from mid-June to mid-September. Now diesel-powered ferries, airplanes, and private yachts provide the same service from early spring to mid-fall. The island airline continues to operate throughout the winter, the old Ford or modern Cessna island-hopping over frozen Lake Erie.

Islander and visitor alike refer to the island as Put-in-Bay, although the correct name is South Bass Island. Local legend has it that "Put-in-Bay" is a contraction of an order that Perry gave his captains, "Put your ships in the bay." This is not true. Lake captains long before the 1813 naval battle knew that when they were in western Lake Erie they could "Put-in-the-Bay" for protection from storms.

The Village of Put-in-Bay was incorporated in 1876 and is centered around the bay area. The remaining part of the island plus North Bass, Middle Bass, and five smaller islands make up Put-in-Bay Township. The village is governed by a mayor and six councilmen, the township by three trustees. No matter whether they live in the village of Put-in-Bay or in the township portion of South Bass, residents give their address as Put-in-Bay, Ohio 43456.

1

Redskins, Redcoats, and Pioneers

The earliest visitors to Put-in-Bay and the other Lake Erie islands were American Indians. One of the ancient Indian trails called the Warrior's Path ended at Lake Erie in present-day Port Clinton. It was also known in Ohio as the Sandusky-Scioto Trail and connected Lake Erie with the Ohio River at the mouth of the Scioto River. The trail was used by the French explorers of the Ohio country and by the French and Indians in their wars with Great Britain for the control of North America. In the struggles between the native American and the on-rushing American settler such frontiersmen as Daniel Boone and Simon Kenton or such missionaries as the Moravians John Heckewelder and David Zeisberger were hurried along the trail as prisoners of the Indians. It was a supply route for General William Henry Harrison during the War of 1812. The Lake Erie end is marked by a stone pillar at the intersection of Fulton Street and East Perry Street in Port Clinton.

The Indian upon reaching Lake Erie proceeded eastward by canoe along the shoreline to Niagara Falls or he paddled westward to the Detroit River and the upper lakes. The more venturesome shortened their journey to Detroit by island-hopping across the lake. Put-in-Bay or some other island provided shelter if a sudden Lake Erie squall arose.

Many Indian arrowheads, stone axes, and other implements of blue and white flint have been turned up by farmers plowing their vineyards on the island. Some stone axes were so small as to suggest their use as a children's toy or as ornaments. Stone pestles for grinding grain have also been found. Some of the caves have held human skeletons, and in one instance it appeared that the unfortunate individual was caught in the rocks and was unable to escape. A large quantity of human bones was discovered in a fissure in the limestone near the United States Coast Guard lighthouse. A crude tomb of black stone slabs, of a formation not known on the island, was found many years ago beneath

1

the roots of a huge stump. Eight skeletons were found, one measuring over seven feet in height. The Matthias Burggraf, Sr., home was built on an Indian mound, and a skeleton buried in charcoal was found when the cellar was dug.

Indians visited Put-in-Bay in the winter when ice conditions allowed the crossing of the lake to hunt raccoons. There was little other game except ducks and pigeons. Early-spring and late-fall storms made travel in canoes hazardous. Summertime brought many kinds of snakes to the island but very, very few snake-fearing Indians.

Probably the last Indian resident of Put-in-Bay was the one reported by Karl Ruh. Ruh came to the island in 1853 when only the Philip Vroman and Archibald Jones families were there. The Indian was accused of stealing a quantity of maple sugar, that Ruh had made; the scared old native left Put-in-Bay the next day.

The Erie Indians lived in Ohio until they were defeated by the Iroquois Confederation in the mid-seventeenth century. About a century later such tribes as the Shawnees, Miamis, Wyandots, Delawares, Ottawas, Mingoes or Senecas, and the Tuscaroras came to Ohio. It is possible that most, if not all, of these tribes visited Put-in-Bay.

Lake Erie was the last of the Great Lakes to be discovered. The French explorer and fur trader Louis Jolliet was the first white man to travel on the lake. This was in 1669, although some unrecorded *coureur-de-bois* may have preceeded him. René Robert Cavelier, Sieur de La Salle built the first ship, the *Griffon*, to sail on Lake Erie The Franciscan missionary and explorer Louis Hennepin accompanied La Salle, and it is recorded that Hennepin said Mass at Middle Bass Island. The explorers cruised among the islands before setting sail for Lake Huron. The first Englishmen on Lake Erie were a group of fur traders led by Johannes Rooseboom in 1685. Their expedition was successful, but further trading trips met with opposition from the French and Indians, and the English were forced to cease operations. Rooseboom apparently followed the north shore of the lake.

An unidentified group of explorers sailed among the Bass islands and Kelleys Island in July 1789. They made charts of the islands, naming of one them "Pudding Bay" because the shape of the harbor (of Put-in-Bay) resembled a pudding bag. A 1798 log book of a British vessel sailing among the islands notes the harbor as "Puden Bay" as do other log books. Lieutenant Robert Pilkington, Royal Navy, mapped the harbor in 1794 and called the anchorage "Hope Cove" after the British schooner *Hope* which had been frozen-in for the winter at the bay. The missionary David Zeisberger in his *Diary* also called a bay, probably North Bay, at Kelleys Island "Hope Cove" in describing a journey in 1786.

When they were still British colonies, the states of Virginia and Connecticut claimed certain territories to the west. These claims were finally settled after the American Revolution with the states giving up jurisdiction to the federal government but retaining ownership of these lands. The Lake Erie islands were included in the tract claimed by Connecticut and which was known as the Western Reserve. That state retained a strip of land 120 miles west from Pennsylvania, between 41° and 42°2′ north latitude. Roughly, this was a forty-to sixty-five-mile-wide area running from the Pennsylvania border to the eastern boundaries of Seneca and Sandusky counties. The Connecticut Land Company was formed to sell the land. In the 1807 draft of land, Pierpont Edwards drew Put-in-Bay, Middle Bass, Sugar, Gibraltar, Ballast, and Starve islands. Edwards also drew a township on the lakeshore which later became Avon Township in Lorain County. Because his allotment was on the indented shoreline, not a straight rectangle like the other townships, Edwards was awarded the islands to "equalize" the territory.

The earliest white inhabitants known to have occupied the Bass islands were French. Accounts vary as to the numbers; one source says six families, another one that two Frenchmen, Vanocher and Colon, lived on Put-in-Bay prior to the War of 1812. These squatters were driven off by Seth Done, agent for the Edwards family. Done brought to the island a number of laborers who cleared over one hundred acres of land and planted wheat in the summer and fall of 1811. He also imported 400 sheep and 150 hogs to graze on the acorns and hickory nuts which were abundant on the island. This first effort to settle on Put-in-Bay ended with the coming of the War of 1812. The workers were busy threshing grain when British soldiers drove them off in the fall of 1812 and destroyed the remainder of the crop. Several days before that, the men had taken 2,000 bushels of wheat to Catawba Island (now a peninsula) where they stored it in a large log pen. This too was destroyed by the enemy.

THE WAR OF 1812

Western Lake Erie and the surrounding land areas in Ohio, Michigan, and Canadian Ontario were the scenes of skirmishes and battles during the War of 1812. The American cause suffered a series of humiliating defeats at the outset of the struggle. General William Hull's invasion of Canada failed, and Hull, in disgrace, surrendered Detroit to the British in August 1812. The force under General James Winchester was annihilated at the river Raisin (Monroe, Michigan), in January 1813. British and Indian invasions of Ohio at Fort Meigs (Perrysburg) and at Fort Stephenson (Fremont) were repulsed in May and August. The turning point of the war in the Old Northwest came with Oliver Hazard Perry's victory over the British fleet in the Battle of Lake Erie, 10 September 1813. The naval victory made it possible for General William Henry Harrison to invade Canada and defeat the British and Indians at the river Thames in October 1813.

Put-in-Bay Harbor was used by Perry as a base of operations. From the Bass islands he could quickly sail to Sandusky Bay for conferences with Harrison or scout the British forces at Fort Malden (Amherstburg, Ontario), in the Detroit River. When the men and ships were not so engaged, there were training duties such as preparing the ships for action and gunnery practice. The American fleet had sailed from Erie, Pennsylvania, on 12 August 1813 and arrived off Sandusky Bay on the sixteenth. Perry conferred with Generals Harrison and Lewis Cass regarding the next step to take in prosecuting the campaign. The British fleet under Captain Robert H. Barclay was sighted by a lookout in the masthead of Perry's flagship, the brig *Lawrence*, at 5:00 A.M., Friday, 10 September 1813. The Battle of Lake Erie began at 11:45 A.M. and ended a few minutes after 3:00 P.M. British supremacy on the lake came to an end with the capture of the entire enemy fleet of six vessels. The conflict began eight miles northwest of Put-in-Bay and reached its climax at West Sister Island fourteen miles away. The triumphant American captain dashed off a short note on the back of an old letter to William Henry Harrison:

> U.S. Brig Niagara, Off Western Sister Island head of Lake Erie, Sept. 10, 1813, 4 P.M.
> Dear General—
> We have met the enemy and they are ours. Two ships, two brigs, one schooner and one sloop.
> Yours with great respect and esteem,
>
> O. H. Perry

The enlisted men killed in action were buried at sea off West Sister Island in their hammocks with a thirty-two-pound shot at their heels. Chaplain Thomas Breeze read the Episcopal service over the fallen sailors. The two fleets, American and captured British, sailed for Put-in-Bay the next day, arriving in the harbor at noon. Three American and three British officers who had been killed in the battle were brought to Put-in-Bay for burial. Sailing Master Daniel Dobbins described the September 12 ceremony which took place on the shoreline:

> At ten A.M., the colors of both nations being at half mast and all things ready, the bodies were lowered into the boats, and then, with measured stroke and funeral dirge, moved in line to the shore, the while minute guns being fired alternately from the "Lawrence" and "Detroit." On landing the procession was formed in reverse order, the corpse of the youngest and lowest in rank first, and so on,

alternately American and British, the body of Captain Finnis coming last. As soon as the corpses were taken up by bearers and moved on, the officers fell into line, two American and two British, and marched to the solemn music of the bands of both squadrons. On reaching the spot where the graves were prepared they were lowered into the earth in the order in which they had been borne, and the beautiful and solemn burial service of the Episcopal Church rendered by the chaplains of the respective squadrons: "Earth to earth, ashes to ashes . . ." The volley of musketry followed, and all was over, the heroes were at rest.

For nearly one hundred years a willow tree stood on the spot where the six officers were buried. Since the area had been cleared of timber before the war, the tree was called the "Lone Willow." The story is told that a lake captain came to Put-in-Bay with supplies a few days after the battle. He cut a walking stick from a green willow limb and when he visited the grave he stuck the willow cane into the soft earth. The shoot took root and grew into a sturdy tree which was the only marker over the tomb for almost a century. By the year 1900 it had become decayed and fell on April 17 when scarcely a breath of air was stirring. The willow was replaced by a pyramid of Civil War cannon balls.

Put-in-Bay became the scene of much military activity as Perry and Harrison planned the invasion of Canada. The British prisoners, confined in their own ships, were taken in four vessels to the mainland (Port Clinton). More than three hundred men were debarked. They were marched to the state capital at Chillicothe under an escort of Harrison's soldiers. The ships and bateaux then began to ferry Harrison's army to Put-in-Bay. Only one-third of the troops could be carried at one time. The whole army, totaling 4,500 men, were concentrated on the island by September 22. They were moved to Middle Sister Island three days later and finally landed below Fort Malden on 27 September 1813. The campaign was successfully concluded with the American victory at Moravian Town on 5 October 1813.

Although Perry had the greatly superior fleet when he went to Put-in-Bay (The British flagship, *Detroit*, nineteen guns, was not yet in service), there was some apprehension that a British raid might destroy the American flotilla at Put-in-Bay. Harrison stationed a few companies of troops at the island to aid the sailors in repelling a surprise attack. The Canadian mainland was no more than forty miles distant. A dark summer night with a fair wind could bring an enemy "commando" raid. Even the victory in September and the coming of winter could not dispel the possibility of attack.

The resourceful British commander, Sir Gordon Drummond, did plan a midwinter foray on Put-in-Bay. The two largest prizes, the *Detroit* and *Queen Charlotte*, were too badly damaged to be repaired in time to be taken to Erie for the winter. They would be immobile targets frozen in the ice. The enemy general planned an expedition of 1,760 men including 200 sailors which was to move against Detroit, cross the ice, and burn the ships in the island harbor. The Americans had observed the preparations for an offensive, noting that the British had seized a large number of sleighs which would be useful in an over-the-ice raid. The enemy considered an attack on Erie but decided that it was too heavily defended and chose to assault Put-in-Bay instead.

Stephen Champlin, in command of the *Tigress*, arrived at the island 25 December 1813 to assume command of the station. He decided that additional troops were needed to supplement the twenty-three sailors and forty soldiers then on duty. Two hundred soldiers were sent from Detroit. Later in the winter Lieutenant John Packett replaced Champlin.

The *Somers*, one of the small gunboats, also wintered at the bay. But even the best plans go astray. The winter of 1813-1814 was a mild one. The lake was still open on 17 January 1814, and on February 3 Drummond reported that his scheme had to be abandoned. With the coming of spring the prizes were fitted out and taken to Erie on 1 March 1814. The temporary post at Put-in-Bay was vacated with the troops returning to Detroit.

Samuel R. Brown, who wrote an early history of the Northwestern campaign, was an interested spectator at Put-in-Bay at the time of the battle. He observed the naval engagement from South Bass Island until his vision was obscured by the clouds of dense white smoke that the cannon of that day produced when fired. The next morning, Brown went to the opposite or bay side to visit the victorious fleet. While on the island he recorded his observations of Put-in-Bay. The bay or harbor area, he commented, ". . . was the best harbor between Buffalo and Malden." He also noticed the work that Edwards had done in 1811-1812: the deadening of three hundred acres of trees, the building of a house near the bay, the growing of wheat, corn, and potatoes. The British or Indians had destroyed the wheat and burned the house. Harrison had built a large log storehouse in which to keep supplies. Brown discovered that the strait between Put-in-Bay and Middle Bass was deep enough to anchor four hundred-ton ships to within twenty yards of the shore. Perry's ships were shallow draft, while the British vessels drew a little more water. Brown described a cave which was discovered in the center of the island. Just what cave it was would be hard to determine. There are many caves on Put-in-Bay.

PEACE AND SETTLEMENT

After the War of 1812 Aschel "Shell" Johnson lived on Put-in-Bay for three years. Johnson was employed by the Edwards family. A Captain

Hill succeeded Johnson but stayed only briefly. The next settlers were Henry and Sally Hyde who came in 1818. When Sally died in 1830 Henry moved his family to Catawba Island. The Hydes brought five hundred head of sheep to the island. When A. P. Edwards came to Put-in-Bay in 1822, he found a French-Canadian squatter living in a red cedar log cabin near the shoreline. This was Ben Napier, a giant of a man, who disputed Edwards's claim. The matter had to be settled at the country courthouse, then located in Norwalk. Napier had no legal claim to Put-in-Bay and was forced to move. He went to Kelleys Island where he was the cause of similar trouble to the owners of that island.

A. P. Edwards then began to develop Put-in-Bay, bringing in laborers to erect the necessary buildings. Various persons served as his agents: John Pierpont, Jacob Scott, James Ross, a McGibbons, and a Van Rassler [sic]. One of the buildings constructed in 1823 was a summer residence for Edwards. The agents also lived there when Edwards was absent. The house was a two-story structure with wide verandas and a full basement, surrounded by a fence. It was called the "Manor House" or, because it was painted with whitewash, was also referred to as the "White House." The home was located on the site of the first Put-in-Bay House some distance back from the shoreline but not very far from the 1813 burial site of the officers killed in the Battle of Lake Erie. There were numerous outbuildings such as a large barn, a carpenter shop, and a blacksmith shop.

Cash with which to buy essential items from the mainland and to pay taxes was derived from the sale of timber, cordwood, and limestone. No regularly scheduled boats called at Put-in-Bay. When a schooner or steamboat was sighted nearing the islands, the residents would fire a small cannon—a prearranged signal with the lake captains. These boats also brought supplies to the people of Put-in-Bay. Transportation facilities for the island consisted of a small sloop, the *A. P. Edwards*, and a large rowboat called a "zig." It was rowed by ten men, five on a side in a manner similar to the ancient galley.

John Pierpont was the agent for Edwards in the early 1830s. He built a dock in the harbor and another one known as the west dock. When Pierpont and two Frenchmen set sail for Sandusky one day and were caught in a sudden storm, the boat capsized, and all were drowned. Jacob Scott, who became the agent the next year, 1837, continued the work of building more docks and of cutting wood for the steamboats.

The first permanent settler to come to Put-in-Bay was Philip Vroman, a sailor on a vessel which stopped at the island in 1843. Alfred P. Edwards persuaded him to become his agent. Vroman settled on the island the next year and remained until his death sixty-eight years later. At that time there were only the "White House" and a half-dozen log cabins on Put-in-Bay. Middle and North Bass had a single cabin each. The islands were a hunter and fisherman's paradise. Because the lake supplied abundant quantities of fish, many islanders combined the occupations of farmer and fisherman. Waterfowl, fox, and raccoon were hunted. Strangely, the squirrel was not a native to Put-in-Bay and only a few deer were seen. Hogs which had been brought in earlier by the first settlers ran wild in the woods. They were hunted but occasionally got their revenge by treeing a hapless islander. Luther Nelson, the first physician to settle on the island, came in 1854. He owned five hundred head of sheep.

In 1845 Gibraltar Island in the harbor was occupied by a group of government surveyors and engineers who were engaged in making charts of the lake. They found it necessary to cut a strip forty-feet wide running through the woods on Put-in-Bay so that they could sight their instruments properly. The strip, used as a road by the islanders, was called "Sight Road." Today it is referred to as the airport road although officially it is Langram Road.

JOSEPH DE RIVERA ST. JURGO

Alfred P. Edwards thought that he had cut and sold most of the good timber by 1852 and lost interest in the islands. He wanted to sell them as a group, not piecemeal. When the United States government inquired about buying land on Put-in-Bay for a lighthouse Edwards sold the government Green Island instead. A lighthouse was built on that nearby islet in 1854.

Edwards's daughter, Alice Glover Edwards, was about to be married in 1853 and needed a dowry. Her father gave her Put-in-Bay, Gibraltar, Starve, and Ballast islands, but her new husband, Elisha Dyer Vinton, wanted ready cash, not a quartet of islands in Lake Erie. A Spanish merchant of New York City, Joseph de Rivera St. Jurgo, had visited the islands, liked them, and wanted to buy them. The Edwardses and the Vintons obliged him—for a price of $44,000. By 22 August 1854 all the legal technicalities had been completed; de Rivera became the owner of South Bass, Middle Bass, Sugar, Gibraltar, Ballast, and Starve islands. The other Bass Island, North Bass or Isle St. George, was sold by Abigail Dunning of Hartford, Connecticut, to Horace Kelly of Cleveland. This purchase also included the smaller island called Rattlesnake.

De Rivera, who had interests in Vermont, Kentucky, and in West Indian sugar plantations, as well as at Put-in-Bay, began to develop the islands. The new owner built a sawmill and a stave mill in the fall of 1854. These structures were located on what became the Valentine Doller Estate. He had the county engineer, Ernst Franck, come to the islands during the summer to survey the area into ten-acre lots and plot the necessary roads. The surveying took from 1858 to 1862. The lots marked by cornerstones with "RSJ" cut into them are still used by surveyors today.

Philip Vroman and Andrew Wehrle were put to work building more roads and selling wood for steamboat fuel. De Rivera sold the wood for seventy-five cents a cord, and Wehrle received sixty cents for cutting, hauling, and shipping the logs. Great amounts of cedar timber were shipped from Middle Bass. Gravel from Ballast Island was sold for ten cents a ton. Also, sheep raising was tried as an agricultural pursuit. As many as 2,000 sheep were grazed on Put-in-Bay, then shipped to New York markets. The most lucrative island industry, however, had not yet been found.

The Lake Erie pioneer lived a hard life isolated from mainland. Daniel Vroman, son of the first permanent settler, Philip Vroman, related some of his experiences as a child. He was, for a while, the only youngster on the island. His playmates were a couple of family calves. When the family moved from their first location, they moved into a hewed log house not far from the Edwards "White House." When Archibald Jones became the agent for Edwards, Daniel had a chum— the Jones boy. The Jones family left the island when de Rivera purchased South Bass. Simon Fox then became the agent and Philip Vroman was foreman. Others in the work force were: Theodore Lauenstein, Lorenz Miller [Muller], Joseph Miller, Andrew Wehrle, George Hinger, and John Mitchell.

One of the early burial plots was the front lawn of the E. J. Dodge home at Bay View and Victory avenues. Some of the remains were moved to Crown Hill cemetery after 1867; others still lie there. Daniel Vroman recalled the first funeral he ever attended. The family who operated the sawmill lived in a wood-frame house that later became part of the Valentine Doller home. Their baby died and was buried, not on South Bass, but on Gibraltar. The body and mourners were rowed over to the island in one boat.

Another island pioneer was Karl Ruh who had immigrated from Baden, Germany, coming to Put-in-Bay in 1854. When he came to the island there were only the Philip Vroman and Archibald Jones families and an old Indian who fled after being accused of theft. About four years later Ruh purchased a farm on East Point. His funds were exhausted but he was determined to buy some grape roots to start a vineyard. Ruh worked two days plowing on the farm of Louis Harms in return for which Harms gave him four roots. His first efforts as a wine producer ended in disaster. Ruh had learned the tanner's trade in Germany so as a novice winemaker he had much to learn about the fermentation of grape juice. A cask, too tightly corked, burst, spilling about five hundred gallons of juice. He eventually learned the business and was a successful winemaker for the rest of his life.

Some other early settlers were Mattias Burggraf, Sr., who developed a vineyard on East Point after coming to South Bass in 1859. Lorenz Miller, a watchmaker, came to the island in 1854 and became a grape grower. After spending eight years in Sandusky, where he was a clerk in a hardware store, Valentine Doller came to Put-in-Bay in 1859. Ruh, Burggraf, Miller, and Doller all came from Baden and all grew grapes.

In the first ten years after his purchase of the islands in 1854, de Rivera sold forty-two parcels of land on South and Middle Bass. His first sale of one-fourth acre was to the South Bass Board of Education. The sale was really a donation. De Rivera received only one dollar. This first school was located just above the hill where Cooper's Restaurant now stands on Catawba Avenue. A glance at the list of buyers reveals names familiar to older islanders: Harms, Smith, Lauenstein, Anthony, Webster, Holly, Dodge, Brookner, Brown, Miller, Stone, Chapman, Beebe, Cooke, Murrary, Palmer, Schmidt, Cooper, Meyer, Wehrle, and Lutes. A William Spaulding leased some land from de Rivera in 1857. Louis Harms, who helped start the grape industry, bought a thirty-five acre farm on East Point for $1,175, on 11 August 1859 and Philip Vroman purchased a ninety-three acre plot on 25 November 1859 for $3,000.

Land could be purchased outright if the buyer had sufficient finances. De Rivera would also lease land or make other arrangements. Philip Vroman leased additional land in 1869 and again in 1879. The agreement listed what crops were to be grown, payment to be made in crops, and other conditions such as the right to conduct tours through the cave on the property. A time payment plan could be worked out. Wyman Dodge bought six acres on East Point for $450.00 on 9 May 1862. De Rivera received $112.50 in cash with further installments of $112.50 payable in 1863, 1864, and 1865. Dodge paid 7 percent interest annually on the remaining debt plus taxes.

TOWNSHIP AND VILLAGE GOVERNMENTS

The few settlers on Put-in-Bay were more concerned with the life and death matters of making a living for themselves than debating the niceties of formal government. Except when they had to pay taxes, vote, or register a deed, the matter of which county the Bass islands were in probably was of little concern to the island farmer. For the record, though, the Bass islands were in Trumbull County from 1800 to 1815 and in Huron County from 1815 to 1840. Ottawa County, organized on 12 March 1840, was made up of the northern parts of Sandusky and Erie counties and the eastern part of Lucas County. Included in the county were the Bass islands and, for five years, Kelleys Island. The town of Port Clinton was selected as the county seat. South, Middle, and North Bass islands were in Van Rensselaer Township which also included the Catawba peninsula on the mainland. After Put-in-Bay Township was formed in 1861 the name was changed to Catawba Township because of the grape-growing interest there, the Catawba grape being the most popular at the time.

The grape-growing and wine-making industry began in the Lake Erie islands in the 1850s, and Put-in-Bay's attraction as an historical island resort was being developed. Large celebrations were held in 1852, 1858, and 1859 honoring Oliver Hazard Perry's victory over the British in 1813. Put-in-Bay was becoming known for its delicious grapes and excellent wines and as a place where the vacationist, via the steamboat, could "get away from it all' for a few hours. The population grew as farmers came to the island to plant vineyards and as others became involved in the resort business. About five hundred persons were permanent residents of Put-in-Bay by the early 1860s.

Local island government was now desired, and, to this end, John Stone, Simon Fox, and others from the three Bass islands petitioned the Ottawa County commissioners for permission to organize Put-in-Bay Township. Their petition was approved and the new township was made up of "South, Middle, and North Bass, Rattlesnake, Sugar, Ballast, Gibraltar, Strontian or Green Island and waters adjacent thereto to include Starve Rock Island. Above named islands to be called Put-in-Bay Township." On 22 June 1861 the electors selected their township trustees. Named were: John Stone, William Rehberg, and Peter Fox. Simon Fox became justice of the peace and Valentine Doller, clerk; Philip Vroman, treasurer; William Axtell, constable; and George Caldwell, road supervisor; a total of twenty-five votes were cast in the new township. The year before, 1860, a post office had been established at Put-in-Bay with Valentine Doller as the first postmaster.

An 1866 story in the Sandusky *Daily Commercial Register* told of the growth of Put-in-Bay Township. Islanders owned 103 horses, 165 cattle, 206 hogs, and 1 mule. The fields were planted in wheat, oats, buckwheat, rye, barley, potatoes, sorghum, tobacco, hay, and clover. The vineyards were a main source of income; 72 acres of vines had been planted in 1865 to bring the total to 422. Grape production for 1865 totalled 1,117,801 pounds, and 33,805 gallons of wine were pressed. The future looked bright for the island farmer.

Fifteen years after the three Bass islands were organized as a township, action was begun to incorporate a portion of South Bass as a village. Under the township form of administration, three trustees, usually one from each island, governed South, Middle, and North Bass. Put-in-Bay was continuing to develop as a summer resort and the vineyard industry was booming. An incorporated type of government would provide a local administration sensitive to the needs of Put-in-Bay alone and to which the affairs of the other two islands would be of no concern.

Initiating action was begun 5 May 1876 when thirty-eight islanders sent a petition requesting incorporation to the county commissioners. Among those businessmen favoring incorporation were: John Brown, Jr., Henry Beebe, Charles Hollway, C. H. J. Linskey, Fred Gill, J. Wigand, Charles H. Engel, Louis L. Engel, G. W. Orr, C. P. Engel, J. S. Gibbens, C. Idlor, William Bing, George Doller, John Doller, W. H. King, A. H. Hunker, and A. Hunker.

The area of the proposed village was larger than the present village limits. Beginning at the lakeshore at Mitchell Road on the west shore, the line ran to Catawba Avenue, to Thompson Road and extended on to the lakeshore on the opposite side of the island, then followed the shoreline to Chapman Road on East Point to a point 1,000 feet from the intersection of Chapman Road and State Route 357, then down Chapman to the bay on Bay View Avenue, to include Gibraltar Island and on over to Peach Point, then along the shoreline to Mitchell Road.

Not all islanders were in favor of incorporation, and fourteen residents signed a remonstrance sent to the commissioners early in July [exact date unknown], claiming that the incorporation would benefit only a few property holders near the bay at the expense in taxes to the other inhabitants. A second remonstrance was signed July 26 by thirty-two persons including Philip Vroman, Joseph de Rivera St. Jurgo, Ann C. McMeens, B. B. Chapman, George W. Orr, William F. Lockwood, Mrs. H. S. Gibbens, Louisa Riedling, James Morrison, and Daniel P. Vroman. In their protest they stated that the proposed village boundaries would "include a large amount more than one hundred acres of agricultural and unimproved land . . . unplotted into town lots . . . and where there are no residents."

An amended petition reducing the size of the proposed village was submitted July 26 to the commissioners. The village line began at the present Perry's Victory Monument, included all of Gibraltar Island, ran to the present downtown Miller Ferry dock, then to Lakeview Avenue, down Lakeview to Catawba Avenue, then on a line crossing Catawba and Langram Road to the lakeshore and back along the shoreline to the monument.

Valentine Doller and A. H. Hunker, agents for the petitioners, presented the legal papers and maps to the commissioners for action. The commissioners approved of the petition 8 August 1876. The incorporation of the Village of Put-in-Bay was finally recorded by G. William Bader, county recorder, on 28 June 1877. The court appointed Andrew Hunker to serve as interim mayor, from April 1877 to April 1878, until a mayor could be elected.

There were a number of attempts to increase the size of the village. The first of these was begun in November 1893 when Councilman E. J. Dodge offered for passage "an ordinance to enlarge the corporate limits of the Incorporated Village of Put-in-Bay . . ." Included in the proposal was that part of South Bass not already within the village, Rattlesnake, Ballast, and Starve islands "to the low-water mark of Lake Erie." The council approved the ordinance unanimously and a petition requesting annexation of the specified territory was sent to the county commissioners. In May 1894 the council amended the petition, asking to annex only that portion of South Bass not included in the village, excluding the other smaller islands.

George E. Gascoyne, acting as agent for the village, presented the amended petition to the Ottawa County commissioners in June, and the commissioners ordered that a meeting to discuss the annexation be held at Put-in-Bay on 8 August 1894. The commissioners met in September to deliberate on the results of the meeting and decided against the annexation of additional territory to the village.

A not-so-ambitious annexation project was successful in 1915. The council sought to annex the section now known as Shore Villas. A petition was presented to the commissioners in August and was approved without opposition on 1 November 1915. The village boundary was extended from Perry's Victory Monument to include the Shore Villas, a real estate development of the Put-in-Bay Resort Company.

The last unsucessful atttempt to incorporate the whole island of South Bass into the village was made in March 1968 when Mayor James A. Poulos sent a letter to all of the island residents suggesting that the village be expanded. He cited such benefits as a more efficient management of the police and fire departments and administration of the island park.

THE VILLAGE OF PUT-IN-BAY

The first meeting of the elected mayor, councilmen, and officers of the newly created village took place on Saturday, 6 April 1878. C. H. J. Linskey was sworn in as the first mayor of Put-in-Bay Village. The mayor then administered the oath of office to his officers: Caspar Schraidt, treasurer; and Orlande Foster, marshal. Clerk W. H. King had been sworn in by Valentine Doller, notary public. The six councilmen were then qualified for office and their terms of office, one and two years, decided by lot. This was done so that three councilmen would come up for election each year. F. J. Magle, William Bing, and Valentine Doller were chosen for the two-year term. Fred Gill, George E. Gascoyne, and L. Osborn received the one-year appointments. A meeting room in the Clinton Idlor (Doller) store was rented for $30 per year.

South Bass Island was now governed by two political units: the village government, consisting of a mayor and six councilmen, and the township trustees, who governed the unincorporated part of South Bass and all of Middle and North Bass. Trouble for the new village came from within when in the spring of 1879 fifty-one petitioners led by John Brown, Jr., and Henry Beebe asked for the surrender of the corporate rights of the village. The council decided to hold an election in the fall to decide the issue. Brown and Beebe were elected to the council at the April election and acrimonious debate developed over the surrender of the corporate rights petition. The election was then held in May; sixty-six votes were cast, thirty-six favoring "No Surrender of Corporate Rights" and thirty supporting "Surrender of Corporate Rights". John Brown, Jr., and Henry Beebe then resigned from the council. A. H. Hunker and Clinton Idlor were appointed to fill the vacancies until the next election.

More routine, but very essential, affairs also occupied the attention of the mayor and council. The source of income for a village government is taxes, and the council lost little time in passing a levy. Action was taken 13 May 1878 with the following rates agreed upon: General Purposes—one mill, Police—two mills, Streets—one mill, Sanitary—one-half mill, Prison—one-half mill, Bridge—one-half mill, Embankment —one-half mill for a total of six mills. The first moneys received amounted to $494.10. By 1882 the rate had declined to five mills and remained at that level through 1885. After the town hall was built in 1887 the rate was raised to eleven and one-half mills where it remained for some time. The present rate is thirty-seven and six-tenths mills. Other moneys were collected through an imposition of fines and the sale of carriage and wagon licenses.

In the twentieth century Put-in-Bay Village continued under the mayor-and-council-form of local government, the only change being the extension of the terms of office from two to four years in the early 1970s. That portion of South Bass Island not within the village limits is still administered by the three township trustees.

LAW ENFORCEMENT

Orlande Foster, the village marshal, was also appointed Special Policeman for a term of two months during the summer of 1878. His tour of duty began at 11:00 a.m. and extended to 1:00 a.m. the following day. Foster was paid $50 a month for his services from July first to September first. The mayor was given the power to appoint extra policemen, not to exceed ten, when the need arose.

The law enforcement officials on South Bass today are the village chief of police and the township constable; but, for efficiency and economy, one man presently holds both positions. Franz Schillumeit has jurisdiction within the village as police chief and outside the village limits and on Middle and North Bass and the smaller islands as township constable. Additional policemen are hired during the summer, usually for the big holidays such as the Fourth of July, Regatta Week, and Labor Day.

Put-in-Bay had no regular jail in 1878, so the council rented part of the cellar of the Valentine Doller building for a temporary "Lock-Up" for $25 per year. Council records reveal that jailing prisoners was "expensive." Once J. Wigand, who ran a restaurant in the Doller building, furnished six meals for jail inmates. Total cost was $1.50.

THE TOWN HALL

Before the town hall was built, the mayor maintained an office and the council held meetings in the Idlor (Doller) store. In 1881 they changed their meeting place and rented a room from Mrs. John Doller. She was paid $50 a year and was to provide lighting and a stove. Mrs. Doller must have been a bit lax in fulfilling the agreement, for the council warned her and her husband, John, that the contract would be continued only if she would furnish a stove from September "until the following spring" and if John S. Doller kept the room and lamps "in good clean order."

It must have been too cold in February 1884 for the council to meet at Doller's, because they held their regular session in the Round House, a popular saloon near the present Park Hotel. Mayor Valentine Doller, Clerk William Wigand, and Councilmen F. J. Magle, G. F. Smith, and George E. Gascoyne took action on only three pieces of village business before leaving the bar of justice to practice before another bar.

The mayor's office and council room were in a private home, the jail was in the basement of a store, and the fire engine was kept in a temporary shed. A town hall combing all three facilities was very much needed. This need was met in 1887 when Valentine Doller donated "for good will and $1.00" a 55-foot by 150-foot lot on Catawba Avenue to the village of Put-in-Bay. Doller specified that the "Town Hall, Prison and Fire Engine Room" was to cost not less than $10,000 and if the building were to be destroyed by fire "or otherwise" it would have to be rebuilt within fifteen years or the property would revert to him or his heirs.

The village council accepted the donation "with its privileges and reservations" in an ordinance passed 14 March 1887. The new town hall is a three-story—basement, first and second floors—building constructed of stone and brick, 44 feet by 102½ feet. Four cells for prisoners were installed in the basement, also a cistern large enough to hold 2,000 barrels of water to be used in case of fire. On the first floor there is the fire engine room, an office used by the mayor and council, the township trustees, and the police chief. A large room called the Assembly Room is used for public meetings. The second floor consists of a dance floor basketball court and a stage. This upper story was once called the Opera House.

George E. Gascoyne submitted plans for the new structure which were accepted by the council after provisions for a town clock were made. James B. Monroe of Toledo loaned the council $5,000 at 6 percent interest and the council issued bonds in that amount. Bids were sought for the construction and Gascoyne was successful with a bid of $10,127. He sublet the stonework to John Vaith, Sandusky; the stone came from Kelleys Island. He also had the brickwork done by Charles Buford and Company of Toledo. Work had progressed far enough by November that the council sent Valentine Doller to Detroit to purchase a "Gas Machine" and lighting fixtures. On 22 December 1887 the council accepted the new town hall stating that it was completed according to specifications.

With such excellent facilities now available for public gatherings, a number of organizations were eager to rent space in the hall. One of the first was the township trustees who rented a room adjoining the council chambers for $60 a year, the council to furnish lighting and heat. Six years later in 1894 the trustees informed the council that they would not lease the meeting room unless the charge was reduced. This intergovernmental bickering was settled amicably, and the trustees now paid $30 per year. The township constable also had the use of the village jail whenever the need arose. Four years later the rent was raised to $40. The town hall construction was financed by the village.

The Eureka Club leased the Assembly Room for a six-month period from November 1891 to May 1892 requesting the council to extend the gaslights to the room. The council agreed to do so, also to allow the club to sublet the room to the Philharmonic Society two nights a week. The club was charged $50 rent for the period. The society received free lighting but paid for the coal they used for heating at a rate of 20c per cubic foot. When the contract expired in May the society had used 150 cubic feet of coal and was billed $30.

The Social Enterprise Club also rented space in the town hall and had installed various items of "Merchandise." Dr. O. T. Sears, club manager, presented bills for these items in the amount of $200.00 to the council and they duly authorized payment. Andrew Hunker outbid George E. Gascoyne for the use of the upper floor or Opera House, bidding $165.00 to Gascoyne's $126.50. Hunker then leased the upper hall to various groups hoping to make a profit.

A necessary outer structure was built in December 1889 as authorized in the words of the council:

> Said closet to be 4 x 8 feet divided into two compartments, and of proper height, to be built of dressed barn boards and battened, with a shingle roof, and that the mayor appoint a committee of one to make contract for same and see that it be put up immediately.

Council minutes do not reveal whether the traditional insignia was cut on the two doors.

EAGLE FIRE COMPANY NO. 1

Even before there was a fire department in existence, the village purchased a fire engine. The mayor appointed George E. Gascoyne, D. P. Vroman, and Fred Gill to solicit subscriptions to buy a "hand engine" or pumper in June 1881. They were successful, and Gascoyne was paid $118.74 to build a temporary engine house. An ordinance establishing the Put-in-Bay Village Fire Department was passed 6 March 1882.

The mayor appointed a fire committee of three councilmen, a fire "Engineer" or chief, and "such Fire Engine men, Hook & Ladder, & Hose & Bucket men" as required. George E. Gascoyne was named "Chief Engineer" of Eagle Fire Company No. 1. A bell was purchased for the engine house, also six lanterns. Fred McCormick was hired in 1884 to take care of the fire engine and keep it in good working order. He received $30 a year for his services.

Financial support for the department came from the village with some donations from the township and private individuals. The department was put on a sounder monetary footing when a Special Fire District for South Bass Island was created in 1969. The fire trucks and equipment were transferred to the township and the department receives tax money from all of South Bass. From time to time, professional fire fighters come from mainland to train the volunteer members of the local department or the islanders go to the mainland.

When the town hall was built provisions were made to house the fire equipment in it. An extension was added to the rear of the building to house a new truck in recent years. An attempt to build a new, larger fire station on the hill above Cooper's restaurant failed when the bond issue failed to pass in the May 1974 primary election by a vote of 102 against to 84 for the $50,000 issue.

ROUTINE BUSINESS

The village organized, the police and fire departments established, and the town hall built, the mayor and council engaged in the routine task of governing the village, passing sundry ordinances and regulations. George E. Gascoyne was paid $2.50 a week for the eight summer weeks for sprinkling the dusty, unpaved streets. He also took care of the kerosene street lamps. Since the fire engine was now housed in the town hall there was no need for the old fire house which was given to Valentine Doller in lieu of rent (it was on his property). Iron bunks were purchased at a cost of $15.90 for the prison cells in the basement. Details are lacking, but council minutes authorized the payment of $2.20 "for a boarding and shipping a tramp." Doller was paid $1.00 for having a dead horse removed from the bay. Ordinance No. 18 prohibited nude bathing in the bay or lake within the village limits "anytime after the rising of the sun and before dark." The fine was not to exceed five dollars and those unable to pay could be confined in the county jail at Port Clinton.

GOD'S ACRE

As noted earlier, Indian graves have been discovered in various sections of the island; the six officers killed in the Battle of Lake Erie were buried near the shoreline of the bay in 1813 and early settlers interred their dead in what became the front lawn of the E. J. Dodge property at Bay View and Victory avenues. Joseph de Rivera St. Jurgo gave South Bass its first formal burial ground when he deeded Crown Hill Cemetery at Catawba and Meechen avenues to Louis Harms as Trustee of Put-in-Bay Township on 27 September 1867. Crown Hill Cemetery is not very large, and it is not feasible to expand it because it is on the crest of a hill. Twenty-six years later the township purchased land from Valentine Doller and Clinton Idlor for a new place of burial —Maple Leaf Cemetery. Purchase price was $1,200. Additional property adjoining the new cemetery, as it is sometimes called, has been acquired since. Maple Leaf is located just off Langram Road between the airport and the Lime Kiln ferry dock.

ISLAND POPULATION

Since South Bass Island is within the jurisdiction of two political units, the village and the township, the arrangement creates a number of problems. One of the lesser ones is how to determine the population of the entire island. Ted W. Brown, Ohio secretary of state, in compiling the "Ohio Population Report" from the Nineteenth Federal Census, 1970, lists the population of Put-in-Bay Township as 507 and Put-in-Bay Village as 135. The township also includes Middle and North Bass, and the village does not include the unincorporated part of South Bass.

The Chamber of Commerce directory, 1974, gives the South Bass Island population as 350. Island population was double that figure in 1880. United States Bureau of the Census Tally sheets for that year give South Bass—village and township sections—a total of 700 residents. Middle Bass had 308, North Bass 208, Rattlesnake 6, and Sugar Island 5. The local minister reported the island census to Jay Cooke in 1899. There were 554 residents. A St. Paul's Episcopal Church brochure of 1913 reduced that figure to 500.

THE PUBLIC LAWN

In fair weather the popular meeting place for tourists is the lakefront village park. The Lawn or Grove as it was called in the early days was given to the people of South Bass Island by Joseph de Rivera St. Jurgo on 14 June 1866. Louis Harms, John S. Gibbens, and F. W. Cooper were made trustees for life, their replacements to be elected by the islanders. De Rivera wrote out certain specifications as to the use of the park. No church, public, commercial, or private building, booth or tent was to be erected in the park, but the trustees could plant trees or shrubbery or build walks, fountains, or benches or erect statuary. An iron fence was to surround the Lone Willow on the 1813 gravesite, and the park was to be fenced with gates or turnstiles where needed.

He retained two acres of land at the east end of the park for himself. After de Rivera died in 1889 the village sought to purchase those two acres which had been used as a part of the "Public Lawn" for many years, but the village lacked sufficient funds. The council hoped in vain that some civic-minded person would buy the property and hold it in trust until the village could pay for it.

In 1896 Thomas E. Webb and William P. Stimmel bought the desired two-acre area for their own purposes. They were going to build a dance hall, operate a saloon, and erect an aquarium near the shore. The council's reaction was to appropriate the land. An election was held on the issue: forty-nine votes were cast for appropriation and twenty-four against. Webb and Stimmel brought suit in the court naming Mayor Henry Fox, the six councilmen, and the election officials as defendants, claiming that the election was fraudulent. The court upheld the village in its condemnation proceedings. A bond issue in the amount of $9,039 was passed to pay for the land appropriated.

STREET EXTENSION

Not all of the streets within the village were public roads. An important artery of communication along the bay front was still a private lane as late as 1889. This was the section that ran from the corner of Bay View and Catawba avenues at the Doller building to the westerly limits of the village (present Miller Ferry downton dock). Petitions to make it a public thoroughfare were presented to the council in February 1889. The proposed public road passed through property owned by Mayor Valentine Doller, and he replied with a remonstrance against the petition. Doller had put a gate across his section of the road and occasionally locked it, preventing others from using the road. The next morning he sometimes discovered the locked gate uprooted and thrown in the nearby bay. The other property owners, Mrs. Hermine Burggraf, John S. Gibbens, and E. J. Dodge, favored the extension. The Bay View extension was approved.

Private property was again appropriated when Victory Avenue was created by ordinance in 1890. The new road connected the Bay View Avenue extension and Lakeview Avenue. No opposition to Victory Avenue was expressed by the property owners.

The landowners along the village streets were required to build sidewalks according to specifications laid down by the council:

> All of such sidewalks to be four feet in width (except Delaware Avenue which was to be six-feet wide), and to be built of one-by-six-inch fence boards, with three two-by-four-inch stringers running under same, said stringers to be well bedded upon the ground, before laying the boards upon the same, the boards to be laid crosswise and securely nailed to the stringers.

The cost varied from twenty and one-half cents to twenty-three and one-half cents per lineal foot depending upon the grade of sidewalk. Every spring the council minutes were filled with notices to property owners ordering them to repair or build new walks. On 26 January 1905 the council passed Ordinance No. 54, which provided that all sidewalks after that date were to be built of stone or cement.

2

Growth and Progress

ST. PAUL'S EPISCOPAL CHURCH

A place of worship was a necessity for many frontiersmen. Just as a school was necessary for educating future citizens, souls needed cultivation also. Some early communities were a bit slow to organize a recognized church. Such was the case at Put-in-Bay. The island had few inhabitants in the 1840s and 1850s.

Jay Cooke, the financier, bought Gibraltar Island in Put-in-Bay harbor in 1864. He was an ardent sportsman and the Bass islands were aptly named, as they were a fisherman's paradise. Cooke was a fisherman of souls too. One of the things that led him to buy Gibraltar for the site of his vacation home was that it "offered an inviting field for Missionary and Christian labors . . . on this Bass and other islands . . ." Until then only an occasional clergyman had come to Put-in-Bay from Sandusky. The Reverend John Mills Kendrick of Gambier came to Put-in-Bay in the spring of 1864 and held services in the school.

Cooke met with island citizens in September 1864 and suggested that they raise what funds they could to build a church, and he would furnish the rest. Joseph de Rivera St. Jurgo donated the lot on the corner of Catawba and Lakeview avenues on which the church was erected. On 3 October 1865 the islanders organized a "religious society to be connected with the Protestant Episcopal Church under the name of St. Paul's Church." They adopted a constitution and the canons of the Episcopal Church and elected a vestry. The first services in the new building were held in October 1865 with Kendrick, the rector, officiating and assisted by R. J. Parrin, rector of Cooke's own church in Chelton Hills, Pennsylvania. In the congregation, besides the islanders, were Salmon P. Chase, chief justice of the United States Supreme Court, and the Honorable Richard Parsons, former minister to Bolivia.

Kendrick served the church until July 1866. He was succeeded by a J. W. Duerr who remained about a year. A problem was created when a Methodist minister from North Bass, a Mr. Disney, held meetings in the church. He tried to establish a Methodist church but failed. The Reverend S. R. Weldon, an Episcopalian minister, became rector in April 1868.

When Jay Cooke came to Gibraltar in the spring of 1868 he found the church doing quite well. It had an Episcopalian minister, 150 children in Sunday school, and a very active vestry. When he returned to Gibraltar for fall fishing it was his custom to be host at an annual party for the Sunday school children. There were games and singing, gifts of religious books and cards and ice cream and candy after which the children were taken back to Put-in-Bay. Cooke felt that he was something of a missionary. He entered into his "Records" an account of an excursion to Pelee Island, Ontario, Canada. "We found ample market for our supply of tracts testaments books & with the children of the island & also with a ship-wrecked crew of 8 or 10 men—wrecked schooner 'Contest' of Chicago."

Although an Episcopal church had been established on Put-in-Bay, there were only six church members living on the island when Weldon arrived in 1868. There were about a half-dozen other Protestant denominations and persons professing those faiths attended St. Paul's Church. Weldon was aware that few islanders were of his faith and that many of them belonged to no church at all. He felt that he would be more successful if he avoided trying to convert them to strict Episcopalianism and tried to get them to love a Christian God. Besides this, Cooke in his early years at Gibraltar was in the habit of inviting various Protestant ministers to spend several weeks at Gibraltar. They were expected to conduct services at the island church and most of them were not Episcopalians. The ministers followed their own faith in the celebration of religious services.

A visiting Episcopal minister in the summer of 1868 noted the deviations from the prescribed ritual. He was surprised, he wrote, to see as many as four different denominations of clergymen in the chancel "in citizen's dress, of every variety of cut from frock to curtail," and that there were grave omissions in the forms of worship. Mr. Weldon, the rector, as well as the visiting clergy participated in these "mutilations" of the church service.

Bishop Charles P. McIlvaine wrote to Weldon that winter and asked him to describe in detail where he had departed from the prescribed forms. The island minister's reply did not satisfy the bishop and he reminded Weldon that although the church at Put-in-Bay had not been consecrated, it was a regularly organized parish subject to the same laws as any other Episcopal church. He advised him that it was "not lawful" to leave out portions of the evening service nor to omit words

Battle of Lake Erie, 10 September 1813. *(Top)* Library of Congress.　Brig *Niagara* in Put-in-Bay harbor, 1913. *(Bottom)* Otto G. Herbster-K. K. Jennings Collection (OGH-KKJ).

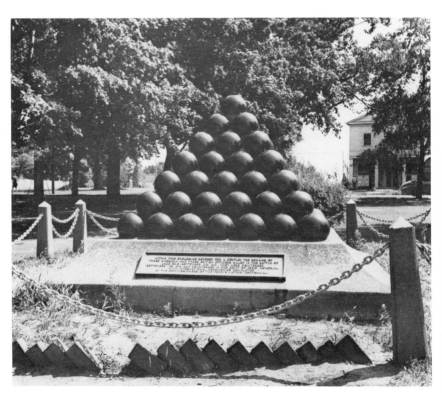

Master Commandant Oliver Hazard Perry. *(Top)* Library of Congress.
Original 1813 burial site. *(Bottom)* R. J. Dodge (RJD).

Town Hall, 1952. *(Top)* RJD. Art, antique, and boutique shops serve the visitor. *(Bottom)* RJD.

St. Paul's Episcopal Church. *(Top)* RJD.
Church. *(Bottom)* RJD.

Interior, St. Paul's Episcopal

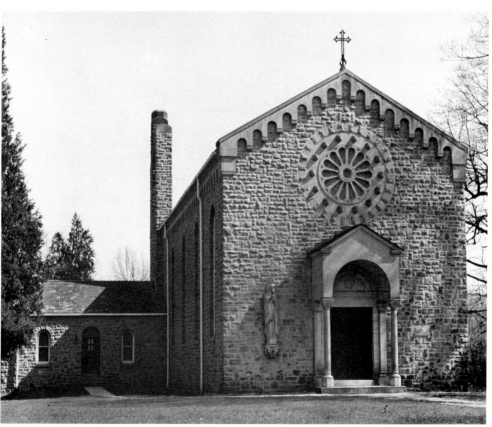

The first Catholic church was on Put-in-Bay Road. *(Top)* OGH-KKJ.
Mother of Sorrows Catholic Church, Catawba Avenue. *(Bottom)* RJD.

Mother of Sorrows Church—a wedding, 1949. *(Top)* RJD.   Philip and
Amelia Vroman—pioneer settlers. *(Bottom)* OGH-KKJ.

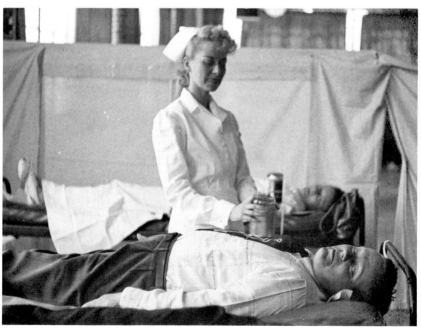

American Legion Doughboy statue. (Top) RJD.   American Legion Blood
Donor Drive, 1956. (Bottom) RJD.

Heading for the starting line, I-L. Y. A. regatta. *(Top)* RJD.　　The docks
are crowded at regatta time. *(Bottom)* RJD.

Awarding trophies at the yacht club, 1952. (Top) RJD.　The first sports broadcast was made from the yacht *Thelma* on 18 July 1907. (Bottom) OGH-KKJ.

The Lighthouse was built in 1897. (Top) RJD.   The former U.S. Fish Hatchery is now a research center of Ohio State University. (Bottom) RJD.

The Ohio State Fish Hatchery. (*Top*) RJD.   One jar could contain 420,000 fish eggs—Ohio State Fish Hatchery, 1950s. (*Bottom*) RJD.

Interior, Crystal Cave. (Top) RJD.   Interior, Mammoth Cave, 1951. (Bottom) RJD.

Island drama group, 1953. (Top) RJD.   Sports car races—the pit—1952.
(Bottom) RJD.

Sports car races—the airport corner. (Top) RJD. Sports car races—the
cemetery corner. (Bottom) RJD.

The first grapes were planted in 1858. *(Top)* RJD.   Many islanders pick grapes at harvest time. *(Bottom)* RJD.

Heineman Winery—Louis (L.) and Harry Heineman pressing grapes in the 1950s. (Top) RJD.   1950 Grape Festival—Cleo Webster, Queen Audrey Klopp, King James Thompson, and Claire Kindt. (Bottom) RJD.

in the baptismal ritual. The bishop also expressed his regret that Weldon wore neither gown nor surplice.

Weldon corresponded with Cooke before he replied to the bishop. Cooke knew of the deviations from the ritual and gave his approval. The rector in his second letter to the bishop held steadfastly to his views. McIlvaine wrote that he could not sanction the omission of parts of the baptismal service nor allow ministers who were "not Episcopally ordained" to preach in Weldon's place. These things were unlawful and a breach of ordination vows, the bishop warned. Weldon then resigned as a minister of the Protestant Episcopal Church.

Jay Cooke was present at a meeting held 20 June 1869 in which the action of the rector was endorsed and the church members unanimously voted to withdraw from the Episcopal Church and form an independent church. A church constitution was written and signed by Weldon and fifty-one others including six who were not island residents. Church services, in general, followed the Episcopal form.

The independent church struggled along experiencing some setbacks and some progress, as Jay Cooke noted in 1885:

> The church work does not progress as fast as could be hoped . . . The fact is the Islands are fast becoming depleted of the original native population. Many who used to take an active interest in the church have gone away & their places purchased by Germans—some of whom care not for God and the Sabbath.

Five years later things looked brighter. ". . . I am cheered & delighted to find the church work prospering I have never doubted that God would fulfill his promise . . . I confidently expect He will soon pour out a Blessing upon the Islands."

St. Paul's Church followed the independent path for twenty years, when in 1889 the members decided to affiliate with the Reformed Episcopal Church. In 1912 the congregation petitioned the Protestant Episcopal bishop of Ohio to receive them back into the fold. This was done officially at a special visitation and service at Put-in-Bay on 25 October 1912. The Reverend J. M. Forbes was appointed rector a month later.

MOTHER OF SORROWS CHURCH

French explorers of North America penetrated the Great Lakes area in the seventeenth century. Father Louis Hennepin accompanied Robert de La Salle in 1680 when that explorer sailed among the Bass islands. Father Hennepin said Mass at Middle Bass and the expedition proceeded to Lake Huron. The first missionary work done in northwestern Ohio took place in 1749 when the Jesuit priests Pierre Poitier and Joseph de Bonnécamp sought to Christianize the Indians living along the Vermilion and Sandusky Rivers. The first permanent religious chapel in Ohio was built in 1751 by Father John de la Richardie of Detroit. The missionaries were forced to flee from the Sandusky area at the time of Pontiac's Conspiracy. The Reverend Edmund Burke was sent from Detroit in 1796 to work among the Indians living near Fort Miami (Maumee). He had little success.

The Mother of Sorrows Roman Catholic Church was established in 1866 with the Reverend Charles Kueman as pastor. A chapel was set up in the Henry Burggraf home on East Point. The church at Put-in-Bay was, and is, a missionary church with St. Michael's Church on Kelleys Island being the mother church. Both churches were in the Diocese of Cleveland from 1866 until 1912 when they were transferred to the Diocese of Toledo.

Martin Barsch in October 1875 donated a lot in the central part of South Bass, on Put-in-Bay Road between Thompson and Meechen roads, on which to build a small wood-frame church. The structure was not completed until the pastorate of the Reverend John Mertes (1880-1885). Construction, begun about 1876, was slowed by the destruction of the Put-in-Bay House by fire in 1878. This hotel which housed eight hundred guests employed islanders and other summer help who could be expected to contribute to the building fund, as well as the hotel guests. Once completed, the church served Put-in-Bay for fifty years.

The pastor of the two churches, Mother of Sorrows and St. Michael's, resided at Kelleys Island. In the early days transportation by steamboat was readily available in the summer. Several boat lines made one or more trips daily between Put-in-Bay, Middle Bass, Kelleys, and Sandusky. Mass was said once a week at 5:30 A.M. When there were large conventions at Put-in-Bay the priest said Mass in the hall at the Hotel Victory. In the spring and fall the pastor could not easily commute between islands. Fewer boats made the inter-islands trip so church services were held only once a month. Once winter set in the priest came only to officiate at funerals.

Father John Schoendorff and the Reverend Charles Alfred Martin of Cleveland conducted in February 1903 an eight-day non-Catholic mission in the town hall and the church, which was well received. They came to the island in an ironclad rowboat through broken ice. A difficult and somewhat hazardous journey, perhaps, but that was the way in which the islanders traveled and received mail and supplies in the depths of winter before the advent of the airplane.

In winter when there was no priest on the island the Catholic congregation would assemble at the church on Sunday and say the Mass prayers. Lay teachers conducted catechism classes when the priest was unavailable. Confirmation ceremonies were held during the summer at the mother church on Kelleys Island. Many of the early parishioners were German and some of the services were said in their language.

The old wooden church was located in the center part of the island outside the village limits and away from the center of population. With the increasing numbers of summer visitors, it proved to be much too small. A new and larger church was built in 1927 on Catawba Avenue across the street from St. Paul's Episcopal Church. The pastor, Joseph E. Maerder, designed the Lombardic Romanesque structure after a similar church in Lombardy, Italy. It was built of Kelleys Island limestone and dedicated in 1928. The altar weighs ten tons and is carved from Florentine marble. Howard Gorman was the architect for Mother of Sorrows Church and Gerhart Lamar painted the various religious scenes in the interior.

Wintertime communication between the islands and mainland was vastly improved with the coming of the airplane in late 1930. Several years earlier Father Maerder had flown from Kelleys Island to North Bass to administer the last rites to a dying parishioner. His pilot was John W. Parker. Father Maerder recognized the need for such service on a scheduled basis and was an early supporter of Milton Hershberger when that flier sought to inaugurate an airmail and passenger route from the Lake Erie islands to the mainland. Even before there was an airport at Put-in-Bay, Father Maerder had Hershberger fly him to the island. It seemed as if the entire wintertime island population had assembled to watch the two-seater plane land on the ice. With the coming of the airplane the pastor could commute between Kelleys Island and Put-in-Bay, saying Mass at one church, then in a matter of minutes, saying a second Mass at the church on the other island. These flights were actually charter trips, there being no scheduled flights between Kelleys and Put-in-Bay. Emergency flights to the sick or dying were made even at night. The coming of the airplane meant that parishioners on Put-in-Bay, Kelleys Island, and occasionally on Middle Bass, could attend Mass on Sunday and holy days more routinely.

When the new church was built in 1927, the stained-glass rose window in the front was installed; but due to lack of funds, such windows were not put in the side. These windows were glazed with translucent glass. In 1966 the old side windows were replaced with a type of colored glass known as faceted glass. A piece of glass is shaped in a manner similar to that of a mason cutting stone with a hammer and chisel. After the piece is shaped, the artisan cuts a facet on the surface to allow the sunlight to be refracted as in a prism. A filler or matrix is put between the pieces of glass and a picture is formed. The new windows were donated by twelve families of the parish.

Neither the old church nor the new one at Put-in-Bay had living quarters for a resident priest. Makeshift quarters were set up when the pastor had an assistant priest to help him serve the two churches. The assistant usually lived at Put-in-Bay during that period, 1932-1942. The bedroom was in the present parish meeting room, while kitchen and dining room were in the basement boiler room. After the furnace was converted to fuel oil, the coal bin became the living room. In 1969 a rectory was built in the lot adjacent to the church. It is a two-piece modular, five-room house. A two-car garage was added in 1972. The parishioners of St. Paul's Church across the street had replaced their original rectory with a modern new one in 1959.

UTILITIES AND FACILITIES

In the early days of settlement, communication between Put-in-Bay and the mainland was by boat during the navigation season and on foot, horse and sleigh, or iceboat in the wintertime. The resort business was growing and a telegraph station at Put-in-Bay was commercially feasible.

The Put-in-Bay Telegraph Company was incorporated in 1873 with a capital stock of $10,000. Sandusky was the mainland terminal and Idlor and Foye's store in the Doller building was the island station. Connections were made with Western Union, the company leasing eight miles of Western Union wire and maintaining twenty miles of its own. Cable was laid from Sandusky, across Sandusky Bay, Marblehead and Catawba peninsulas, and from Catawba Point two and seven-eighth miles across the lake to South Bass Island. Later on, a third office was located in the Hotel Victory. After World War II, an automatic machine replaced the old hand-operated key but service was discontinued shortly thereafter.

RING TWO SHORT, ONE LONG

The telegraph provided good communication with the mainland. The telephone did not only that, but allowed the islanders to talk with each other as well. Conversations were person-to-person and only as private as a party line would allow.

The first underwater telephone cable was laid in 1899 by the Central Union Telephone Company. The island terminal was located in the Hollway store in the Schiele building next to the town hall. There were initially only three telephones in use, one at the Hotel Victory power house, one at Perry's Cave, and one in Doller's store. Their chief use was to start the street cars at either end of the line so that the cars could pass each other at the cave bypass without delay. The line ran from the Hotel Victory to the boat docks in the harbor.

The switchboard was moved a number of times—from the Hollway store to a second-story alcove between the store and the town hall, and then to several residences. Service at first was provided only until 9:00 P.M. with a direct line to the doctor's office for use in emergencies. When the exchange was in the operator's residence twenty-four hour service was possible. Although the operator retired at a respectable hour, he or she could be aroused by a bell. Some of the early operators were William Schnoor, Emil Ritter, Mame Ladd, Clara Anton, Emilia Heuchle, Jessie Ritter, and Rose Senne.

The manual exchange was replaced by an automatic one in the mid-1930s and dial phones replaced the old hand-cranked wall instruments. Calls to the mainland were long-distance calls and a cable charge was added to the bill. In recent years a microwave tower has been erected near the exchange building and since January 1968 Put-in-Bay residents have been able to dial to mainshore. Telephone service to the island still had to go through the Port Clinton exchange until 15 September 1973 when it became possible to direct distance dial into Put-in-Bay and the cable charge was eliminated.

LET THERE BE LIGHT

Pioneer island homes were lighted by candles and kerosene lamps. The Hotel Victory had its own powerhouse which supplied electricity to the hotel, streetcars, and to the caves. Some island homes had acetylene gas-making plants and, later on, their own electric generating systems. The village streets were illuminated by coal oil lanterns and the town marshal or some other islander had the task of lighting and hanging the lanterns in the lampposts. The lanterns were apparently inadequate because fifty-four residents petitioned the mayor and council "to dispense with the services of one policeman and use the money . . . in lighting up the park and principal streets of the village."

The village council granted the Put-in-Bay Improvement Company a franchise to "establish, operate and maintain an electric light system" in May 1906. The street lighting system was converted to electricity and seven arc lights were put in service for the three summer months at a cost of $175. Island-produced electric power was expensive, costing twenty-nine to thirty-one cents per kilowatt and was uncertain at best. Power was not supplied on a twenty-four hour basis at first, nor every day. The current for nighttime lighting came on about 4:00 or 5:00 P.M. and was turned off in the morning except that power might be furnished during daylight hours once a week so that those households with electric washing machines could do the laundry.

A floodlighting system was installed at the Perry's Victory Memorial in 1928 by the Ohio Public Service Company of Sandusky and the Put-in-Bay Improvement Company distributed the power at first. The company was paid $1,770 for electric power furnished the monument for the 1928 season.

An underwater cable, two and seven-eighths miles long, was laid between Catawba Point and Put-in-Bay in 1929, and the Ohio Public Service Company now undertook the distribution of power for the entire island. Rates were cut substantially; for example, the light and power bill for the monument for the August 1930—July 1931 season was only $500, and the entire column, not just the top, as was previously done, was floodlighted.

Steam and several types of internal combustion engines were used to drive the generators in the powerhouse on Erie Street. The Ohio Public Service Company maintained two diesel engines on a standby basis to provide emergency service if there was a power failure. These engines were operated once a year and their "chug-chugging" could be heard all over the island. The island is now served by two underwater cables. The Ohio Public Service Company merged with the Ohio Edison Company in 1950.

SEWER AND WATER

Progress was made in providing other utilities in the first decade of the twentieth century. The village council hired an engineer in 1904 to draw up plans for a sewerage system. The landowners to be served by the facility were assessed varying amounts ranging from $37.50 to $600.00. Extensions to the system were made but only the businesses and residences in the center of the village are served by the sewer.

The village issued bonds in the amount of $8,000 for the construction of a water-pumping station and distribution system in 1909. A 30,000-gallon wooden tank which is still in use was erected in the park. Most, but not all, households in the village and some beyond are served by the water system. A Board of Trustees of Public Affairs administers the water system.

W.C.I.A.

The Womens' Civic Improvement Association was organized in April 1912; the initial officers were Mrs. F. Gross, president; Mrs. G. Heineman, vice-president; Mrs. J. J. Day, secretary; and Mrs. T. B. Alexander, treasurer. The primary duty of the association was to operate and maintain the women's restroom in the village park. Some funds were provided by the village council; other moneys were raised by subscription, card parties, and once T. B. Alexander put on a play in the town hall which netted the association $182.65.

In 1915 the organization also contributed $200.00 toward the purchase of the town clock which cost $301.68. A new restroom with facilities for both men and women was built in 1920. In March 1939 the association disbanded, turning the operation of the restroom over to the village.

REBELLIONS AND WARS

REBELS AFLOAT

The Civil War had its effect on the islands in the same way as it had in the small towns and large cities on the mainland. The young men served in the Union army, although several islanders hired substitutes to fight in the battles in their place and one went as a paid substitute. After the war a number of veterans made Put-in-Bay their home. Jay Cooke, the financier who sold government bonds during the war, bought Gibraltar Island in 1864 and was a summer resident until 1905.

The battles and skirmishes of the Civil War took place hundreds of miles from the Lake Erie islands. The horrors of war were only read about, not experienced, at peaceful Put-in-Bay. One event in September 1864 did bring to the islanders the excitement of possible battle with the enemy. This was the Lake Erie Conspiracy which had as its goal the freeing of the Confederate prisoners of war on Johnson's Island in Sandusky Bay. The Confederate secret agent, Charles H. Cole, planned to capture the gunboat USS *Michigan* on guard off the prison camp, and John Yeats Beall was to seize the island steamer *Philo Parsons*, take the vessel to the camp, and free the prisoners. The rebels took possession of the steamer shortly after the *Parsons* left Kelleys Island enroute to Sandusky. Beall was informed that there was not enough fuel on board to carry out his plan, so he returned to Middle Bass for more wood. While at Middle Bass, the steamer *Island Queen* was captured and towed behind the *Parsons* before being set adrift in a sinking condition. Beall again lay just outside Sandusky Bay, awaiting a signal which never came. Cole had been arrested before the plot could be put into action. The *Parsons* steamed back to the starting point, Sandwich, Ontario, and the rebels escaped into Canada.

The passengers and some of the crew of the two boats were put ashore at Middle Bass and were warned not to communicate with the mainland for twenty-four hours. There was no telegraphic service to the islands in 1864. Two groups of eight men each obtained rowboats and went to Put-in-Bay. An attempt to sail to Ottawa City (Catawba) failed because of rough seas. Four of the men did manage to row to Kelleys Island, arriving at daybreak. The *Michigan* also arrived at Kelleys at sunrise and her captain, John C. Carter, learned of the fate of the *Parsons* and *Island Queen*.

John Brown, Jr., son of the abolitionist, and other islanders noted the unusual activity at Middle Bass, the return of the *Parsons* and the towing away of the *Island Queen* in bright moonlight. John Brown and three others set sail for Ottawa City and, despite the bad weather, made the passage safely. Brown walked in the dark across the peninsula to a point opposite Johnson's Island and rowed across the narrow channel to report what he had seen to the camp commander, Colonel Charles W. Hill.

The unsuccessful attempt to free the rebel prisoners on 19-20 September 1864 created much excitement and apprehension in the Lake Erie area. John Brown, Jr., wrote to Colonel Hill and offered to raise a company of militia for the defense of the islands and the protection of lake commerce. His offer was accepted and the company enlisted. Brown was elected captain and Governor John Brough signed his commission November 24. The unit, "Brown's Independent Company of Infantry," was composed of fifty men and boys between the ages of thirteen and fifty years. Equipment—rifles, bayonets, slings, and belts—was sent from Columbus to arm the group. The men were not to serve beyond the islands or immediate vicinity unless an emergency forced the governor to call out the entire enrolled militia of the state.

A BRIEF ENCOUNTER

The Spanish-American War in 1898 had little effect on the island. Only two islanders served in the armed forces, Joseph Meyer, who enlisted in the army and went to Cuba, and Hugo Wagner who was a sailor on the USS *Baltimore*.

A boom in the tourist trade was expected because of the war. The Sandusky *Daily Register* reported that the conflict would scare many people away from the Atlantic coast resorts and to inland vacation areas such as Put-in-Bay. Eastern port cities were rumored to be the target for bombardment by the Spanish fleet. Such attacks did not occur. The enemy fleet was destroyed by the United States Navy on July 3 at the battle of Santiago.

THE BIG WAR

When the United States entered World War I in 1917 thirty-two men of the Bass islands answered their country's call to arms. Eight were from Middle Bass or North Bass and the remainder from South Bass. Two islanders, Albert Scheible, a soldier, and Rex Downing, a sailor, died in service.

The Put-in-Bay Auxiliary of the American Red Cross was organized on 24 June 1917 and the officers elected were: Grace Williamson, president; Mrs. J. W. Forbes, vice-president; Meta Ingold, secretary; and Marion Whitsey, treasurer. The local unit, expanded later to include Middle and North Bass, was affiliated with the Ottawa County Red Cross Chapter at Port Clinton. A junior auxiliary in the school was formed in January 1918. Peak membership at Put-in-Bay reached 156 plus forty-two in the junior branch. Middle Bass had thirty-nine and North Bass thirty.

The members made such items as sweaters, socks, and mufflers. Christmas boxes were sent to island servicemen in 1917 and 1918. After the January 1921 meeting the Put-in-Bay Auxiliary became inactive. The unit was reactivated on 23 January 1942 when the United States became involved in World War II. Mayor Henry Fox called an organizational meeting. The mayor was elected chairman; Lena Phillips, vice-chairman; Gerta Cooper, secretary; and Dorothy Tancock, treasurer.

The unit performed services similar to those in World War I. Red Cross fund drives were oversubscribed by a wide margin. There were scrap metal and rubber collections. The bronze Liberty statue which had stood on the Hotel Victory lawn was a contribution to one of these drives. The statue, which had been damaged by vandals, brought $37.76 to the coffers.

The last meeting of the auxiliary was held on 13 November 1951. The officers were: Lena Phillips, chairman; Kay Market, vice-chairman; Gerta Cooper, secretary; and Edith Herbster, treasurer. The unit returned to an inactive status.

Island World War I veterans organized an American Legion post at a meeting held 8 December 1921. The new organization was named the Scheible-Downing Post No. 542 in commemoration of the two local servicemen who died during the war. There were sixteen charter members: Nathan H. Ladd, Maurice F. Arndt, Arnold F. Burggraf, Emil S. Wiesler, Norman V. Heineman, Raymond J. Truscott, Arthur G. Duggan, Carleton L. Meyer, Jack Clifford, Jake Market, Howard V. Doller, Roderick A. Miller, Ervin Heidle, William A. Market, Jr., Arthur O. Kuchner, and Henry F. Gottlieb. Bimonthly meetings were held in the rooms above the Rittman Meat Market.

The post put on a musical, *Sitting Pretty*, to raise funds for a statue to be put in the park in commemoration of the two islanders who lost their lives in the war. The doughboy statue was made by the Fremont Monumental Company and was erected in 1923. A ladies auxiliary of the American Legion was also formed.

A BIGGER WAR

World War II saw seventy-seven men and one woman of the Bass islands enter the military service of their country. Eight of these were from Middle Bass and four from North Bass. Two World War I veterans also served in the second international conflict: Nathan H. Ladd and Roy Thompson. Two islanders were killed in action: Richard Sampson, a sailor, and Ralph H. Sanford, a soldier. Their names were placed on the pedestal of the doughby statue in the park after the war. Islanders also served in the Korean police action and in the Vietnam—Southeast Asia theater of war. A Veterans of Foreign Wars post, Sampson-Sanford 8999 with thirty-four members, was organized in January 1947 but became inactive after a few years of existence.

The island location of the American Legion post made it difficult for the members to participate at the district, state, and national levels although some members did attend various conventions. Several First District (comprising ten northwestern Ohio countries) Conventions were held at Put-in-Bay.

PEACE CEREMONIES

A small-scale international peace memorial service was held at Perry's Victory and International Peace Memorial in 1949. The local post and the Canadian Legion post at Pelee Island, Ontario, sponsored the event. A slightly larger observance was held in 1950.

A much larger United States—Canadian peace ceremony took place in 1953. It was not only a peace memorial but also a state of Ohio sesquicentennial celebration and a First District of Ohio American Legion convention. The convention was held on Saturday, June 20 and on Sunday morning, June 21. The joint Canadian—American International Peace Memorial Service and the Sesquicentennial program commemorating 150 years of Ohio statehood was held that Sunday afternoon on the plaza of the monument.

Secretary Douglas McKay of the United States Department of the Interior was the principal American speaker and General E. L. M.

Burns, deputy minister of Veterans' Affairs, represented Canada. Other orators were Milo J. Warner, former national commander of the American Legion, and Major T. A. M. Hulse, president of the Ontario Command, Canadian Legion, British Empire Service League. Lieutenant-Governor John Brown of Ohio was the master of ceremonies. Major Hulse and William O. McClelland, Department of Ohio American Legion commander, placed wreaths over the crypt in the monument rotunda. The ceremony concluded with the Delta Legion firing squad firing three rifle volleys and the Canadian bagpipers sounding the mournful "Lament."

CIVIC SERVICE

The local American Legion post has been involved in island civic projects since its founding. In conjunction with Port Clinton Post No. 113, the island veterans arranged transportation to the mainland so that islanders could donate blood when the Red Cross Bloodmobile visited either Port Clinton or Marblehead on the mainland. Island Air Service planes took the donors, free of charge, to mainshore. Post No. 113 members drove them to the collection center and returned them to the Miller Boat Line Catawba dock or the Erie Isle dock where they returned, gratis, to Put-in-Bay. It would be too expensive and time-consuming for the Bloodmobile unit to go by ferry to Put-in-Bay. Scheible-Downing Post also sponsored for a few years the annual visit of the tuberculosis X-ray unit.

The post has participated in many island civic projects such as building and maintaining a tennis court in the school recreation area, putting up the village street Christmas decorations, sponsoring the annual children's Easter Egg Hunt, and decorating the veterans' graves on Memorial Day and Veterans' Day. The post listed fifty-nine members for 1974.

SAIL HO!

Commercial steamers and sailboats were not the only watercraft to visit the Lake Erie islands. Yachts of all sizes and descriptions sailed to Put-in-Bay. It was natural that sailing yachts would compete in races. The Sandusky *Daily Register* reported such an event in September 1871 titling the race "The First International Regatta of the Lake at Put-in-Bay." Thirteen boats varying in length from thirty to fifty-two feet competed over a thirty-mile course. The apparent winner was the *Ina* of Toronto, Ontario; coming in second was the *Zoe* of Toledo; third, the *Coral* of Detroit; and fourth, the *Mystic* of Cleveland. First prize consisted of a purse of $125 and a silver epergne; second, $100 and a barometer; third, $75 and a marine glass. A protest was lodged against the *Ina* and the Canadian yacht was disqualified. The protesting yachtsman claimed that the *Ina* did not follow the rules when rounding a stake boat.

Other races were held and the regatta closed with a grand ball at the Put-in-Bay House. The International Regatta Association was organized with W. F. Lockwood of Toledo being named president; W. H. Baxter of Detroit, secretary; and Merit Sweeney of Put-in-Bay, treasurer. A second International Regatta was held in 1872. This time the *Ina* came in first, followed by the *Zoe* and the *Restless* of Sandusky.

This first attempt to form a yachting association of more than a local nature was not successful, for another attempt was made in July 1884. Henry Gerlach, a Cleveland yachtsman, invited a small group of friends for a Lake Erie cruise on his sloop, the *Lulu*, and while they were anchored in Put-in-Bay harbor, and later at Toledo, the Inter-Lake Yachting Association was conceived. George W. Gardner, who had founded the Cleveland Yachting Association, was a leader in the formation of the I-L.Y.A. which was formally organized at a January 1885 meeting of the Cleveland Yachting Association and the Cleveland Canoe Club. Gardner became the first commodore and held that post until the Panic of 1893, which temporarily disrupted the association. [Gardner was mayor of Cleveland.]

The Inter-Lake Yachting Association held its first regatta at Put-in-Bay in 1885. After its reorganization in 1894 the I-L.Y.A. has held the regatta each year since, despite wars and depressions. Charter members were the yachts clubs from Put-in-Bay, Sandusky, Toledo, Cleveland, Buffalo, Erie, and Detroit. Put-in-Bay has been the site of the sail and power boat events except for two years—in 1909 when the regatta was held at Toledo and in 1920 when Erie, Pennsylvania, sponsored the races. Although the regatta is primarily a program for sailing yachts, it is claimed that the world's first motor boat races were held at the 1895 regatta. Two naptha launches, the *Restless* and the *Sweetheart*, competed, with the *Restless* being named the winner on a time allowance.

E. W. Radder, secretary-treasurer of the I-L.Y.A. met with East coast yachtsmen in 1897 to form a national governing body for yacht racing. Radder, speaking for ten clubs, met with representatives of ninety-nine other clubs in New York City and the North American Yacht Racing Union was founded. The union establishes yacht racing rules for North American yachtsmen.

Whether there was a formal racing organization or not, sail races were held at Put-in-Bay. A local boat took the honors in 1883, 1884, and 1885. The *Fanchon*, twenty-six feet long, was built about

1878 by the Southard Brothers of Marblehead peninsula for John Doller of Put-in-Bay. The gaff-rigged sloop was used to haul light freight and passengers in the island area and was raced very successfully in various regattas.

The *Fanchon* won in its class in 1883 defeating a favorite, the *Alert*, and was victorious again in 1884. There were forty to fifty boats, representing yachts clubs from Chicago to Cleveland, entered in the 1885 regatta. The *Fanchon* won for the third successive year defeating twelve other boats including the *Alert*, *Cora V*, and the *Lulu*. The boats sailed a twenty-one-mile course, triangular, and to the westward of Rattlesnake Island. In the crew of the *Fanchon* were Captain Virgil Ennis, George Wilds, George Orr, Charles Hollway, Charles Niele, and Patrick Saddler. Doller claimed that his sailing success was due to the fact that he rubbed shoe polish on the hull of the *Fanchon!*

Interest in the sailing races was so great that in 1906 the newspapers used carrier pigeons dispatched from a boat at the finish line to fly the results to the mainland. Although there were telephone and telegraph cables to mainshore, a trip back to the island would take too long. A much more modern means of communication was successfully tried out the next year. Lee De Forest, inventor of the modern radio tube, conducted the first ship-to-shore conversation in the world at the 1907 I-L.Y.A. regatta. The land-based station was located in Ladd's Boathouse on Fox's (Erie Isle) dock. The water-borne equipment was installed in Commodore W. R. Huntington's seventy-two-foot yacht, the *Thelma* (renamed *Electra* for the occasion).

De Forest and Frank E. Butler encountered difficulty in securing sufficient electrical ground for the radio on the wooden-hulled yacht. They purchased two large copper sheets and large-headed nails at a hardware store and secretly fastened them to the hull and ground was obtained. Huntington was taken aback, to put it mildly, when he discovered that nails had been pounded into the highly-polished hull of his yacht, but he was sportsman enough to allow the experiment to continue. The first broadcast was made on the morning of 18 July 1907, "9:57.5 . . . I will tell when the first boat crosses the line. First boat crossing at 9:59. The *Spray* crossed the line about twenty-five seconds after 9:59 (official time was 9:59.5"). When he was not reporting the race results, De Forest played phonograph records over the transmitter.

PUT-IN-BAY YACHT CLUB

Island businessmen, noting the organization of the Inter-Lake Yachting Association, met at the Idlor and Foye (Doller's) store to found a yacht club. The date was 13 February 1886 and Valentine Doller was elected commodore; Walter Ladd, vice-commodore; John S. Doller, rear-commodore; George H. Bacher, secretary; Clinton Idlor, treasurer; and George E. Gascoyne, yacht measurer. The island association became a charter member of the I-L.Y.A.

Meetings were held in one of the local boathouses only once or twice a year, the main purpose being to invite the I-L.Y.A. regatta to Put-in-Bay each summer and having an island delegate attend the I-L.Y.A. meetings. The club made a substantial monetary contribution to the larger organization in the early days. At the present time the island yacht club is the I-L.Y.A. headquarters during the regatta.

Membership in the Put-in-Bay Yacht Club was not restricted to permanent island residents. Summer cottage owners and visiting yachtsmen joined the club. There was a great increase in membership in the centennial year of Perry's 1813 victory in 1913. One hundred fifty-seven names were listed in the roll book in that year. Membership dropped to forty in 1914 and to twenty-eight in 1915. It was not until 1949 or 1950 when membership again exceeded one hundred (184 in 1950).

The yacht club was founded as an organization for profit but this was changed in 1960 to a nonprofit charter. In 1952 an eleven-week, Saturday sailing series was inaugurated by Commodore Frank Miller. Improvements were made to the club building and pavilion, more land was purchased and a dock built. In addition to hosting the I-L.Y.A. regatta, the club has hosted many district and national class regattas such as the Highlander, Lighting, Rhodes Bantam, Interlake, and Shark Catamaran sailboat races.

A major event of the summer is the annual I-L.Y.A. regatta held in August. The island club offers its clubhouse and other facilities to the I-L.Y.A. Regatta week begins with the various deep water races from Cleveland, Sandusky, Toledo, Vermilion, Port Clinton, and Detroit. Sail yacht races are held on Monday, Tuesday, and Wednesday. Twenty-one types of sailboats were registered for the 1973 regatta. There are usually about two hundred craft entered in the contests. The race courses are laid out around South, Middle, North Bass, and Rattlesnake islands and vary in length from four to fifteen nautical miles.

Other events include services at the local churches, the Commodore's Banquet, a memorial service at the Commodore's Monument in the park, a ladies' party, and the climax of the regatta—the awarding of trophies and pennants on the yacht club lawn on Wednesday afternoon.

One hundred and one yachts clubs are affiliated with the I-L.Y.A.: thirty-two are from Michigan, three from Pennsylvania, one from

New York, two from Indiana, and five from Ontario, Canada. The remaining clubs are from Ohio and include such inland cities as Columbus, Fremont, Worthington, Dayton, Mansfield, Akron and Parma. Many of the larger cities have more than one yacht club.

FEDERAL AND STATE INSTALLATIONS

THE LIGHTHOUSE

The United States government wanted to buy land on South Bass from the Edwards family on which to build a lighthouse but purchased Green Island for that purpose instead. A lighthouse was finally erected on South Bass in 1897. It is a two-story brick building —both a residence and a lighthouse. Harry H. Riley was the first lighthouse keeper and Paul F. Prochnow was the last. When Prochnow retired in October 1962, the old light was retired too. An automatic light on a steel tower near the old house now flashes its signal—a red and white alternating beam.

FISH HATCHERIES

The United States Commission of Fish and Fisheries announced in 1889 that Put-in-Bay had been selected as a site for a new federal fish hatchery. The island was located near major Lake Erie fisheries where the spawn of fish eggs could be collected quickly and inexpensively. Also the water used in the hatchery would be pumped from the lake and the temperature change would be slight. Joseph de Rivera St. Jurgo sold .60 acres of land on Peach Point to the federal government on which to build "a fish hatching house."

The state of Ohio experimented with the propagation of fish in small hatcheries at Castalia, Kelleys Island, Toledo, Cleveland, and Sandusky at various times. In 1907 the state built a wood-frame hatchery next to the federal facility but on 31 May 1914 this building was destroyed by fire. It was replaced by a brick structure that is still in use.

Commercial fishermen supplied the spawn or eggs of whitefish, herring, and lake trout in the fall and the spawn of pickerel and perch in the spring. The fishermen were paid for the spawn, sometimes the federal and state hatcheries competed against each other but an agreement between the two was reached. The federal hatchery processed pickerel spawn and the state hatchery, whitefish.

J. J. Stranahan was the first superintendent of the United States Fish Hatchery. It was through his efforts that the American Fisheries

Society met at Put-in-Bay in 1893. Stranahan was well qualified for his position and published an article on fish hatching, "The Method, Limitations and Results of Whitefish Culture on Lake Erie," in the Bulletin of the United States Fish Commission for 1897 (XVII).

The federal hatchery ceased operations in the mid-1930s and in 1940 the facility was transferred to the state of Ohio and is now used as a research station by the Franz Theodore Stone Laboratory of the Ohio State University. The two hatcheries at one time employed a total of twenty-five to thirty men during the peak spawning period. Two steamboats, the *Shearwater* and the *Oliver H. Perry*, were used by the federal and state hatcheries, respectively, to gather the spawn and distribute the fry or newly-hatched fish. The capacity of the state hatchery was reduced and at present there are two full-time employees. Whitefish and pickerel were hatched until the late 1960s when the hatchery switched to coho salmon, then to chinook salmon and steel-head trout.

SOUTH BASS ISLAND STATE PARK

The state of Ohio operates more than sixty state parks. Two of these are on the Lake Erie islands, one at Put-in-Bay and one at Kelleys Island. The state acquired the property of the United Fisheries Company at a bankruptcy sale in 1938. From the original ten acres located at Stone's Cove the state has expanded the park to include the old Hotel Victory site. Tent, truck, and motor home campers now have 150 campsites available in the thirty-two acre facility.

The park has such utilities as tap water and vault-type latrines but no electricity or sewer hook-ups for camper trucks or trailers. Docks and a boat ramp are reserved for the use of park guests only. There is one two-bedroom and one three-bedroom cabin for rent. The Oak Point lot, owned by the state since 1938 and used by the Ohio State University and the Division of Wildlife, was put under the jurisdiction of South Bass State Park in July 1972. Oak Point has docks for small boats but no campsites. During the summer, park personnel present programs on nature, conservation, and ecology.

THE CAVES

One of the great tourist attractions on South Bass Island are the caves. Perry's, Crystal, Daussa's (or Mammoth), and Paradise caves provided the visitor with a thrilling journey underground where it was cool and a refreshing drink of cold pure water can be had from the "Wishing Well." Perry's Cave, so named because Oliver Hazard Perry supposedly discovered it in 1813, is fifty-two feet below the surface and is 208 feet long, 165 feet wide and the 42° temperature varies little. A small lake, the Wishing Well, rises and falls with the level of Lake Erie. Estwick Evans who made "A Tour . . . Through the Western States . . . during 1818" probably was the first white man to explore Perry's Cave despite the belief of Perry's discovery. He found no evidence of previous exploration. The entrance to the cave was small, only three feet wide and a foot and a half high. Later, a Mr. Faber, candle in hand, conducted occasional tours making as much as $100 a day. Joseph de Rivera St. Jurgo leased the cave to Philip Vroman in 1869 and Vroman built a shelter over the entrance, displayed stalactites, fossils, and crystals and acted as guide for ten cents a person.

Daussa's Circular and Labrynthic Cave, later renamed Mammoth Cave, is sixty feet underground. The entrance led to an eighty-by sixty-foot lake, from which the tourist followed a six-hundred-foot natural and circular tunnel to a large cavern and the exit. The last cave to be discovered was Paradise Cave, noted for its stalactites, six to thirty-two inches long, hanging from the ceiling.

The most unusual cave on the island, and perhaps in the United States, is Crystal Cave located at the Heineman Winery. Workmen were digging a well on the Gustav Heineman property in November 1897 when they broke into the cave. Upon examination, they found a solid mass of a dazzling mineral—crystaline strontia. The sidewalls are solid strontia and the ceiling is arch-shaped and has prismatically formed crystals that emit brilliant colors. Strontia crystals have ten faces and the angle on each face of one crystal is the same as the like face of another. The cave has the only sizable deposit of strontium sulphate found in the United States. It has the largest strontia crystals in the world—eighteen inches long. The crystals are blue-white in color.

The four caves are located in the center of the island near the junction of Catawba Avenue and Thompson Road. Crystal and Perry's caves are the only ones open to the public today and guided tours are available during the summer. There are many other caves on the island but these are on private property and are not open to the general public.

The strontia found on the islands had a commercial value. Salts of strontia produce a crimson color when burned and were used in the manufacture of fireworks. Green Island was once called Strontian Island because of the deposits found there.

A German visitor, Emil Venator who was a graduate of a school of mines, came to Put-in-Bay in 1882 and leased various areas for twenty-five years. A large amount of strontia was found two years previously when a well was opened on the Herbster property. Venator brought in miners and about seventy-five tons of strontia was extracted, but the costs of shipping the mineral to Germany were too great to be practical. The company had a mine in Italy and the American enterprise was closed until such time as the European source became exhausted. Venator gave John Brown, Jr., a power of attorney and left the island, never to return. Brown aided both Venator and State Geologist J. S. Newberry in their geological explorations of Put-in-Bay.

LIME KILNS

The Bass islands and the nearby mainland are made up of various types of limestone. Many lime kilns were built to burn the stone to produce the lime needed to make mortar. Two lime kilns were built at Put-in-Bay. The ruins of one at the south end of the island near the lighthouse gives its name to the Miller ferry dock—the Lime Kiln dock. The second one was built on East Point near the former Yachtmen's Club. Lime manufactured in this kiln by Peter Bernhardt was used in the construction of the Burggraf home. Owners of the kilns found the dolomite stone too hard to burn well and soon went out of business. Records are vague but it seems that the kilns were in operation in the 1860s and 1870s.

THE BLACKSMITH SHOP

William Kiinzler operated a blacksmith shop on Put-in-Bay for almost sixty years. His first shop was on Concord Avenue but he later built a new shop on Catawba Avenue. His statements advertised that he did "General Blacksmithing-Horseshoeing-Carriage Work-Pipe Fitting- Bicycle Repairing," and he followed the trend of the times when he added "Automobile Repairing" in 1913. When Kiinzler retired in 1954 at the age of seventy-nine there were only three horses left on the island.

The blacksmith shop was acquired by the South Bass Island Company in 1965, and in 1972 it became a gallery and boutique selling sculpture, pottery, jewelry, leather goods, and paintings.

THE PLAY'S THE THING

A number of theatrical and musical groups came to Put-in-Bay during the summer. The Sandusky *Daily Register* reported that "the Brown Company is playing to full houses at Put-in-Bay." Eagan and Wall's Comedy presented *Chick, The Octoroon,* and *The Vagabond's Wife* at the Opera House in the town hall. Twenty gypsies from Budapest—The Royal Hungarian Band—played in the Opera House and then moved to the Ward Summer Resort (Crescent Hotel) for several weeks.

There was homegrown talent on the island. J. C. Oldt, school superintendent and mayor, recalled that there had been a drama group at Put-in-Bay before he came in 1890. The leading figure in island drama at that time was Thomas B. "T.B." Alexander, a leading man in stock companies around Chicago. "T.B." visited the island during the summer when he was "between engagements." He married Edith Brown, granddaughter of John Brown the abolitionist, and eventually settled on the island and served as mayor for many years.

Oldt joined the drama club which "T.B." organized and gave such plays as *Pearl of Savoy*, *Queenie*, and *Ranch King* with the proceeds donated to the Episcopal church. *Saved by the Enemy* and *Master and Man* netted the school $38.65. Alexander also put on plays in 1910 to help the school out of financial difficulty. The group gave performances in 1899 to raise money to emplace the Civil War cannon and the cannonball pyramid in the park.

A number of stars of the vaudeville circuit built summer homes on Put-in-Bay. So many of them resided on Peach Point that it was called the "Actors' Colony." The Ross Lewises, John Hemingways, Fred Whitfields, Martin Sandses, Frank Willingses, the Murdock brothers, Harry and Crystal Bannister—all had cottages on the island.

Jack and Sue Snyder are well remembered by older islanders. When the Carl Nixons entertained servicemen overseas in World War II, a number of islanders in uniform wrote home that they had seen the Nixons. The members of the "Actors' Colony" put on many performances for the benefit of island churches, lodges and the school.

NEWSPAPERS

Island ventures into journalism ended in disaster. The *Herald*, Volume One, Number One, appeared on 25 August 1898 declaring "Everybody Wants It—First Newspaper for Put-in-Bay." C. N. Whittaker, editor and publisher, had an office for the weekly in the basement of the Graves House. Subscription rates were $1.00 a year, fifty cents for six months, and to attract the summer residents, thirty cents for three months. After accepting money for subscriptions and advertising in December 1898 Whittaker took the mail boat to Port Clinton on the seventeenth and disappeared. People on all three Bass islands lost whatever they had paid.

A second attempt at newspaper publishing was made the next year when the Put-in-Bay *Tribune* was printed. The failure of the *Tribune* was announced to its readers by Editor Shipaugh in late June 1899. He thanked the islanders for their encouragement but said that as there were only 137 families on Put-in-Bay, the island was too small to support a paper. He returned the money which had been advanced to him, paid all his bills, and ceased publication.

SPORTS CAR RACES

Although the waters around Put-in-Bay have been the site for sailboat races for one hundred years, a twentieth-century sport was introduced to the island scene in 1952 when sports car races were held in September. The small, two-seat, open roadster-type of vehicle, usually of foreign make, became popular in the United States after World War II, and various types of races were devised to test the skill of the driver and the quality of the car. An estimated 2,000 persons came to Put-in-Bay for the 1952 event. Unfortunately rain caused the cancellation of the races after only four laps of the first race. Thirty cars were registered for the four scheduled races.

Better weather prevailed the next year when the races were held in June. The rectangular three-mile course followed four connecting roads on the island with the start-finish line in front of the Crescent Hotel on Delaware Avenue. From there the racers made a right turn on to Toledo Avenue, a turn to the right on Langram Road, a right turn on to Meechen Road at the airport, another sharp right at Crown Hill cemetery down Catawba Avenue, and a right turn to the Delaware Avenue finish line.

Various makes and sizes of sports cars competed in the races. A few of the well-known makes entered were the English M.G., Siata, Lotus, Saab, Fiat-Abarth, Sprite, Turner, Morris, Elva, Porsche, Lester, Morgan, Triumph, and Arnolt-Bristol. Entries were limited to one hundred cars in this, the last remaining, true, United States road race in which the racers sped over regular streets through inhabited areas. The event was conceived by vacationing members of the Cleveland Sports Car Club.

An estimated 15,000 people attended the 1959 race. Then no races were held for the next four years, for the state legislature passed a law aimed at those persons who drove at excessive speeds on state highways and the law could be applied to such well-regulated affairs as the Put-in-Bay road races. A new law was passed restoring the races to the island. Although the start-finish line was moved to Concord Avenue eliminating the leg of the race that ran through the business district, the two-and-one-half mile course was still a true road race.

The new races were under the sponsorship of the Central Ohio and Put-in-Bay Road Enterprises, Incorporated. The event held on 5 October 1963 was the last sports car race on the island. Sport Car Club of America officials wanted the entire course to be fenced off, with no front yard spectators and they also wanted trees and utility poles adjacent to the course removed. The Chamber of Commerce felt that such demands could not be met.

O.S.U. MUSIC CAMP

The Ohio State University founded the Franz Theodore Stone Laboratory for biological studies on Gibraltar Island in Put-in-Bay Harbor in the late 1920s. Another branch of the university sponsored summertime activities on South Bass Island when the O.S.U. School of Music established the Island Opera Workshop. The workshop was directed by Dr. Theron R. McClure, School of Music Opera Department. Professor Eugene J. Weigel, director of the School of Music, and Professor Dale V. Gilliland, chairman of the voice faculty served as advisors.

Operas or scenes from such operas as *Seraglio*, *La Traviata*, *La Perichole*, and twenty-four other scenes or short operas were presented in the town hall. After three years at Put-in-Bay the summer opera workshop was transferred to the main campus at Columbus where there were larger facilities available. The workshop, begun in 1958, was a success.

In 1960, a chamber music festival sponsored by the American String Teachers Association was held on the island. The Music Camp, as it is now called, continues to grow with students coming not only from Ohio but from twenty-four other states, Washington, D.C., and Ontario, Canada. Elementary, junior high, and high school students attend the camp during July and August as well as college-and adult-level students. Although the camp features string music, other instruments are used. There have been harpsichord, clavichord, and recorder programs, also programs for marimbas, woodwinds, brasses, and the classical guitar.

Such artists as Dr. Boyd Neel, dean of the Royal Conservatory of Music, University of Toronto, Canada; Giorgio Ciompi, and Robert Gerle have conducted workshops. Hilda Jonas has presented harpsichord concerts and William Fierens of Buenos Aires conducted a classical guitar program.

NATIONAL PARK SERVICE SLIDE TALKS

Another program of education and entertainment available to visitors and islanders in the summer season are color-slide presentations by the staff of Perry's Victory and International Peace Memorial. These evening programs held on the monument plaza cover such topics as the past and present on Put-in-Bay, other Lake Erie islands, the War of 1812 and the Battle of Lake Erie, the building of the monument, Lake Erie, and the National Park Service. Talks on the islands and

the War of 1812 are given several times daily on the plaza. An open
house is held one evening each summer and is well attended. The
color-slide programs, first held in the town hall, began in 1957.

DOCKS

The majority of tourists traveling to Put-in-Bay come on the ferryboats or on the airplane from the mainland. There always have been
numbers of visitors who come in their own boats; they have been doing
so for one hundred years. After World War II there was an increase in
boating on Lake Erie. The small-boat owner can trail his boat from
inland cities and villages and launch it on the lakeshore for a cruise to
the islands. Owners of larger yachts harbor their craft in various mainland marinas and yacht clubs and drive back and forth between home
and club.

Sailors from the time of Oliver Hazard Perry and before have
anchored in the harbor of Put-in-Bay. Dockage facilities at the island
are limited inasmuch as the piers built for the steamboats and ferries
are not generally available to the yachtsman. The village park dock
can be used by boaters as well as some privately-owned docks. After
World War II the village expanded facilities and built a dock at the
west end of the park. A larger dock was constructed at the east end
in 1971. Both the village and the state provided funds for this new
wharf. Dockage is charged at these three facilities. There are also
several marinas where dock space can be rented. During the regatta
and weekends the docks are crowded with boats ranging in size
from fourteen feet to over fifty feet in length and numbers of sailboats and cruisers anchor in the bay close to Gibraltar as did Perry in 1813.

Put-in-Bay harbor provides a generally safe refuge for yachts
during severe storms. Although the craft may be safe from wind and
waves, they are subject to the danger of a rise in the water level of
five feet or more. This rise usually lasts less than twenty-four hours.
Boatsmen have to shift their vessels to other locations until the
water returns to normal. The level of Lake Erie in the fall, winter,
and spring of 1972/73/74 was the highest in the memory of the oldest
island residents.

On 14 November 1972 a severe storm swept over Lake Erie. All
the docks in the harbor area—Miller's, Crew's Nest, Doller's, the three
public docks, the Erie Isle dock, and the Perry monument grounds
were inundated. The people living on East Point could not drive
into the village because of flooding at the monument. Bay View Avenue
was impassable from the V. Doller Estate to Oak Point State Park
and the bridge over Smith's Pond was under water. There was exten-

sive erosion along much of the shoreline. The water pumping station and several cottages were damaged, some of the cottages irreparably. The state park and Lime Kiln docks in the lee of the wind were also flooded.

Another storm hit the island on St. Patrick's Day, 17 March 1973. There was general flooding although the water was not as high as the previous November. Still another storm came up during the night and day of 8-9 April 1973. The water level reached and exceeded that of Novempber 14, but the winds were not as strong. The fourth high-water period of 1973 occurred on 16-17 June when the water rose suddenly but remained high for only a few hours. The island again experienced periods of very high water in 1974. There were severe storms and flooding on 12, 28-29 March and 8 April.

An examination of Lake Survey bulletins reveals that Lake Erie had record-breaking high-water levels in 1886, 1952, and 1969, as well as in the recent 1972/73/74 floods. Low-water records established in 1934, 1935, and 1936.

Islanders who suffered flood and erosion damage to their property received federal aid in the form of grants and low-interest loans. Additional private funds had to be used to repair the eroded shoreline or wrecked buildings. The storms affected people not only in the island area but also thousands of persons living in the low-lying shoreline areas in the western end of Lake Erie.

3

"Wine Makes
the Heart of Man Happy"

OUR VINES HAVE TENDER GRAPES

Although the early settlers of Put-in-Bay raised wheat and other grains, brought in sheep and hogs, cut timber for steamboat fuel and for shipbuilding, they also noticed that wild grapes grew well on the Lake Erie islands. About 1842 Datus Kelley of Kelleys Island brought some Isabella and Catawba vines from Rockport, Ohio, where he formerly had lived and successfully planted the roots in his garden. Charles Carpenter, also on Kelleys Island, the first to set out an acre of grapes as a field crop, produced his first wine in 1850.

Grape culture did not start on Put-in-Bay until 1858 when Joseph de Rivera St. Jurgo, Philip Vroman, Louis Harms, and Lorenz Miller planted vines. Thus it can be said that the basis for the agricultural prosperity of the island dates from 1858 when the first grapes were planted and it was discovered that the combination of limestone soil and the lake climate was favorable to the grape culture.

A correspondent for the Sandusky paper wrote that Lorenz Miller got an unbelievable eight and one-fourth tons of Catawba grapes from one acre. This was twice the usual yield. Lorenz Anthony was paid $1,070 for grapes grown on seven-eighths of an acre. Land which had been selling for ten dollars an acre a decade before now sold, when in vineyard, for $1,500. The Sandusky *Daily Commercial Register* reported in July 1862 that "Put-in-Bay Island is improving with marvelous rapidity . . . The grape fever is striking root with all the intensity that it prevails on Kelleys Island." Louis Harms had four acres in full production, J. W. Gray put in seventeen, and Lorenz Anthony fifteen.

A total of seventy-four and one-half acres were planted on the Bass islands with fifty being on Put-in-Bay. Other islanders became grape growers: George Bickford, Casper Schmidt, Conrad Brookner, Chris

Brick, Lucas Meyer, Mattias Burggraf, Karl Ruh, Joseph Miller, William Rehberg, John Stone, Milan Holly, Wyman Dodge, and Valentine Doller. The grape industry was only beginning in 1862 with twenty-six and a half acres bearing a crop. Twenty years after the first plantings there were seventy-one grape growers on Put-in-Bay cultivating 550 acres of vineyard producing 1,231,000 pounds of grapes. The most popular grape was the Catawba with 393 acres; fifty-four were in Delaware, ninety in Concord, and twelve in such types as Ives, Norton, Clinton and others.

After experimentation with various methods the nineteenth century island grape grower planted his grapes in rows about eight feet apart with a space of four or five feet between the vines. Cedar posts were used to support the vines on wires strung from post to post. This system is used in Germany and France. Many of the island vineyard owners came from Germany although farming may not have been their original occupation. Grape picking began in late August and lasted into November. First to ripen were the Champion, Niagara, Wilder, Warden, Massasoit, Salem, Golden Pocklington, Noah, and Hartford grapes. Concord, Delaware, Norton, and Ives matured next. Last, and the greatest in acreage and value, was the Catawba which needed the island's long growing season to fully ripen. Even today the ripening grapes impart a delicious scent to the air near the vineyard.

Grapes were picked by hand, a procedure which required a large labor force. Every island resident who could be spared—man, woman, and child—went into the vineyards with a special pair of shears, a basket, and a small stool to pick grapes. Schoolchildren were given a two-week grape picking vacation in late September and early October so that they could be employed in the vineyards. Several pickers worked a row. Table grapes were packed in various-size baskets for shipment to mainland on the steamboats. Other grapes were pressed for the juice, some of which was sold as juice but much more was processed into excellent wines.

Once the frantic period of grape picking was over, work in the vineyards continued at a more leisurely pace. The vines required pruning, which was done in the fall and winter. Posts raised by the winter frost were driven back into the ground in the spring. Then came the tying of the vines. For the first tying, yellow willow shoots were used and, for the second, rye straw. There was always some plowing, gathering of brush, and spraying to do. Practically every bit of arable land on Put-in-Bay was used for grape growing. There were a few home gardens, some pasture and orchards, but to paraphrase a phrase, "The Grape was King."

The beginning grape grower purchased his vines from the mainland. An 1887 price list from a Dr. H. Schroeder, Bloomington, Illinois, quotes the following prices per 1,000 vines: Concord, Champion, Ives, and Isabella—one-year vines, $12, two-year, $25; Catawba—one-year, $22, two-year, $35; Niagara—one-year, $200, two-year, $250. Three-year vines were one-half more than two-year because they were closer to their crop-bearing period. About 1,000 vines per acre were planted in a vineyard.

WINERIES

At least a dozen islanders had press houses where the juice could be squeezed from the grapes. Some juice was sold as grape juice with a preservative added to retard fermentation. Most of the juice, however, was processed into various types of wines—sweet, semisweet, and dry. At one time there were five distilleries for the manufacture of Catawba brandy; none are in operation today.

There were a number of small wine cellars on Put-in-Bay. One such cellar was that of Lungren and Rotert whose advertisement stated that they grew forty varieties of grapes on twenty-four acres. The cellar was a three-story masonry building having a capacity of 30,000 gallons of wine. This cellar also shipped table grapes to Boston, New York City, and as far away as Kansas and Nebraska. The site of the winery was at the present Skyway Lodge on Langram Road. The Henry Pfeiffer cellar, with twelve acres in vineyard, had a capacity of 25,000 to 30,000 gallons. Schraidt's Wine House and Garden advertised that it served "native wines, ice cream, cobblers, mineral waters and ginger ale" thus pleasing those who enjoyed the nectar of the grape and those who preferred a nonalcoholic drink.

The largest winery on the island was the Put-in-Bay Wine Company, which had a capacity of 150,000 gallons. It was organized in August 1871 with a capital of $100,000. The incorporators were W. E. Sibley, Captain Amander Moore, Joseph M. Beckstead, Valentine Doller, and Fred Rotert. Sixteen years later on 24 January 1888 the winery was totally destroyed by fire. A worker started a fire in an office and then went down to the cellar to clean wine casks. One of the island schools was on the hill just above the winery and some of the students noticed flames coming through the roof near the chimney and gave the alarm. The village fire engine—a hand pumper—was rushed to the scene but was of little use. The winery was too far away, a half-mile from the lake, for water to be pumped on the fire. The winery did furnish its own fire-quenching liquid. Huge wine casks burst and thousands of gallons of wine flowed into ditches; the wine was pumped onto the blaze but to no avail. The loss was estimated at $65,000. Only 75,000 to 80,000 gallons of wine were in storage at the time. A distillery was in a separate building and was not damaged. The officers of the company in 1888 were Philip Vroman,

J. S. Gibbens, Valentine Doller of Put-in-Bay, and George Whitney of Sandusky. About forty island-grape growers and businessmen suffered losses with the destruction of the cellar. Cooper's Restaurant was built on the site of the old winery after World War II.

Thomas H. Langlois in *South Bass Island and Islanders* lists the date of arrival and economic activity of residents from 1811 through 1945. For the period 1811 to 1900, 195 persons are listed, of whom sixty-seven are grape growers or grape growers and wine makers. Included in the list are semipermanent and summer residents such as Jay Cooke, hotel employees, the doctor, the teachers and preachers, and others who could not be considered as islanders. About thirty persons could be placed in this latter group as of 1899. The list is not a census, just a listing of occupation. One cannot tell whether the individual is single or married with a family. It does serve to point out that almost half of the wage earners for the period 1858-1899 were engaged in the grape and wine industry. The period 1900-1945 shows only four persons who regarded themselves as newly-arrived grape growers. Of course, many of the older vineyard owners were still in business but the rush to grow grapes was over. There were 103 heads of households named in this latter listing and forty-one were semipermanent or summer inhabitants.

The fame of the island grapes and wine spread rapidly in the 1880s and annual production reached 1,500,000 pounds. Shortly after the turn of the century both a reduction in production and acreage was noted. Eight tons of grapes per acre was recorded in the earliest days although four tons was the average yield. In 1890 there were six hundred acres of land out a total island area of 1,382 in grape production. By 1930 there were less than three hundred acres.

The island location of the grape growers worked to their disadvantage. Grapes and wine could be shipped easily and cheaply by steamboat to lake port cities such as Sandusky, Toledo, Cleveland, and Detroit, but shipment to inland cities meant an additional handling of the merchandise. Competing grape growers and wine makers in Michigan, New York, and even California could send their products directly to the market by train, and later, by truck.

ONE SIP TOO MANY

Put-in-Bay began developing as a summer resort about the same time that the vineyard industry got its start on the island. A big celebration commemorating the forty-fifth anniversary of the Battle of Lake Erie was held in September 1858, the same year de Rivera St. Jurgo, Vroman, Harms, and Miller planted their first grape vines. Access to the island was by steamboat. The tourist could get away from the city for a few hours or days. Once on the island the nine-teenth-century visitor toured the caves, the museum, bowling alleys, and billiard rooms. Warm summer days invited the sampling of locally-produced wines or other alcoholic beverages. Those not so inclined could quench their thirst at a Tuft's soda fountain.

An occasional visitor, then as now, imbibed too well of the fermented juice of the grape as reported by the Sandusky *Daily Register* in 1892, "A man who had on a very heavy load of booze at Put-in-Bay yesterday (July 12) tried to whip all the deck hands of the steamers along the docks. The men turned a stream of water on him . . . and after he had been thoroughly washed he was locked up by the village marshal."

Vacationers were not the only ones to worship at the altar of Bacchus. Some islanders sampled the product of the vineyard too freely and were put on a blacklist, usually by an irate wife but in one case a father blacklisted his son. The official form went thus:

> Personally appeared before me, F. W. Burggraf, Township Clerk, . . ., a resident of Put-in-Bay, Ottawa County, Ohio, who under oath says: That her husband . . . is a habitual drinker, and she therefore demands that no one shall sell, give or otherwise convie [sic] to cause him to obtain any intoxicating drink of whatever nature, the same being prescribed by law. (signed) . . . In the presence of John Rehberg, William Schnoor. F. W. Burggraf, Town-ship Clerk, July 15, 1910, 8:30 o'clock A.M.

Later the clerk received a note, "Mr. Burggraf: Take . . . name off the list this morning and we will pay you your time, Mrs. . . ., Sept. 14, 1910." Then at the beginning of the next summer,

> June 22, 1911, F. W. Burggraf, Township Clerk, Dear Sir: I want you to go to every saloon and wine cellar owner on the island and have . . . put on the blacklist, and tell them that they will be prosecuted if they give or sell him any intoxicating liquors. Please do this immediately. Yours truly, Mrs. . . .

From the records it would appear that the errant husband could not withstand the temptations of the numerous saloons which were in operation during the summer. The summer hotels and taverns were closed during the winter but there were some establishments that catered to the local residents all year round.

PROBLEMS—COMPETITION AND PROHIBITION

The grape growers and wine makers of the Bass islands continued to enjoy the good times which began during the Civil War; however, the twentieth century brought problems which many of them could not solve. Island-produced grapes and wines had to compete with the large wineries in Sandusky, Toledo, and Cincinnati. A grape growers cooperative was set up in 1906 and for several years operated at a profit. Growing more ambitious, the locally-owned Bass Island Vineyard Company built a winery at Sandusky and sold stock to outsiders. The new venture failed. The winery eventually became the property of the Meier Wine Company of Silverton.

As far as the crops were concerned, the years 1921-1924 were good, Catawba grapes brought $100 per ton to the farmer. Prohibition was in effect and wineries could not legally make wine so many of them suspended operation. A few continued to produce grape juice and were allowed to make sacramental wine for religious use.

Surprisingly, there was a market for unfermented grape juice. The Lonz Winery at Middle Bass sold 100,000 gallons of juice a year, sometimes as much as 20,000 gallons at one time. Grape juice was shipped as far away as Utah and Florida. Playwright George S. Kaufman bought island grape juice. Wine fanciers whose supply was cut off by Prohibition did not really switch their tastes to grape juice. They knew that untreated juice would, in time, ferment and become wine. It was not a violation of the Volstead Act for wineries to press grapes and sell unfermented grape juice. Printed instructions were give to the buyer as to what to do if the juice, unfortunately, started fermenting before it was consumed.

DIRECTIONS

Immediately upon receiving Grape Juice, enough should be taken out of the barrel and put into another container to allow room for sugar to be added, also water if so desired. Keg or barrel should not be more than 9/10 full, or some of the juice will work out of the top of the barrel and thus be wasted.

Sugar should be added dissolved in warm water. Not more than **one gallon of water should be used to each three pounds of sugar.** We find that most of our customers use one pound of sugar to each gallon of grape juice, if you wish a more sour juice use less sugar, if a sweeter use more. The Bung hole must be left open until the juice is thru fermenting unless a fermenting bung is used. After fermentation keg or barrel should be corked tight and opened only when some juice is drawn out.

The usual time it takes to ferment is about three weeks. Juice may be taken out at any time without injury to remaining contents as long as keg or barrel is immediately corked up again. Juice will ferment much faster if it is warm; therefore do not put same in too cool a place until it has fermented. However, when thru fermenting it should be kept in a fairly cool place.

It is not absolutely safe to bottle juice until about the following May. [The juice as purchased in the fall]

Grape growers shipped grapes in baskets to the markets but the profit had been in wine. Fourteen island-viniculturists struggled along during Prohibition, most of them eventually giving up and abandoning their vineyards.

Although the manufacture, sale, and transportation of alcoholic beverages in the United States was banned by the Prohibition Act, Americans were not to be denied liquor, beer, or wine. Various types of spirits could be made at home, i.e. "bath tub" gin or American-made whiskey and beer served in speakeasies. Another source was foreign produced liquor and beer. Americans in foreign countries could buy any quantity they wished. They broke the law only when they crossed the international boundary and entered the United States.

Put-in-Bay is only eight miles by boat from Middle Island, an islet just across the border in Canada, ten miles from Pelee Island, Ontario, and twenty-eight miles from Kingsville on the Canadian mainland. Yachtsmen on their way to Canada stopped at Put-in-Bay to refuel and rest before proceeding beyond the American borders. On the return trip, if they had contraband on board, they could be intercepted by the Coast Guard when they crossed the line into the United States. Docked and on land, they risked arrest by customs agents if they had illegal alcohol in their possession. The enforcement officers had to seize a boat with the liquor still aboard. If seizure seemed imminent, the crew threw the evidence overboard. There are many cases of well-aged Canadian whiskey at the bottom of Lake Erie.

Put-in-Bay was not unlike many other American communities during the Prohibition era. Alcoholic potables were available to the tourist and native alike. Some islanders might conceal a small keg of grape juice in a dark corner of the basement. The juice, unfortunately, would begin to ferment. Beer lovers made potent home brew. The homemade product was usually destined for personal consumption although in the depression years any source that would produce an extra dollar or two was welcome. Whiskey and beer could be obtained surreptitiously from the nearby Canadian islands.

REPEAL BUT LIMITED REVIVAL

The repeal of the Eighteenth Amendment in 1933 did not bring back the "good old days." There was a demand for whiskey and beer but the taste for wine did not return and the country was in the midst of the Great Depression. Vineyards untended for thirteen years, unused presses, and old skills forgotten were other handicaps for the Ohio grape grower. Norman Heineman, Roy Webster, and Fred Cooper continued to operate wineries on Put-in-Bay; the other grape growers sold out.

Those establishments which had stayed in business by pressing grape juice had maintained their vineyards and equipment. Yet the small, family-operated wineries faced competition from the larger Ohio concerns as well as out-of-state wineries. Also, the federal and state regulations were much stricter. In addition, all Ohio wineries faced a challenge from the huge wineries of California whose products were widely and expensively advertised and were sold for less than that of the small wineries.

During World War II grain was required for food and the manufacture of explosives, so the production of hard liquor was restricted and wine became moderately popular spurring the cultivation of grapes. Engels and Krudwig Wine Company of Sandusky bought about 300 acres on Put-in-Bay and put the old vineyards back into production. The company sold its island holdings to the Lonz Winery in 1973.

Fred Cooper had planted grapes which were just beginning to bear when Prohibition went into effect but he stayed in business, pressing out grapes for juice. He was the first islander to get a license to produce wine after repeal. In 1946 Cooper and his sons, Gustav and Edward, built a new winery and restaurant on the site of the old Put-in-Bay Wine Company cellars. The restaurant opened in May 1947 and is still in operation. The winery was closed in 1955. Charles and Mary Lou Fleming bought the restaurant at the end of the 1973 season.

Roy Webster also owned vineyards and a winery on the south end of South Bass. He converted the old Andrew Schiele residence into a restaurant—the Castle Inn—and after many years in the business sold the restaurant but continued as a wine maker. After his death in 1958, the company continued operations for seven years before finally closing in 1965. The Castle Inn was sold to Wilbur E. Holley and George Putz at a sherriff's sale in 1973 and became a private residence once again.

HEINEMAN WINERY

Gustav Heineman came to the United States from Baden, Germany, in the 1880s, worked in the vineyards, and bought his own vineyard in 1896. He built a winery building in 1901 on the site of the Crystal Cave. That structure was replaced by a separate winery and salesroom after World War II. Heineman Winery is the only winery still in business on Put-in-Bay.

Heineman Winery produces ten different wines from five varieties of island-grown grapes; Concord, Catawba, Delaware, Niagara, and Ives. Sauterne wine, moderately sweet, is a blend of Catawba and Niagara grapes; Sweet Belle is a proprietary wine unique to Heineman's and is their best seller; the Claret is a bit drier than their Burgundy; Rosé is modrately sweet; Delaware, Sweet Concord, and Dry, Pink, or Sweet

Catawba are varietal wines, that is, made from a specific variety of grape. Concord and Catawba grape juice are also bottled.

Grape growing methods have changed over the years. The earlier yield per acre declined from an average of four tons to two and one-half tons. The present yield, using different methods of cultivation, pruning, and the use of insecticides and fertilizers, is five to six tons per acre. The old willow shoot and straw ties to support the vines have been replaced by thin wire and twine ties. Tractors have taken the place of horses. Although grapes are still picked by hand on Put-in-Bay, Meier's Wine Company uses mechanical pickers on North Bass. The Heineman Winery founded by Gustav Heineman passed to his son, Norman, and is now under the management of a grandson Louis. The cellar produces about 30,000 gallons of wine and grape juice a year.

MIDDLE AND NORTH BASS VINEYARDS

Middle Bass has two producing wineries. Lonz Winery dates back to 1884 and has a capacity of 150,000 gallons. It is built on the site of the old Wehrle, Werk and Sons winery which had a capacity of 500,000 gallons. The winery is now owned by Philip A. Porteus of Toledo and is the third largest in Ohio. Still a family operation, the much smaller Bretz Winery was founded in 1867. Lonz and Bretz make champagne as well as still wines.

Meier's Wine Cellars of Silverton own 570 acres on North Bass (area 740 acres) and have 350 acres under cultivation; 80 percent of the crop is in Catawba grapes. No wine is made at North Bass, processing is done at Silverton near Cincinnati.

The future of Ohio wineries is bright. There are now twenty-two wineries producing 4,000,000 gallons annually, and American wine consumption has risen to an average of two gallons per person per year, four times that of fifty years ago but far below the thirty-gallon rate of the French.

GRAPE FESTIVALS

The Put-in-Bay Chamber of Commerce sponsored the first grape festival in 1948 and festivals were held annually, except for 1958 and 1959, through 1960. The event celebrated the beginning of the grape harvest and usually took place the weekend after Labor Day. There were free samples of wine and grape juice, a stage show, band concerts, street dances, and various games. A Put-in-Bay High School girl was crowned Grape Festival Queen. The first queen was Barbara Traverso, followed by Jo Ann Zura, Audrey Klopp, Paula Webster, Betty Ann Parker, Sonya Market, and Irene Hales.

4

Island Education

THE FIRST SCHOOL

After he had built his home, planted his crops, and settled down to the hard life of the frontier, the pioneer Ohioan thought of the education of his numerous children. Some schooling was necessary if the children were to read the Holy Bible and conduct such business affairs as their small farms required. The island settlers were no different from their mainland cousins in this respect. The islanders had to go to mainland to vote (the Bass islands were in Van Rensselaer Township). When Philip Vroman, along with two others, went to cast his ballot in 1844, he was appointed school director for the three islands. There was no school at Put-in-Bay at the time.

The first schoolhouse was built by Vroman in 1855 in the center of the main part of the island on land donated by Joseph de Rivera St. Jurgo. It was located near the junction of Mitchell Road and Catawba Avenue on the hill above the present Cooper's restaurant. Vroman also built a wood-frame school on North Bass in 1857.

A. I. Jones, the first teacher, had about a dozen pupils enrolled in his classes but only about a half-dozen attended school with any regularity. Once when Director Vroman inspected the school, he found that his son, Daniel, was the only student in class! The building was modestly equipped with large desks and benches, some chairs, a few textbooks, and no blackboard. There were winter and summer terms, usually of four and three-months' duration. Rose Neader taught the 1852 summer term.

After Put-in-Bay Township was organized in 1861, a school district was established for the three islands—South, Middle, and North Bass in 1863, and a board of directors composed of John Stone, Valentine Doller, Philip Vroman, Alexander Hitchcock of Put-in-Bay, and Simon Fox of North Bass was chosen. The board met in the spring and fall to decide on school policy, bond issues, and tax levies.

As the school population grew, the need for a larger building arose. The old small building was sold and moved away. The township provided the funds for the new school, popularly called "The school on the hill."

Even the new school was soon filled to capacity and the newly-constructed St. Paul's Episcopal Church was used as a temporary school. Space was rented in the church basement and a Mr. Gorem taught classes there for which tuition was charged. Some of the wealthier parents took their children from the regular school and sent them to Mr. Gorem. This was done so that there would be room in the public school for those children whose parents could not or would not pay tuition. The church school was equipped with small desks and little red chairs.

EAST POINT SCHOOL

In order to relieve the pressure on the school on the hill and perhaps because it was a two and one-half mile walk for some children living on East Point, a second school was put in operation on that part of the island in the 1860s. The East Point School Board was organized on 15 April 1867 and L. R. Webster, Lawrence Miller, and Charles Ruh were the initial board members.

The first classes, begun in December 1868, were taught by L. F. Webster for a four-month term in a log cabin furnished by Louis Harms. Harriet Haskins taught the summer term, a three-month period beginning 21 June 1869. Haskins held classes in a shed. Omri Webster was engaged for a three-month term and offered to teach an additional month without pay if the board would furnish fuel for the stove.

The East Point school had a winter term—December 1 to April 1—and a summer term—May 1 to September 15—with a two-week vacation in the first part of July. The periods when there was no school coincided with the grape tying and picking seasons, allowing the children to work in the vineyards.

The Board of Education of Put-in-Bay Township bought one-eighth acre of land each from Charles Ruh and Louis Harms on East Point. The deeds, dated 16 October 1869, had some interesting clauses. The land was to be used for educational purposes only, not for religious or church purposes; the board was to erect and maintain a five-foot high picket fence, and the grantors had the privilege of buying back the land for the original price of $25. This last clause was a source of irritation when the East Point school property was sold in 1918.

The Put-in-Bay Township Board of Education made the required report to the State Board of Education in 1868 and disclosed the following information. A total of forty-three pupils were enrolled in school on the three islands, average daily attendance was twenty-five. They went to school five days a week during a twenty-five week session studying such texts as the McGuffey Reader, Webster Speller, Spencer Handwriting, Ray Arithmetic, Brown Grammar, and Monheath Geography. The male teachers received $31.66 a month and the women teachers $19.89!

THE SCHOOL ON THE HILL

A new school building was needed and the original plot donated by de Rivera St. Jurgo in 1855 was not large enough, so he again gave land "to build a schoolhouse and to be used for public and gratuitous education and for no other purposes whatsoever." He gave three-fourths of an acre adjacent to the 1855 grant. The deed was recorded on 30 July 1878. The new school was called the Central School by the board but was more popularly known as "the school on the hill."

A SPECIAL SCHOOL DISTRICT

The population of South Bass grew rapidly after 1860, and the two schools were brought under common management with the creation in 1880 of the Special Put-in-Bay School District. The District included not only South Bass but the smaller, nearby Ballast, Rattlesnake, Gibraltar, Buckeye, and Starve islands. Children from Rattlesnake, Ballast, and Gibraltar have always attended school at Put-in-Bay. The other islets are too small to support a permanent population.

The district report for that year now listed 112 students with an average monthly attendance of 111 in the two schoolhouses (three classrooms) for the thirty-six-week session. The one male teacher was paid $65 per month and the two women $40.

Valentine Doller headed the school board in 1880; Dr. C. H. J. Linskey was clerk, and Charles Ruh was the other member. Various improvements were made as time went on. The board purchased the first encyclopaedia in 1882; German was added to the curriculum in 1890; and a ten-month term was adopted for the 1890-1891 school year. A fence was built around the school in 1880; in 1885 a boy was paid to carry drinking water to the building, but he lost his job in 1888 when a well was drilled at a cost of $235. Financial problems arose in 1890 and the island citizens responded by subscribing $165 to keep the school operating.

JOEL C. OLDT

Joel C. Oldt came to teach at Put-in-Bay in August 1890 and remained for eighteen years. The school session began on August fourth but the building needed cleaning because repairs had been made. Island help was not available because the islanders were at work in the resort hotels. Oldt managed to clean one room over a Saturday and Sunday and opened for classes on August fifth. He had been hired to teach algebra, so he assumed that there would be other teachers on the faculty. Eighty-two students registered that day, and Oldt found himself to be the one and only teacher in the entire school.

To make matters worse, Le Roy Webster, a board member, told him that the board was bankrupt because of the repairs and would not receive any money from the county auditor until October. Oldt had less than ten dollars in his pocket! More problems plagued the new teacher; school was closed from the end of September to the middle of November for the grape- and fruit-picking vacation. The board secured a loan and paid Oldt his salary for two months—$120. He went back to college to take a business course for seven weeks. The board hired two other teachers and Oldt returned to the island and did not leave until 1908. He also served as mayor as well as superintendent of schools. It was under his management that the school was graded, a high school established, and the first high school graduation ceremony held in 1895.

The number of pupils enrolled in the school for the years 1890 through 1895 averaged 151 with the average daily attendance about thirty students fewer. There were two pupils in high school in 1892, seven in 1893, eighteen in 1894, and twenty-five in 1895 when one student was graduated.

The Board of Education maintained two schools and employed a faculty of four: one high school teacher at $64 per month, one male elementary teacher at $40, and two women elementary teachers at $38. The elementary faculty taught a thirty-nine week session and the high school a forty-week one.

The 1895 curriculum included the basic courses of Reading, Writing, Spelling, Language, Geography, and History and had been expanded to include high school subjects: American and English Literature, United States and World History, Algebra, Geometry and Trigonometry, Botany, Zoology, Geology, Physical Geography, Astronomy, Chemistry, Civil Government, Political Economy, Drawing and Mechanical Drawing, Rhetoric and Ethics, Music, Latin, and German. Students could select the German course at a textbook cost of $15.36 for the high school years or the Latin course at $18.45 for the same period.

Matthias Burggraf was president of the Board of Education in 1895. Other members were: Edward Keimer, clerk; Philip Vroman, treasurer; and E. J. Dodge. The school faculty consisted of Joel C. Oldt, superintendent; Mrs. Adelaide Babcock; Lillie Doller; William V. Lamb; and the first graduate of the Put-in-Bay High School, George J. Linskey. Adam Heidle was truant officer

THE FIRST GRADUATE

The first annual commencement of the Put-in-Bay High School was held on a Saturday evening, 29 June 1895, in the town hall. The awarding of the diploma was preceded by a number of student recitations. Orators and orations presented were: Mary M. Linskey, "Honesty is the Best Policy"; Ollie J. Morrison, "The Yosemite"; Tena Herbster, "The Old Man Goes to Town"; May Brady, "Handsome is that Handsome Does"; Madge M. Connors, "On Board the Cumberland, March 7, 1862"; Mina Bickford, "Filled Is Life's Goblet to the Brim"; Inez Dodge, "The Death of Leonidas"; and, reflecting the Germanic origin of many of the islanders, Annie Keimer with "Des Saengers Fluch." Susie Brown read the class history and Jay C. Idlor the class prophecy. The lone graduate, George J. Linskey, then gave the valedictory address, "Upward," and was presented with his diploma by J. C. Oldt. The Reverend W. C. Sheppard gave the benediction and Lucy Rittman closed the program with "The Addenda." Graduate Linskey was given a set of James Fenimore Cooper's works, *Webster's* Unabridged Dictionary, and Emerson's *Essays* by friends.

EAST POINT SCHOOL CLOSED

The Board of Education continued to operate the school on East Point, although some of the parents of the children were not satisfied with the short seven-month term. William Breither, Henry Burggraf, H. V. Warren, S. W. Downing, Robert Shortliff, and G. F. Ingold petitioned the board in 1901 to "continue our school . . . without vacation and extend the school term four weeks." The board accepted the suggestion and Leila Ennes was hired to teach the extra month. She was rehired for the 1901-1902 school year for a nine-month term at $35 per month.

The operation of a separate building on East Point required additional funds for maintenance and the teacher's salary. In 1904 the board decided that the East Point children should attend the school on the hill and that transportation would be provided during the winter months. They specified that a fifteen-passenger closed wagon be used and that blankets be available to cover the children. Bids were sought, and George E. Gascoyne was awarded a contract to bus the children from 14 November 1904 to 14 April 1905 for a fee of $129. The students arrived at school at 8:15 A.M. and left for home at 3:30 P.M. In the fall and spring the children walked to school.

The transportation of the East Point students continued through the year 1918. Financial difficulties in 1910 almost caused the cancellation of busing but it survived on a reduced schedule—a twelve-week period instead of the previous twenty. Gascoyne was the successful bidder, except in 1913 when L. E. Schraidt won on a bid of $90 for the January 13 to April 7 period. When there was sufficient snow in the winter, a sleigh was used instead of the wagon.

With the East Point children attending the school on the hill, the second schoolhouse was no longer needed. The board sought to sell it in 1914, but the bids received were too low. Also, they discovered that according to the terms of the deed, the original owners of the land or their assigns had to be given the first chance to buy the property back at the 1869 price.

The board could rent the land and building for a limited period, which they did. John Lay of the Port Clinton Fish Company leased the building for two years with the understanding that the structure was to be removed at the end of the lease. After some delay the schoolhouse was moved to the present Lime Kiln dock in 1919 and used to store fishnets. It was torn down when the concrete and steel ferry dock was built. It wasn't until 1927 that the East Point school lot was returned to the adjoining property holders, William and Henry Gram, Marie Ruh Oelschlager, and Herman Ruh.

OLDT RESIGNS

Superintendent Joel C. Oldt made his last report to the school board in 1908. The school had two schoolhouses, the one on the hill and the shuttered East Point school. A faculty of two men and two women taught a thirty-six-week school year. There were eighty-seven elementary students and twenty-four in high school for a total of 111. Oldt submitted his resignation 14 August 1908, and R. J. Alber was hired to succeed him as superintendent.

The school was in financial difficulty in 1910 as witnessed by the forced reduction in the busing of the East Point students. This was done to avoid an additional school tax. Only one teacher taught in the high school, and some classes were doubled up. Superintendent Alber suggested that the Chemistry and Physics courses be dropped from the curriculum because of the lack of equipment or of a separate classroom. The board further economized by hiring only three teachers, instead of the usual four. Four teachers were hired in 1913, but the school term was reduced to eight months. The Island Drama Club, directed by T. B. Alexander, offered to give two plays in September and October with the proceeds applied to school repairs. The board accepted the offer.

GRAPE-PICKING VACATION

Since the principal agricultural pursuit on the island was grape growing, a large labor force was needed to pick grapes in the fall and to tie the vines in the spring. For this reason, the school children were given vacations so that they could be employed in the vineyards. This practice continued through the nineteenth century and into the twentieth. According to the records of the Board of Education, the year 1911 was the last year that a spring grape-tying vacation was allowed. Grape picking began in October and extended into November for a two week-period. The actual starting date varied depending on when the grapes matured. The last grape-picking vacation began on 8 October 1928. Grape production was adversely affected by Prohibition, and later, by the Depression, and a large labor force was no longer needed.

ISLAND SCHOOL ROUTINE

When Superintendent B. E. Koonce made his monthly report to the board in December 1914, there were sixty elementary and twenty high school students enrolled. The curriculum included the usual Reading, Writing, Arithmetic, History, and Science courses. New courses such as Shorthand, Typing, and Bookkeeping had been introduced to meet the needs of a commercial America.

Pictures of the old-time schools often show the potbellied stove, which not too efficiently warmed the room. The school on the hill was a typical old-time school in this respect. The sanitary facilities were out back. Wood for heating could be obtained on the island but coal had to be shipped across the lake from Sandusky. A typical fuel bill was the statement of 15 June 1910 of the C. A. Nielsen Coal Company, Sandusky:

61,824 lbs Egg Hard coal @ $5.65 per ton	$174.65
FOB Capt. Dodge Lighter	
Interest on above for two months	1.75
	$176.40

Additional expenses were incurred. E. J. Dodge was paid fifty cents a ton for lake transportation from Sandusky to Put-in-Bay, and the V. Doller Estate (Put-in-Bay Dock Company) received seventy-five cents a ton for dockage and delivery to the school. The total cost of the coal was $6.90 per ton, making it more costly for the island schools than for the mainland schools which did not have the lake freight and dockage charges to pay. Various island and mainland companies bid on supplying the school. Among them were the C. A. Nielsen Company of Sandusky,

Put-in-Bay Dock Company, E. J. Dodge, and Nicholas Fox and Sons of Put-in-Bay. The Put-in-Bay school has converted to an oil-fired furnace in recent times, but fuel oil still has to be brought from the mainland.

In 1898 the opening of school was delayed because a few cases of smallpox were discovered among the black employees at the Hotel Victory. Classes did not begin until September 26. The board had Dr. A. A. Hessell fumigate the school in 1908; in 1915 it recommended that all children be vaccinated when a case of smallpox was found on the island.

The nation-wide influenza epidemic which followed World War I had its effect on Put-in-Bay when the school was closed in December 1918 for several weeks. The board sent letters to the parents suggesting that the students study "out of school hours," and the high school pupils met on Saturday morning after school had resumed to make up lost time. Classes had to be shut down again for two weeks in March 1920 because of illness.

A NEW SCHOOL

The wood-frame school on the hill was many years old and lacked adequate facilities for the teaching of Chemistry and Physics when the board passed a resolution in 1913 recommending that a new four-room building be erected at a cost of $16,000. No action was taken on the resolution. The board appointed a committee in 1919 to promote a new school and to select a site within the village limits. The old school was in the township section of South Bass Island and would be abandoned.

A special election was held in June 1919 to vote on a bond issue for the school. Funds in the amount of $25,000 were required to purchase the site, build and equip the school, and provide a playground for the children. The issue passed with a vote of eighty-four yeas and forty nays. The site selected was on the corner of Catawba and Concord avenues within the corporation line which meant that village water and sewerage facilities were available. Property was purchased from W. T. Tyler for $1,100 and from Margaret Fuchs for $300. Later, in 1928, a miniscule bit—three hundredths of an acre—was acquired from Matthias Ingold.

J. A. Feick of Sandusky was awarded the general contract to build the two-story brick school. Feick's bid of $23,850 in September 1919 did not cover the expense of electrical wiring or heating and plumbing equipment, so an additional bond issue of $5,000 was needed to complete the school.

Construction on the building began 1 May 1921 and was completed by 1 October 1921. G. E. Scott was the architect. The school contained ten rooms—classrooms, an office, restrooms, science laboratory, and a library.

A dedicatory program was held in the town hall on Friday, 14 October 1921. Addresses were given by S. M. Johannsen, president of the Board of Education; A. O. Dehn, County Superintendent; Superintendent A. B. Lynn; Principal Raymond Truscott; Henry Fox; Mayor T. B. Alexander; and in behalf of the students, Myra Anton. The Reverend I. F. Jones and the Reverend Joseph E. Maerder gave the invocation and benediction. An inspection of the new school preceeded the program.

School began in the old building on 6 September 1921 because the new school was not yet completed, but the children were able to move to the new facilitiy after grape-picking vacation ended in October. The old school on the hill was sold to John Feick in September 1921 on a high bid of $2,500.

A class of three seniors was graduated from the new school in 1922. Leona Keimer [Brown] was valedictorian; Edwin Smith, salutatorian; and Edmond Miller, the third member of the class. Leona Keimer's address was entitled "Heroes of Yesterday"; Edwin Smith and Edmond Miller also gave brief speeches. The class address was given by the Honorable George T. Morris, and S. M. Johannsen awarded the diplomas.

The 1922 Board of Education consisted of S. M. Johannsen, presient; George A. Fox, vice-president; Jobe Parker; John Rehberg; William Kiinzler; and Frank Fuchs, clerk. On the Put-in-Bay school faculty were Superintendent A. B. Lynn, Principal Raymond Truscott, Edna Esselbach, and Margaret Webster [Fox].

The boys' basketball team of 1922 was given a banquet in the new school in April and six boys—the entire team—were awarded letters. The six so honored were: Edwin Smith, Carl Keimer, Anthony Kindt, Edward Market, George Stoecker, and Robert Parker. The team had to travel by boat to play their opposition, or the visitors, in turn, came to Put-in-Bay by boat. Put-in-Bay beat Kelleys Island twice, won against Port Clinton, then lost to Port Clinton, and lost to the Sandusky Business College.

The girls' team, eight members, defeated Kelleys Island and Sandusky Business College. On the way to Kelleys Island by boat the regulars on the girls' team got seasick, and the substitutes played the first half and were losing 8-4 when the regulars recovered sufficiently to come in and win 9-8. Weather is still a problem. Once in a while the team has to cancel a game because bad weather prevents the plane from flying to mainland or to one of the other islands.

The course of study had not changed appreciably; German was no longer taught, being replaced by French. Students still struggled with Caesar, Cicero, and Virgil in the Latin classes. The Home Economics course gave the girls a chance to practice their homemaking skills. Literature, History, Civics, Science, and Mathematics continued to provide a base for a sound education in the Put-in-Bay High School.

A lack of funds caused the school to close at the end of eight and one-half months in 1924. The students were rehearsing a musical comedy when the classes came to an abrupt end on May 18. They continued rehearsals and presented the play, "College Days," in the town hall May 23. Twenty-six students and adults were involved in the production. The school does not have an auditorium, so the commencement programs, school plays, and indoor sports activities are usually held in the town hall.

STUDENTS FROM OTHER ISLANDS

The Put-in-Bay Special School District has had a high school since 1891. All twelve grades, elementary and high school, are housed in the brick building on Catawba Avenue. Middle and North Bass islands have elementary schools only. Prior to 1926, Middle and North Bass students had to pass the Boxwell examination to qualify for tuition-free admission to any Ohio high school. At times, the state paid toward the board of students attending school on the mainland. Some children had relatives on mainshore, but others could not go to high school because their parents could not afford to pay room and board. Rattlesnake Island has no school, but is in the Special District. Early in the twentieth century the Hammond children from that island were taken in a rowboat to school at Put-in-Bay. The rowing distance between Rattlesnake Island and Peach Point where they landed is just under one and three-fourths miles. Lake storms kept them out of school occasionally. Many students from the other two Bass islands attended school on the mainland, but now most of them come to Put-in-Bay.

The school boards at Middle and North Bass pay tuition for their students enrolled at Put-in-Bay. The charge for the 1926-1927 year was $12 per month per pupil. The present rate is $51.67. Victor McNeely was the first North Bass student to go to Put-in-Bay High School but left after three and one-half months. Elizabeth Kuemmel [Parker] was the first Middle Bass pupil to complete a full year at Put-in-Bay in 1927-1928.

The students returned home by boat during the navigation season. In the wintertime the mail carrier took them to Middle Bass or returned them to Put-in-Bay. One winter, Elizabeth Parker recalls, she drove back and forth over the ice between the islands in a Model T. Ford for about two or three weeks. That mode of transportation was used only when the ice was heavy enough to support a car.

Students from the other islands came to Put-in-Bay by boat; they stayed with relatives or roomed at a boarding house. With the coming of inter-island air transportation it is now possible for the students to commute daily from Middle and North Bass and Rattlesnake Island. The State Board of Education reimburses the local board for transportation expenses. Usually about a half-dozen students from the other islands commute to school at Put-in-Bay. Their bus is usually a modern single-engine Cessna airplane although the vintage Ford Trimotor could be used. Should they be fogged-in, arrangements have been made for over-night lodging at Put-in-Bay. Sometimes fog or other weather conditions keep them at home, thus providing the boys and girls with the most unusual excuse for missing classes, "Sorry, teacher, but the weather kept the plane grounded."

THE CLASS OF '42

Joel C. Oldt left the island in 1908 but came back to deliver the class address at the commencement program in 1942. It was one of the larger classes in school history: nine graduates awaited their diplomas— Dorothy Anna Fox, Richard W. Vroman, Edward N. Cooper, Margaret E. Fuchs, Lawrence W. Reinhard, Arthur J. Traverso, Jane Webster, Richard Sampson, and Wayne F. Ingold. Oldt gave the class address, "Looking," and Board President Eugene Ingold awarded the diplomas. All the men of the class of 1942 and one faculty member, William Dean Cochran, served in World War II. One graduate, Richard Sampson, was killed in action during a naval engagement in the Pacific.

ISLAND EDUCATION IN THE '70s

The Board of Education usually has no difficulty in finding teachers for the island school. The class load is light, island life is appealing, and the men have an opportunity to go fishing almost at will. Some, however, do not stay long. C. W. Codding liked Put-in-Bay, but resigned to accept a more advanced position; Helen Pennell left to teach in a school nearer her home; Mary E. Frantz, in a letter dated on 5 November 1928, asked to be released stating that she had no social life and was in poor health.

The board does not always have to go to mainland to secure teachers. Fourteen islanders who attended the local school have returned to teach for varying periods of time. They were: Lillie Doller, George J. Linskey, Mary A. Rittman, Leila Ennes, Edna Esselbach, Edith Schiele Herbster, Ruth Webster Hallock, Margaret Webster Fox, Verda Herbster Jenkins, Justine Heineman Bianchi, Jane Webster Garofolo, Linda Crowe Frederick, Robert J. Dodge, and Edwin J. Market who served twenty years in the army, then went to Bowling Green State University for a degree in education and is now teaching at the Put-in-Bay school.

An examination of the 1974 *Islander*, the school yearbook, discloses that there have been seven classes with only one graduate: George J. Linskey, 1895; Henry Weisler, 1914; Eloise Ruh Burgess, 1930; Eva Brown Rietz, 1932; Joseph J. Parker, 1937; Sonya Market Dress, 1956; and Daniel J. Zura, 1957. The commencement program was carried out just as if there had been hundreds of graduates as in a large mainland school. There have been years when there were no graduates: 1897, 1899, 1900, 1918, and 1921. The largest class in the history of the school, eleven members, was graduated in 1974. The total number of graduates from the Put-in-Bay High School is 343, distributed among seventy-five classes. Enrollment in all twelve grades at Put-in-Bay has averaged ninety in recent years.

Many mainland schools have that many and more in one senior class, but how many of them can claim that 100 percent of the graduating class attended college and received their bachelor degrees? Put-in-Bay can. Daniel J. Zura, the lone member of the class of 1957, was graduated from Bowling Green State University and is teaching in Fremont, Ohio.

The teaching staff numbered eight teachers for the 1973-1974 year, although several taught only part time. On the staff were: Kelly E. Faris, superintendent; Linda Erne, grades 1/2/3; Edwin J. Market, grades 4/5/6; Justine Bianchi, Music, Art, English; Susan Duff, Sciences, Typing, Business; Thomas Eversole, Sciences, Mathematics, Drama; Margaret Naylon, Accounting, Reading, Sociology, Psychology; Joan Booker, Physical Education.

Members of the Put-in-Bay Board of Education are: Gerda Crowe, president; Louis Heineman, vice-president; Nello Bianchi; Joseph Parker; Dennis Naylon; Jeanne Burgess, clerk.

The curriculum at the island school contains the standard courses: English, Mathematics, Science, History, Government, and Languages. There are such other courses as: Psychology, Sociology, Driver Education, Drama and Speech, Home Economics, Art, Typing, Drafting, and Accounting.

Departing from the usual custom of holding the commencement in the town hall, the class of 1973 received their diplomas on the plaza of the Perry's Victory and international Peace Memorial. The class of 1974 was the largest graduating class in the history of the school. The record-breaking members were: Glenn R. Cooper, Kevin J. Hauck, Angela E. Heineman, Christopher J. Ladd, Julene M. Market, Peggy L. Meyer, Charles R. Sweeney, Steven G. Turvey, Mark J. Wilhelm of Put-in-Bay, and David L. Harlan and Vicky L. Jenkins of North Bass.

THE ALUMNI ASSOCIATION

The Put-in-Bay High School Alumni Association was organized in June 1902 when a committee—Carl Oelschlager, Mina Bickford, Mamie Rittman, Mildred Dodge, and Fred Gross—drew up a constitution defining the objectives and requirements for membership in the association. The objectives are two-fold: to bring members together for social and intellectual improvement and to induce pupils to complete their high school education. Members must be graduates of the Put-in-Bay High School.

THE STONE LABORATORY

An educational institution of higher learning is located on Gibraltar Island in Put-in-Bay harbor, the Franz Theodore Stone Laboratory of the Ohio State University. Ohio State has maintained a biological laboratory on Lake Erie since 1896 when the university established, under Professor David S. Kellicott, a facility in the state fish hatchery, then at Sandusky. In 1903 the laboratory was transferred to larger quarters at Cedar Point, near Sandusky, and in 1918 moved to the new state fish hatchery at Put-in-Bay.

Julius F. Stone purchased Gibraltar from the Jay Cooke heirs, and in 1925 gave the island to Ohio State University for use as a biological station. The name was then changed from Lake Laboratory to the Franz Theodore Stone Laboratory in honor of the donor's father. A dedicatory program was held 22 June 1929. Julius F. Stone, chairman of the Board of Trustees, Ohio State University, presented the island to Dr. George W. Rightmire, president of Ohio State, who accepted on behalf of the university. Governor Meyers Y. Cooper of Ohio accepted on behalf of the state. Other speakers were Perry Green, Director of Agriculture; Raymond C. Osburn, Director of the Laboratory; Henry Fairfield Osborn, president of the American Museum of Natural History; and Edwin G. Conklin, Research Professor of Zoology, Princeton University.

Herbert C. Osborn succeeded Kellicott as director and was, in turn, followed by Raymond C. Osburn. Dwight M. Delong served one year and Thomas H. Langlois was director from 1938 to 1955. Loren S. Putnam served as director until the end of the 1973 summer quarter.

Facilities include the three-story brick laboratory; two boats used for research and transportation; numerous rowboats; Cooke Castle, the men's dormitory; Barney Cottage, the women's dormitory; and a cafeteria. The university also uses the former United States Fish Hatchery as a research station. The hatchery was a gift of the federal government in

1940. Julius F. Stone purchased and donated for faculty use a house near the hatchery. The old Cincinnati Fishing Club clubhouse on nearby Oak Point was used as a dormitory for about fifteen years. It was razed in 1956.

A year-round program was instituted in 1938 with the students attending summer classes at Gibraltar and with research carried on in the old fish hatchery in wintertime. During World War II, from 1943 to 1945, no summer classes were held. Classes resumed in 1946. Winter research ended in 1955 but has been reinstituted on a limited basis since 1962. The instructional program was designed by the College of Biological Sciences to meet the needs of biology and general science majors, graduate and advanced undergraduate biological science majors, and professional aquatic biologists.

The courses taught at Stone Laboratory are not those usually found on college campuses: Limnology, Ecological Physiology of Aquatic Plants, Aquatic Microbiology, Aquatic Mycology, Aquatic Entomology, Algae, Fish Ecology, and High Aquatic Plants.

The majority of the teachers come from Ohio State University but many of them are from other institutions in Ohio and elsewhere. While about half of the students are from Ohio State, many are from out-of-state, and a few are foreign students. The enrollment for each of the two summer terms of the quarter is about sixty-five to seventy students, the limit of the accommodations in the dormitories. There are fourteen instructors, usually seven different persons for each term. Students are limited to two courses per term and classes are held six days a week, seven hours a day. Field trips are made to other Lake Erie islands in American and Canadian waters as well as trips to mainland research areas.

State universities found themselves operating on a tight budget in 1973 and this affected the laboratory at Gibraltar. There were no formal classes taught at the island facility during the summer of 1973. Instead, a small group of about a dozen and a half students were engaged in problem study in their particular field of biological science and the research projects in progress were continued and expanded. The 1974 summer quarter saw a return to the normal class load and schedule.

5

Paddlewheel and Propeller

The dictionary defines an island as a land mass entirely surrounded by water. People living on mainland are accustomed to driving for miles and miles without interruption on the expressways. The thought of traveling in a boat or airplane to Put-in-Bay and the other Lake Erie islands is appealing to them. It is a welcome break in the monotony of sitting behind the steering wheel of an automobile for hours on the turnpike. A boat ride on a sunny summer day is relaxing, the scenery—myriads of small boats and the forested island shoreline dotted with cottages—is a relief from the high-rise office building and the industrial park of the city.

The question was, and is, how do you get to the island? American Indians, following the Great Warrior Path to the Lake, paddled their canoes to the Bass islands and on to Detroit. Early French explorers built sailing vessels and cruised among the islands. In the early nineteenth century, sailing ships stopped at Put-in-Bay bringing supplies and taking aboard lumber and stone. The Sandusky *Clarion* reported some of these early trips when the boats arrived at Sandusky: "April 22, 1822, open boat, from Put-in-Bay, Budd Martin, master"; "June 4, 1823, Sch. *Hornet,* Capt. Horton, from Put-in-Bay"; "April 14, 1824 Schooner *Washpokenatta,* Capt. Horton."

The islanders had small sailboats and rowboats which they used in traveling to and from mainland. The first steamboat on Lake Erie, and the third on the Great Lakes, was the *Walk-in-the-Water* in 1818. Wood-burning vessels stopped among the islands to refuel.

The first person to establish regular boat service between the Bass islands, Kelleys Island, Sandusky, and Detroit was Canadian-born Simon Fox. He spent his youth on Pelee Island, Ontario, and in the course of time acquired the *Amherst,* a sloop-rigged sailing craft. Fox came to Put-in-Bay about 1850, became interested in grape growing and, like other island vintagers, was also a fisherman. He moved to North Bass in 1861.

By boat Put-in-Bay is twenty-two miles from Sandusky, sixty-five miles from Cleveland, forty miles from Toledo, and sixty miles from

Detroit. Sailboats depended on the wind for propulsion: too little wind meant a delayed passage, too much wind could make the voyage dangerous. Steamboats, which did not rely on the strength of the wind, could operate on a schedule. Lake Erie storms could delay or even prevent steamboats from sailing but, in general, steamboats were a reliable means of Lake transportation. The boats were propelled by paddle wheels mounted on the side or by a screw or propeller in the stern.

EARLY STEAMBOATS

The first steamboats to make regular stops at Put-in-Bay were the *General Scott* and the *Fashion* of the Detroit-Sandusky line. Those runs began in 1846. That same year Captain Dibble of Sandusky built the steamer *Islander* on Kelleys Island using native red cedar. The seventy-six-foot craft made the first trip 16 October 1846, under the command of Captain George W. Orr. Service to Put-in-Bay did not begin until 1851, and ended in 1854 when the *Islander* was replaced by the *Island Queen*, also built at Kelleys Island by Captain Dibble in 1854. This larger vessel, 120 feet long, made her maiden run in June 1855. Captain Orr was her master until 1866 when the *Island Queen* was sold. The *Queen* is best remembered as being one of the two ships seized by the Confederate plotters in their unsuccessful attempt to free the prisoners of war on Johnson's Island. The rebels tried to scuttle the *Queen*, but the boat grounded on Chicanola reef two miles south of Pelee Island, Ontario, and was back on the inter-island route in less than a week.

Besides the scheduled trips to the islands, the boats often ran special excursions to other ports. The ladies of the Sandusky Methodist Episcopal Church in 1858 chartered the *Island Queen* for an outing to Kingsville, Ontario. The tickets cost one dollar and included dinner. For those who might suffer from *mal de mer* there was the reassuring note that "if the weather is bad" the boat would stop at Put-in-Bay! It was a forty-mile lake journey to Kingsville and only twenty-two miles to Put-in-Bay. Some excursions were too large to be handled by one steamboat as witnessed by this advertisement in the Sandusky *Daily Commercial Register* on 30 July and 12 August 1858:

> Union Excursion and Pic-Nic
> Str. "Island Queen" G. W. Orr, master.
> Sail Yacht "Monarch of the Glen" Capt. Thomas J. Clark.

> Str. "Bay City" Capt. Edwards.
> Tickets $1. per couple.

During the Civil War the Confederate prison camp on Johnson's Island in Sandusky bay was an attraction. The boats did not stop but cruised past the camp.

> Excursion of the 4th (of July) Str. "Whitney."
> Capt. S. F. Atwood. Leave 9 A.M., return in time
> for 6 o'clock train, round trip 50c . . . passing
> by Johnson's Island, giving a near view of the
> Gov't Bldg and the rebel Prisoners' Quarters,
> on her way up and back from Put-in-Bay.

Captain G. W. Orr piloted the *Island Queen* on similar journeys and for the same price, fifty cents a round trip. Captain Atwood also commanded the *Philo Parsons*, a 135-foot steamer, and in 1864 followed the same routine:

> 1864 Season Arrangements   Sandusky & Detroit
> Touching at all the celebrated Grape Islands in
> Lake Erie, pass the famous Johnson's Island Depot
> for Prisoners of War.
> The New Upper Cabin, Low Pressure Steamer
>   PHILO PARSONS   Capt. S. F. Atwood
> Leave Sandusky for Detroit via Malden every
> Tues., Thurs., Sat., 8 A.M., leave Detroit for
> Sandusky every Mon., Wed., Fri., at 8 A.M.

The *Philo Parsons* entered the pages of Civil War history when John Yeats Beall captured her in the abortive attempt to free the rebel prisoners on 19-20 September 1864. Beall took the *Parsons* back to Canada where he landed at Sandwich on the Detroit River. An attempt to sink the ship was made, but the *Parsons* was back in service on the twenty-fourth.

The *Evening Star* replaced the *Island Queen* in September 1866 on the Sandusky-Islands schedule. Built at Saginaw, Michigan, at a cost of $46,000, the 168-foot side-wheeler could carry more than seven hundred passengers. The *Star* remained on the island route until 1873. For two years, 1866-1868, the *Island Queen* traveled between Detroit, the islands, and Sandusky. In July 1868 the new steamer *Jay Cooke*, launched at Detroit in April, took over the run for a ten-year period. Later the *Cooke* was put on the Sandusky/Put-in-Bay route, serving the islanders under that name and as one of the several City of Sandusky's. The *Cooke* was 162 feet long. It might be said that old steamboats, or rather their engines, never die. The steam engine was taken from the *Cooke*, rebuilt, and installed in the second *Arrow* in 1895.

There were a number of steamboats running to the islands from

Sandusky, Detroit, Toledo, Cleveland, and Port Clinton. The *Reindeer*, 162 feet long, made two trips daily from Sandusky to Put-in-Bay, Middle Bass, and Kelleys Island. Every Monday, Wednesday, and Friday the *Reindeer* continued on to North Bass. Captain G. W. Orr was the master and round-trip fares were twenty-five cents in 1869. Toledoans wishing to go to Detroit or Cleveland by boat could board the *Chief Justice Waite* at 8:30 A.M. and make connections at Put-in-Bay with boats going to those two other cities. The *Waite* was owned by the Toledo, Lake Erie, and Island Steamboat Company. The boat was built in 1874 and was 188 feet long. There were accommodations for 1,500 passengers.

The *J. K. Secor*, a small, seventy-seven-foot propeller-driven boat, made daily runs between Put-in-Bay and the county seat, Port Clinton, twelve miles away. The *Secor* left Put-in-Bay at 6:00 A.M. and Port Clinton at 3:00 P.M., a schedule which was convenient for islanders going to mainland on business or to shop. Clevelanders seeking cool lake breezes combined with a short stay at Put-in-Bay could take the side-wheeler *Pearl* at 8:30 A.M. and (with a stop at Kelleys) arrive at the Bay at 2:00 P.M. The boat left on the return trip at 3:30 P.M. Built in 1875, the *Pearl* was 177 feet long and could carry one thousand passengers. Her Fletcher and Harris engine had a cylinder forty-six inches in diameter with a nine-foot stroke giving a speed of fifteen miles an hour.

THE AMERICAN EAGLE

The majority of the steamboats running to Put-in-Bay were in service only during the summer vacation season. A few, on the Sandusky-islands route, operated as early in the spring and as late in the fall as weather and economics would permit. Fewer still tried to cut through the winter ice, until even the stoutest vessel was forced to lay up until the spring thaw. One such steamboat was the *American Eagle*, 115 feet long, built in Sandusky at Monk's Shipyard in 1880 for Wehrle, Werk and Son of Middle Bass. The *Eagle* was sheathed in boiler plate so that the hull would not be damaged by ice and was a propeller-driven craft. Side-wheel ships could not be used for ice-breaking as the paddle wheels would be broken by the ice. Captain Frederick J. Magle of Put-in-Bay was the master of the *American Eagle* during the twenty years the vessel served the islands.

A terrible tragedy overtook the *Eagle* in 1882. Six persons were killed when the boiler exploded on May 18. Such accidents were not uncommon experiences in the early steamboat days. On the day of the tragedy, the *Eagle* and the *Jay Cooke* left Sandusky at the same time on their way to the islands. Sometimes in similar situations steamboats would stage an informal race. A number of passengers on the *Eagle* believed that to be the case this time, although the captains of the two vessels denied that they were speeding. The two boats were about two miles from Kelleys Island when the boiler of the *American Eagle* blew up killing three crew members instantly: Fireman Frank Bittel and deckhands Frank Walter and Lorenz Nielsen. Engineer James W. Johnson and passengers John Lutes and James Fullerton died of injuries a few days later.

The *Cooke* stopped to take off the injured and other passengers; the *Eagle* did not sink and was towed back to Sandusky. Another boat, the *Mystic*, also aided in the rescue. A passenger, John W. Gilbert, told of hearing the engineer Johnson tell the crewmen to "fill her up" (with coal) so that the speed would be increased. He also stated that Captain Magle ordered Johnson to "slack the speed of the boat in order to drop astern of the *Cooke*." A captain in the pilothouse has no direct way of controlling the speed of his vessel except by signals to the engineer in the engine room. Mate Hugo Steiert and Clerk Fred Rehberg supported Magle in his contention that the *Eagle* was not racing. Captain George Brown of the *Jay Cooke* also stated that they were not speeding. Engineer Jacob Weis of the *Cooke* said "we were carrying forty-three pounds of steam of the fifty pounds allowed. . . ."

There was a government investigation of the disaster. An expert machinist, Fred Rinkleff, testified that government inspectors had allowed the boiler to carry too much steam. It had been tested and the safety valve set at 106 pounds the previous September. Before he died of injuries Johnson said that the boiler carried 110 pounds at the time of the explosion. The federal grand jury exonerated Captain Magle and placed the blame for the accident on Johnson, alleging that he put a lump of coal on the safety valve thus preventing it from operating normally. The valve was tested a few days after the accident, it did not open up to relieve the pressure until the 130-pound mark was reached. Repaired, the *American Eagle* resumed the inter-island route.

One of the fatally injured passengers was James Fullerton, the seventy-nine-year-old caretaker of Ballast Island who was better known as "Uncle Jimmie." He usually made but one or two trips to mainland a year. Fullerton planned to return to Put-in-Bay on another boat but joined some friends aboard the *American Eagle* for what was to be his last trip. Uncle Jimmie was buried in Crown Hill cemetery on South Bass Island, the plot is identified by a tombstone inscribed, "To the memory of UNCLE JIMMIE of Ballast Island—a victim of the American Eagle explosion—May 18, 1882, Erected by his friend GEO. W. GARDNER."

MORE STEAMBOATS

Occasionally a boat would interrupt a schedule to make an excursion to another port, such as this one advertised in the Sandusky *Daily Register* on the fifth and sixth of July in 1888: "American Eagle—Excursion to Cleveland—July 7—Saturday. Leave Sandusky 8:30 A.M., Returning leave Cleveland Sunday, July 8 at 8:30 A.M. Round trip 50c."

The steamer carried freight as well as passengers. The *American Eagle* ended her regular schedule early in September and spent the remainder of the navigation season hauling grapes and other fruit from the islands to Toledo. After serving the islands for two decades, the *Eagle* made her last run 25 August 1901. The sturdy old icebreaker was then used at Toledo to keep the river channel open during the winter.

The replacement for the *Eagle*, the steamer *Lakeside*, 128 feet long, was built in 1901 by the Craig Shipbuilding Company of Toledo for the Peninsula Steamboat Company. The hull was steel with heavy frames and plating to resist the pressure of ice-breaking. A fore-and-aft compound engine turned the propeller. Two Roberts Safety Water Tubular boilers provided the steam. Electric lights, relatively new on lake boats, furnished the illumination of the interior. A powerful searchlight was mounted on the pilothouse. The owners chose an old, experienced hand to command the new vessel, Captain Frederick J. Magle. Alex R. Bruce was the clerk.

Besides the large passenger steamers, a number of smaller boats were used as ferries, charter fishing craft, and to haul grapes to the market from the islands. Captain E. J. Dodge bought the forty-two-foot *Ina*—capacity, twenty-five passengers—in 1882. In 1902 Captain Dodge leased the village park dock for a ten-year period. The *Ina* was used as a ferry to carry people from Put-in-Bay to Wehrle's Dance Hall on Middle Bass. The lease could be terminated if the wooden dock burned up or was otherwise destroyed, also if Wehrle's went out of business. Rent was $90 per season.

The old steam yacht *Wayward*, built in 1882, was purchased from A. A. and B. W. Parker of Detroit by Captain Dodge in 1906. The *Wayward* was eighty-nine feet long. Three years later Dodge commissioned the American Shipbuilding Company at the Globe Shipyard in Cleveland to build the steamer *Tourist*. The steel hull, eighty-five feet overall, was designed for ice-breaking. Like the other small steamboats, the *Tourist* saw varied service; charter trips, scheduled runs to Port Clinton, the transporting of grapes to Toledo, Detroit, and other ports, even journeys to Buffalo, New York, were made. Captain Dodge operated as late in the winter as ice conditions would warrant but inevitably the lake would freeze so solid between Put-in-Bay and Sandusky that even the *Tourist* would have to lay up until spring.

The steamer *Grandon* was also used on ferry service between Put-in-Bay and Wehrle's Hall. In addition, the fifty-nine-foot craft made three trips daily to Ballast Island. Valentine Doller had the *Visitor*, eighty feet long, built by the Detroit Boat Works. The *Visitor* was used in the inter-island trade for a few years. Three Middle Bass residents had steamers built for island service. The smaller one, sixty-nine feet, was the *J. V. Lutz*. The largest vessel, the *Andrew Wehrle, Jr.*, was 148 feet long and traveled the route from Put-in-Bay, the peninsula, and Sandusky from 1889 to 1908. Bird Chapman operated the *Leroy Brooks*, seventy-five feet, for William Rehberg of Middle Bass. Rehberg personally ran the *Ganges* on similar ferry service.

The *City of Toledo*, 212 feet long, provided service between her namesake and Put-in-Bay in the 1890s. The side-wheeler could carry 1,500 passengers and, like the *Lakeside*, had electric lighting. Known as the "Flyer of the Lakes," the *Frank E. Kirby* was built in 1890 for W. O. Ashley for the Detroit, Islands, and Sandusky route. The side-wheeler was 195 feet long and cost $150,000. On 8 August 1891 the *Kirby* broke the previous record when she raced between Sandusky and Put-in-Bay, twenty-two miles, in one hour and twenty-one minutes. Average time for the other boats was two hours.

The second steamer *Arrow* was designed and built by Frank E. Kirby in 1895 at Wyandotte, Michigan. Cabin interiors were furnished in Mexican mahogany and were electrically lighted. The *Arrow*, 165 feet, could accommodate eight hundred passengers. On Tuesdays during the summer the steamer made a round trip to Cleveland, fare was fifty cents —George A. Brown was captain; August Foye, mate; and Eugene McFall, clerk.

The *Arrow*, owned by the Sandusky and Islands Steamship Company, served the islands for twenty-seven years. On 14 October 1922 she was destroyed by fire while berthed at Doller's dock, Put-in-Bay. The eight men on board (of a twenty-five-man crew) escaped without injury. Sailors on the *Oliver H. Perry* tried unsuccessfully to put out the fire. Finally, the *Arrow* was set adrift so that the blaze on the dock could be extinguished. The burned-out hull was sold to a Chicago firm in 1923.

Canadian-American international relations were strained in a minor way in May 1894 when the Canadian revenue cutter *Petrel* "captured" the steamers *Visitor* and *Leroy Brooks* off the south point of Pelee Island. The sport fishermen were charged with violation of the Dominion fishing laws. The *Petrel* almost caught another victim. Fishermen from the Cincinnati Fishing Club had chartered the *Ina* and were off Middle Island just across the border in Canada when they saw the cutter approaching. They awoke the sleeping captain, E. J. Dodge, and "escaped" across the boundary line into American waters, reporting the seizure of the *Visitor* and *Leroy Brooks* when they returned to Put-in-Bay. The fifty fishermen from the seized boats were released and brought back to Put-in-Bay on the *American Eagle* at dusk. On June 12, the two boats were returned to their owners on bond. Five weeks later the case was dropped in the Canadian courts after a small fine was paid; however the two steamers could have been confiscated.

In its very first issue the Put-in-Bay *Herald* published a schedule of steamboats stopping at Put-in-Bay in 1898. Persons wishing to travel from Cleveland to Toledo could board a steamboat at Cleveland, lay over at Put-in-Bay for two and one-half hours, and take passage on a different steamer for Toledo. The *Metropolis*, 168 feet, sailed between Toledo and Lakeside with a stop-over at Put-in-Bay. Operating on a more convenient schedule for islanders who wanted to shop in Toledo, the *Ogontz*, a seventy-nine footer, left Put-in-Bay at 9:00 A.M., arrived in Toledo at 1:00 P.M., and left for the island at 3:45 P.M. The *Post Boy*, seventy-eight feet, traveled between Port Clinton and Put-in-Bay with a stop at Catawba Island [a peninsula, not an island] each way. Two round trips were made daily by the *Arrow* between Put-in-Bay, Middle Bass, Kelleys Island, and Sandusky. Excursionists from Detroit could take the *Frank E. Kirby* to the islands and Sandusky. The various steamboats brought tourists to Put-in-Bay, and a few excursionists went from the island to the mainland, as reported by the *Herald* on 25 August 1898:

> Excursion and Dance—Next Sunday Evening there will be an Excursion to Catawba Island and a dance at that place. The Str. LeRoy Brooks will leave Middle Bass at 8:30 and Put-in-Bay at 8:45. The Round House orchestra will furnish the music for the occasion. A nice time is promised to all who may go. The fare to the round trip is only 25 cents.

HAZARDS OF LAKE TRANSPORTATION

Stormy weather and other lake conditions sometimes interrupted boat service, as evidenced by announcements in the Sandusky *Daily Register:* "The Str. 'Louise' left here on Saturday night at 12 o'clock with a party of excursionists bound for Cleveland, but after going about 12 miles, a severe storm occurred and the boat put back to this port." "The excursion advertised to be given on the steamer 'Ferris' to Put-in-Bay yesterday was postponed on account of rough weather." "A high north-east wind yesterday caused the lake to be very rough and the steamer 'City of Sandusky' did not make her second trip. The vessel lay at Put-in-Bay." "A baby boy was born on the steamer 'Pearl' on her return trip Sunday during a storm which almost everyone including a couple of crew members were sick. Mother and son did not seem to be affected by the storm."

Strong winds can blow the water down the lake and lower the level at the western end. For example, "The steamers 'A. Wehrle" and 'American Eagle' did not make their usual trips yesterday on account of low water." As the wind changes direction or dies out, the water level returns to normal, usually in a matter of hours, certainly by the next day. In just the opposite way, a northeast wind can raise the water level five feet or more.

Boatmen plying the waters around the Lake Erie islands must learn the location of the numerous reefs if they wish to avoid running aground. Even the best seamen cannot always avoid such a fate. The *G. W. Warmington* of the Minch Line ran onto a ledge of rock extending out from Starve Island in August 1878. The vessel was carrying nine hundred tons of iron ore but was not badly damaged. The schooner *Harrison* had preceded the *Warmington* in grounding at the same spot.

Another large vessel, the *State of Ohio*, 225 feet long, ran aground at Rattlesnake Island in the early morning hours of 20 September 1906. High winds and fine rain made navigation difficult for the ship on its regular route between Cleveland and Toledo. The forty passengers aboard were removed to the *City of the Straits* and taken to Toledo.

The side-wheeler, six feet out of water forward, resisted the efforts of several tugs to free her. Captain C. H. Sinclair, representing the insurance underwriters, was put in charge of the salvage operations. The captain became ill on October 7, and with two men, Johnson and Moore, rowed in a small boat to Rattlesnake which was uninhabited. Despite a severe northwest storm, the three started out for Put-in-Bay, one and three-fourths miles away. They got about halfway when their boat capsized. Captain E. J. Dodge had been observing the lake and saw the overturned rowboat bobbing around in the waves with the sailors clinging to it.

Captain Dodge and crewmen Wilbur L. Dodge, Harold Dodge, and Peter Peterson set out in the steamer *Wayward* to the rescue. After a desperate struggle with the storm-driven waves they reached the exhausted seamen and Captain Dodge personally pulled Captain Sinclair aboard the *Wayward*. Three years later, on 21 September 1909, Captain Dodge and his crewmen received medals awarded by the United States secretary of the treasury for "heroic conduct in saving life." The captain was presented with a gold medal; the crewmen received silver medals.

The *State of Ohio* was finally pulled off Rattlesnake Island on October 17 and towed to Put-in-Bay, where temporary repairs were made before being taken to Detroit. The old side-wheeler returned to the islands on the Toledo/Put-in-Bay schedule in the years 1919-1924.

THE LAST DAYS OF THE STEAMBOATS

The steamer *Put-in-Bay* plied the waters between Detroit and Put-in-Bay for thirty-eight years. The 226-foot craft was greeted with booming cannon, cheers, and applause when she made her maiden trip to the island on 17 June 1911. Designed by Frank E. Kirby, the steamer could transport 3,500 passengers on four decks—in the cabins, lounges, lunchroom, dining room, private parlors, ballroom, and on the spacious open decks. The propulsion machinery, a four-cylinder triple-expansion engine and four boilers, developed 3,000 horsepower, which enabled the *Put-in-Bay* to speed along at twenty miles per hour.

It was the custom of the islanders to assemble on Fox's dock (Parker Boat Line) on Labor Day, the last day of the summer season, to say farewell and "See you next year" to the *Put-in-Bay*. The ship's orchestra seated at the stern played "Auld Lang Syne" as the vessel pulled away from the pier. The last full season of operation for the old steamer was the 1949 season. In October 1953 the *Put-in-Bay* was burned for scrap on Lake St. Clair.

For a brief two years, 1950-1951, the *Eastern States* and the *Western States*, 350-foot side-wheelers, alternated trips to Put-in-Bay and Detroit. When one of those boats was taken off the run in 1951, the venerable *Put-in-Bay* was pressed into service to finish out the season. With their going, the steamboat service from Detroit to the island ceased.

Steamer service between the islands and Sandusky was interrupted by the destruction by fire of the *Arrow* in October 1922. Her replacement was the *Chippewa*, a 198-foot side-wheeler, built in 1884 as the United States revenue cutter *Fessenden* mounting four guns and with a crew of forty men. The *Fessenden* was converted to a passenger steamer in 1908 at Toledo and renamed the *Chippewa*. The Sandusky and Islands Steamship Company purchased the *Chippewa* from the Arnold Transit Company of Mackinac Island in November 1922 and placed the boat on the Sandusky-Islands run in 1923.

Service to the islands began in late April; for example, the 1924 season began April 28 with the *Chippewa* leaving Put-in-Bay at 7:00 A.M. and leaving Sandusky on the return trip at 3:00 P.M. From June 22 to September 1 two round trips daily were made, leaving the island at 5:30 A.M. and 2:45 P.M. and leaving Sandusky at 10:00 A.M. and 5:00 P.M. On Sundays only a single trip was made. From September 2 until the end of the season only one round trip was scheduled. The boat stopped at Lakeside, Kelleys Island, and Middle Bass on the Sandusky/Put-in-Bay route.

The last run of the *Chippewa* to the islands was made on 5 September 1938. Four years later the old steamboat was cut up for scrap. In 1939 the *City of Hancock,* 104 feet long, took over the route for that one year only, and with the *Hancock,* steamboat service from Sandusky to the islands ended.

Steamboats, side-wheelers and propeller-driven, provided transportation to the Lake Erie islands for over a century. On the Sandusky, Kelleys Island, Middle Bass, and Put-in-Bay route seventeen ships operated in the period 1851-1939. Twelve steamers added Lakeside on Marblehead peninsula to their schedule on the Sandusky-islands run. Put-in-Bay was a stopover on the route from Detroit to Sandusky for nineteen vessels from 1846 to 1951. Toledoans, from 1854 to 1947, traveled on twenty-six different craft on their excursions to the island. Twelve steamers have made the short twelve-mile run betwen Put-in-Bay and Port Clinton, but the route which began in 1869 has not been in continuous operation. Today two diesel-powered ferries, the *Erie Isle* [2nd] and the *Yankee Clipper,* carry passengers and automobiles to Middle Bass and Put-in-Bay on that century-old route.

It was inevitable that the lake passenger steamers would be replaced by more modern means of transportation such as the diesel automobile ferries and the airplane. Federal legislation in the form of the 1915 La Follette Seamen's Bill made it uneconomical to operate the passenger steamers during the short summer season. One of the provisions of the bill required lake, as well as ocean, vessels to carry enough lifeboats to hold all the passengers and crew that the ship was licensed to carry.

The steamer *Arrow,* for example, would have been required to have fifty additional lifeboats and one hundred more crewmen. Her normal crew numbered twenty-five and there were five lifeboats and three life rafts available for emergency use. Life jackets were provided for everyone on board. Mayor T. B. Alexander—representing Put-in-Bay, Middle and North Bass residents—went to Washington to protest the bill to Congress. He pointed out how dependent the islanders were upon the steamboat and that the boats were never more than five miles from land and in water no deeper than forty feet, but to no avail.

Other legislation regulating working hours required the hiring of a second and even of a third crew. When they returned to their home port, some of the boats took out nighttime or "moonlight" excursions with the passengers spending several hours dancing to the music of the ship's orchestra. Those vessels traveling to the more distant cities exceeded the normal eight-hour working day in their schedules; thus, as in a factory, a second or third "shift" was employed.

Another factor that brought about the demise of the steamboat were changes in transportation. The automobile provided the individual or family with land travel that was flexible; one could leave and return home when one desired or even change the destination while enroute. The tourist was not tied to a boat schedule which dictated when and where he went. Also, as the twentieth century progressed, more and more people owned their own boats, and weekend trips from mainland to Put-in-Bay were not beyond the skill of the novice navigator. After World War II there was a tremendous growth in boating, especially in the numbers of small outboard boats that could be towed on trailers from inland points to various Lake Erie marinas. Any office clerk or factory worker, decked out in a new captain's hat, could be the skipper of his own craft.

The beautiful black smudge of smoke on the horizon that heralded the approach of a steamer would be called pollution today; the shrill air horn of the diesel has replaced the melodious blast of the steam whistle. Like the trolley car and steam locomotive, the lake passenger steamer is gone but not forgotten.

NEUMAN BOAT LINE

Until the coming of the auto ferries running to Catawba and Port Clinton, Sandusky was the mainland port which received the bulk of the trade from Put-in-Bay. Steamboats like the *Arrow* and *Chippewa* did not provide service in the early spring or late fall after the grape harvest. Smaller boats were then used. John P. Neuman of Sandusky—the Neuman Boat Line—furnished this out-of-season transportation for thirty-eight years.

Neuman got his start in 1907 with a gasoline-powered, wooden, forty-three-foot launch, the *Alton*. For three years the *Alton* made trips between Lakeside and East Harbor on the Catawba peninsula and then was sold in 1910. Neuman built the fifty-two-foot *Reliance* at Sandusky in 1911. Freighting trips to Kelleys Island and Put-in-Bay were made on a charter basis. A second boat, the forty-five-foot *Cupid*, purchased in 1917, was caught in a heavy sea off Cedar Point. The cargo of gasoline barrels shifted and the boat rolled over and sank. The two crewmen wearing life jackets swam to Cedar Point, but the *Cupid* was not recovered.

The *Alert*, formerly the *Ida L. II*, a fifty-five-foot boat was used briefly on a run from Sandusky to Bay Point at the tip of the Marblehead peninsula across Sandusky Bay to make connections with the electric interurban cars for Toledo. The *Alert* and *Reliance* were sold in 1920.

Scheduled runs to the islands in the spring and fall began when Neuman built the *Messenger* in 1921. The *Messenger* was a sixty-five-foot wooden vessel which was first powered by a gasoline engine. Later, in 1923, a diesel engine was installed. During the summer when the large steamers were operating, the *Messenger* made charter trips to the islands and to Toledo and Detroit. The boat was also used to tow a scow from Catawba to Put-in-Bay loaded with a dozen and a half automobiles. The passengers of this early auto ferry rode in the *Messenger*. The *Mascot*, a sister ship, was built in 1925.

Although not icebreakers like the steamers *American Eagle*, *Lakeside* or *Tourist*, the wooden-hulled *Messenger* and *Mascot* were "ironed-off," that is, metal sheathing on the hull protected the boat from the cutting effects of the ice. The *Mascot* was constructed to break ice; the hull was made of heavy timbers and a watertight bulkhead in the stern allowed a compartment to be flooded and thus raise the bow for easier ice-breaking. The *Mascot* was smaller than the older ships used during the winter months.

The *Messenger* left Sandusky on 11 December 1929 with a dozen passengers and freight for Kelleys Island. Following about a mile behind was the *Mascot*, bound for Pelee Island with a load of gasoline, eighteen tons of anthracite coal, and other supplies desperately needed at that Canadian island. There was ice in the lake although the two boats did not have to break through it. The weather was stormy, and a huge wave hit the *Mascot*, causing the loose coal to shift. Water rushed to the forward end, tore off a hatch cover, and flooded the engine room. The boat rolled over on its side, up-ended, and sank.

Captain John P. Neuman, the crewmen Karl Wobser of Sandusky and Russell E. Smith of Put-in-Bay, and passengers Fred Adams and Fred Ammonite of Pelee donned life jackets and entered icy Lake Erie. The accident was observed by those on board the *Messenger*. Captain Jacob Frederick turned the boat around and, within half an hour, rescued the five men. The *Mascot* was raised from the bottom of the lake and put back on the inter-island route.

The *City of Hancock* was the last steamboat to make the Sandusky/Put-in-Bay run. The next year, 1940, Neuman began to make scheduled trips to the islands during the summer as well as in the spring and fall. Schedules varied to meet the needs of the season. Islanders boarded either the *Mascot* or *Messenger* at Put-in-Bay at 7:00 A.M. for the ride to Sandusky; stops were made at Middle Bass and Kelleys Island; and the boat arrived at Sandusky at 9:30 A.M. The return trip began at 3:00 P.M. and ended at Put-in-Bay about 5:30 P.M. On pleasant days the two and one-half hour journey was uneventful; rough weather made the boat ride a bit more exciting. The craft pitched, tossed, rolled, and lurched; water sloshed over the deck, diesel engine fumes permeated the passenger cabin and those who had not gotten their "sea legs" got seasick. Those unfortunates could look forward to the return voyage—the weather might be better, the same, or even worse!

A new all-steel diesel ferry was acquired in 1945. The *Commuter* was just under sixty-five feet long, like the older boats but beamier (wider), twenty-four feet to the *Mascot's* fifteen. Six or more automobiles could be carried on the lower deck; the passengers rode on the upper deck either in the cabin or on the open deck. Much of the freight was carried on and off the boat by hand. The *Commuter* was sold in 1960. The *Challenger*, similar to the *Commuter* but having a more streamlined appearance, was added to the line in 1947 and is still in use. In the summer two round trips daily were made to the islands.

A departure from the familiar style in lake ferries was made when the Neuman Boat Line purchased the *Corsair*, built in 1955, at Warren, Rhode Island. The all-steel diesel ship was the first open-deck auto ferry designed for use on Lake Erie. It resembles a miniature aircraft carrier, there being no large upper deck. Just under sixty-five feet, the *Corsair* has a thirty-three-foot beam. A similar ferry, the *Commuter* (2nd) was put into service in 1960. A larger boat, one hundred feet long, of the same open-deck type, was put on the Marblehead/Kelleys Island route in 1969. It was aptly named the *Kelley Islander*.

The Sandusky/Put-in-Bay route was abandoned after the 1959 season. There were two other ferry companies, one running to Catawba and one to Port Clinton, both shorter routes requiring less time for a one way journey. Neuman concentrated on boat service to Kelleys Island from Sandusky, and starting in 1955, from Marblehead.

The old *Messenger* was sold in 1947 to the Welch Line at Sault Sainte Marie and used to take tourists through the Soo Locks until 1958 when she was broken up. A sadder fate overtook the *Mascot*. That veteran of the lake was used in towing service from 1947 to 1955 when she was sold to the Key/Erie Boat Line of Cleveland. Moored in the Old River Bed of the Cuyahoga River, the *Mascot* sank twice and was finally covered over with fill dirt and buried under tons of earth in 1960.

The boat lines which ran from Put-in-Bay to Sandusky or Port Clinton served the islanders well until the coming of the automobile. These early ferries could not carry cars although some were later adapted to carry one or two autos. The island passenger had to confine his visit to the port city unless he wanted to stay overnight on mainland. Public transportation had to be used for trips to other than the port city. Also the schedules of the large steamboats were more convenient for the visitor to Put-in-Bay than for the islander having business on the mainland. Then, too, much valuable time was consumed merely in riding on the boat. A round trip from Put-in-Bay to Sandusky on the *Mascot* took at least five hours.

ERIE ISLE FERRY

What was needed was a boat to carry cars and passengers on a short route from the island to the mainland. That need was met with some degree of success when the Put-in-Bay Auto Ferry Company was organized in 1920. William Good piloted the *Messenger* towing a scow loaded with up to eighteen cars between Put-in-Bay and Catawba Point, a distance of seven miles. The passengers rode in the boat. Upon arrival at Put-in-Bay the cars were driven off a ramp on Fox's (Parker Boat Line) dock. Later the *Burger*, Joseph Anton, pilot, did the towing. Sometimes during bad weather the ferry landed at Stone's (State Park) dock.

The ferry service began in late June and ceased operation about Labor Day. Three round trips were made daily from the island at 9:00 A.M., 12:45 and 4:30 P.M.; from Catawba at 10:30 A.M., 2:15 and 6:00 P.M. Passengers paid fifty cents each way and cars were $1.50 one way.

The company was reorganized as the Erie Isle Ferry Company in 1930. Officers and directors of the company were: Henry Fox, president; William Schnoor, secretary and treasurer; Captain A. J. Stoll, general manager; Gordon A. Dodge, Norman V. Heineman, Rudolph Fisher, and George Lonz, directors. To replace the boat-and-scow ferry the company bought the *Fredericka*, built in 1894, at Philadelphia. The 118-foot steamer was rebuilt and renamed the *Erie Isle*. The new ferry could carry thirteen cars and three hundred passengers. Ferry service began in April and ended in the middle of September. Weekly evening voyages to Sandusky were made to "coal up," that is, to fill the bunkers with a seven-day supply of fuel. Many islanders took this excursion to mainland where there was enough time to see a "movie" before the boat returned to Put-in-Bay. Five round trips were made daily between the island and mainshore.

The steamboats and auto ferries brought multitudes of people to Put-in-Bay in the years before World War II. The *Put-in-Bay Gazette* reported that so many tourists came to the island for the Fourth of July weekend in 1939 that the hotels were jammed to capacity and emergency sleeping quarters had to be found for those who had no reservations. Getting the visitors back to mainland was a problem too. So many cars and passengers had been brought over on the *Erie Isle* that Captain A. J. Stoll called upon William M. Miller for help. Stoll had hauled about 140 cars to the island and Miller helped by putting the old scow and tug back into operation in order to get all the people back to mainshore at a reasonable hour.

Business was not always that good for every steamer calling at Put-in-Bay. The *Gazette* told of the excitement that was caused when the steamer *Goodtime*, 268 feet long, did not arrive, as scheduled, at the island. Henry Fox learned the next day that the weekday trip was cancelled; less than ten persons had appeared for the run to Put-in-Bay.

The steamer *Erie Isle* was in service for a decade when she was replaced in 1942 by the *Mystic Isle*—an all-steel, diesel-powered ferry, 103 feet long—capable of transporting eighteen cars and 350 people. The *Mystic Isle* operated on the Put-in-Bay/Catawba route through the 1946 season and then ran from Port Clinton to the islands. Old ferries never die—the *Erie Isle* ended her days as a barge, the forward end was separated from the after section and used to haul coal, stone, and sand to the islands. The Miller Boat Line and then the Neuman Line owned the *Erie Isle*, unofficially renamed the *Fubar*, an acronym taken from the initial letters of a vulgar military phrase used in World War II. The *Fubar* now lies sunken off the entrance to the Lonz Marina at Middle Bass.

The *Mystic Isle* was well suited for the peak summertime tourist trade when capacity or near capacity loads could be carried, but when traffic was light in the early and late summer the ferry proved uneconomical to operate. A smaller, sixty-one-foot boat, the diesel *Erie Isle* (2nd), was built by the Rud Machine Company of Cleveland in 1951 and put on the route in 1952. The *Mystic Isle* was sold. Alfred Parker became the captain of the new boat and the Erie Isle Ferry Company is now better known as the Parker Boat Line, Incorporated. A sixty-two-foot, open-deck diesel ferry was purchased in 1963, and during the summer the *Yankee Clipper* and the *Erie Isle*, together, make six round trips between Put-in-Bay and Port Clinton.

The *Erie Isle* begins the spring schedule in the first or second week of April, depending on when the lake is clear of ice. Two round trips daily are made, then the number of runs is increased as the season progresses. Always dependent on the weather and ice conditions, the *Erie Isle* continues to operate into December. Neither of the two boats is considered to be icebreakers.

MILLER BOAT LINE

Originally called the Miller Boat Livery, the Miller Boat Line was started in 1905 by William M. Miller. A modest start it was. Miller's first boat was an eighteen-foot flat-bottomed wooden craft powered by a one-cylinder, two-cycle Relacco engine. In the summer he delivered ice to yachts anchored in the bay, hence the name *Iceman* for the boat. He rented rowboats to fishermen and entered the charter fishing business when he bought a thirty-two-foot boat in 1912.

The Miller Boat Livery eventually operated six charter fishing boats from Put-in-Bay. The wooden-hulled boats were powered by gasoline engines and ranged in length from twenty-five to thirty-four feet. About six fishermen could be accommodated for trolling, that is, fishing while moving slowly through the water, and ten or twelve for still fishing at anchor. The boat pilots met their fishermen at Catawba and returned

Grape Festival wine booth. (Top) RJD.
1951. (Bottom) RJD.   Cooper's winery and restaurant,

Cellar, Cooper's winery, 1951. *(Top)* RJD.   The School on the Hill served islanders for sixty-seven years. *(Bottom)* OGH-KKJ.

The brick school was built in 1921. *(Top)* RJD.   The Franz Theodore
Stone Laboratory, O.S.U., Gibraltar Island. *(Bottom)* RJD.

Str. *American Eagle*—Sandusky-Islands route. *(Top)* OGH-KKJ.　　Str. *Arrow* —Sandusky-Islands route. *(Bottom)* OGH-KKJ.

Str. *State of Ohio* ran aground on Rattlesnake Island 20 September 1906. *(Top)* OGH-KKJ.   Str. *Put-in-Bay*—Detroit/Put-in-Bay/Sandusky route. *(Bottom)* RJD.

Str. *Western States*—Detroit/Put-in-Bay route. *(Top)* RJD.   Str. *Eastern States*—unloading passengers at Put-in-Bay. *(Bottom)* RJD.

Challenger and *Commuter*—Neuman Boat Line—Sandusky and Islands. *(Top)* RJD.   Put-in-Bay auto ferry, 1920s—Catawba/Put-in-Bay. *(Bottom)* OGH-KKJ.

Str. *Erie Isle*—Catawba/Put-in-Bay auto ferry. *(Top)* OGH-KKJ. *Mystic Isle*—Catawba, later Port Clinton/Put-in-Bay auto ferry. *(Bottom)* RJD.

Diesel ferry *Erie Isle*—Port Clinton/Put-in-Bay. *(Top)* RJD.   Miller Boat
Livery fleet, 1936. *(Bottom)* OGH-KKJ.

South Shore—Miller Boat Line—Catawba/Put-in-Bay route. *(Top)* RJD.
Put-in-Bay—Miller Boat Line—Catawba/Put-in-Bay route. *(Bottom)* RJD.

Lime Kiln dock—Miller Boat Line, 1974. (Top) RJD. Charter fishing boat
Shore-Nuf. (Bottom) RJD.

Unloading grain sacks at Put-in-Bay. *(Top)* RJD.   Gill-net boat *Marie M.*
(Bottom) RJD.

Charles Mahler, Vincent Traverso, and Jack Meyer sort fish on the *Marie M.* *(Top)* RJD.　　A good catch for fishermen George Wertenbach, Norman Heineman, Nello Bianchi, Romer Stoiber, Frank Shane, Joe Prentice, and Nathan Ladd. *(Bottom)* RJD.

The *Mascot* tows the *Fubar* loaded with coal in the 1950s. *(Top)* RJD.
Unloading coal on the Dodge dock in the 1950s. *(Bottom)* RJD.

The Beebe House, renamed the Hotel Commodore, burned down in 1932.
(Top) OGH-KKJ. The Park Hotel in the 1950s. (Bottom) RJD.

Delaware Avenue, 1953. *(Top)* RJD.   The Crescent Hotel was also known
as the Hunker House, Ward House, and the Detroit House. *(Bottom)* RJD.

them there, thus eliminating the time-consuming journey to Put-in-Bay. Charters could be made from the island if desired. There were also a number of independent charter-boat operators such as Gordon Dodge and Charles Mahler. There are many fishing spots around the Lake Erie islands. Some of them are off South Middle, and North Bass, Rattlesnake, Sugar, and Starve islands, West Reef, Buckeye, and Gull Reef; and in Canada near Pelee and Middle islands, East and Middle Sister, Hen and Chicken islands.

William Miller cut ice from the bay in the winter and stored a thousand tons of it in an icehouse on the dock. After the old icehouse was torn down, refrigerated ice was brought from mainland on the Miller ferry and kept in a small icehouse. William M. Miller, aided by his son, William Lee, also began freighting gasoline and other petroleum products to the island. Barreled gasoline was brought by boat or boat and scow until Lee Miller bought a small World War II landing craft, the *Mervine II*, in 1949 and adapted it to carry gasoline and fuel oil. The petroleum business was sold to Ladd's Sales and Service in 1960. The boat livery also operated several Lyman speedboats as water taxis, providing rapid charter service to the other islands and mainland.

Lee Miller entered the auto ferry business in 1945 when the *South Shore* was built at the Stadium Boat Works in Cleveland. The craft, just under sixty-five feet in length, has a beam of twenty-four feet and is similar in appearance to the *Commuter* of the Neuman Boat Line. The *South Shore* ran between the downtown Miller dock and Catawba, a seven-mile, forty-minute voyage. In 1947 the *West Shore*, also an all-steel diesel ferry, was added to the Miller fleet. The *West Shore* has a thirty-foot beam and can carry more cars than the *South Shore*. A third ferry, the *William M. Miller*, was put in service in 1954. William C. Miller, the grandson, was the pilot of the new ferry. He was drowned in a boating accident in 1958.

A new dock, the Lime Kiln dock, was constructed in 1957 at the south end of the island. The running time of the ferries was cut in half, from forty minutes to less than twenty and the distance from seven miles to less than three. The new dock is two miles from the center of town. Visitors in a hurry could take the short, twenty-minute trip from Catawba to the Lime Kiln dock. Others who went to the downtown dock enjoyed the longer ride and the scenery—the forested island shoreline dotted with summer cottages and the many small boats darting about the lake. Islanders usually took the short route; a boat ride is no novelty to them. Eight trips were made daily from the downtown dock and seven from the Lime Kiln.

Ferry service was further expanded in 1959 with the addition of the *Put-in-Bay*, an open-deck diesel vessel similar in appearance to Neuman's *Corsair.* The older Miller ferries carry the cars on the lower deck with the passengers going to the upper deck for the trip. The *Put-in-Bay* can carry large trucks, campers, or motor homes because there is no large upper deck, only a small passenger cabin.

A change in scheduling was made in 1972: the longer runs to the downtown dock have been eliminated, and twelve daily trips are now made to the Lime Kiln dock. An extra evening run is scheduled on weekends. Middle Bass, which had been served on the downtown-Catawba route, is now on a special schedule with four daily trips between Middle Bass and the mainland. The Parker Boat Line also stops at Middle Bass enroute from Port Clinton.

The two boat lines, Miller and Parker, offer the visitor a choice of eighteen trips, between 7:00 A.M. and 7:30 P.M., when cars and passengers can be brought to Put-in-Bay. In addition, Island Airlines makes ten daily flights to Put-in-Bay from the Port Clinton airport during the summer—passengers only, of course. The *West Shore, William M. Miller,* and the *Put-in-Bay* can carry up to eleven automobiles each. The *South Shore* was sold in 1973. The *Erie Isle* can accommodate six cars and the *Yankee Clipper* nine. The number of cars carried on each ferry is regulated by the United States Coast Guard. A balance is struck between the number of cars and the number of passengers; that is, a full load of cars reduces the number of passengers that can be carried. Automobiles vary in size, also affecting the number that can be carried.

E. J. AND GORDON A. DODGE

Captain E. J. Dodge operated the *Ina, Wayward,* and the *Tourist* through the years from 1882 until just after World War I. He owned two scows with which he hauled coal and building supplies to the island. Nicholas Fox and Sons and the Put-in-Bay Dock Company were other dealers in coal and supplies.

In the mid-1920s Captain Dodge retired from active participation in the business, turning it over to his son, Gordon A. Dodge. John P. Neuman built a thirty-eight-foot wooden launch for Gordon Dodge in 1926. It was powered by a four-cylinder Regal gasoline engine of forty horse power. The boat was used for charter fishing parties and for towing a scow.

Most trips to Sandusky for coal were routine and uneventful. Dodge —alone or sometimes with his teen-aged son Robert or nephew Wilbur— would leave Put-in-Bay at dawn for the two-hour journey to the Lower Lake docks for a fifty-ton car of coal. The large lake boats loaded coal at these docks, taking on thousands of tons at one time. The dock machinery could lift an entire railroad car of coal, turn it upside down, emptying it into a chute which directed the coal into the hold—all in one minute. It took a little longer to load the Dodge scow since the load had to be distributed evenly on the scow to avoid listing (tilting) too much to one side or the other. The operation took about five minutes; it took hours to load a lake freighter, of course.

On a calm, pleasant summer day the return trip took four hours with Robert or Wilbur acting as "wheelsman" for part of the journey. Storms could delay the return a day or two or even a week. Sometimes the sailors would get caught out in the lake when a squall suddenly arose. Experience would dictate whether the seamen would continue or return to port. Or they could seek shelter in the lee of one of the islands or lie close to mainshore if a dock could not be found until the storm had subsided enough to proceed. Upon arrival at Put-in-Bay, the scow was unloaded manually, using No. 6 scoop shovels and wheelbarrows. Twenty to twenty-five trips were made to Sandusky for coal during the season.

In 1945 the wooden boat and scow were sold and replaced by an all-steel thirty-eight-foot boat, the *Shore-Nuf*, which was used mainly for charter fishing parties. Grain and fuel oil were also freighted in the Port Clinton built boat. Neuman was engaged to haul coal from Sandusky. The old *Mascot* towing the *Fubar* could bring over one hundred tons of coal at one time. A modern crane or power shovel was used to unload the scow. Fuel oil-burning furnaces were replacing the old coal-fired heating systems when Dodge retired in 1954. The small amount of coal used on the island today is brought over on the ferries in dump trucks from the mainland.

Dodge also hauled stone, sand, cement, fuel oil in barrels, and cattle and chicken feed to the island. Sacks of grain or barrels of gasoline or fuel oil were loaded into the boat at Port Clinton for the hour and a half run back to Put-in-Bay. In the fall a scow-load of grain, straw, and hay was brought over and stored for the winter. By 1954, there was also a decline in the number of horses used in the vineyards and in the cattle and chickens raised on the island. Practically all of the food supplies are now imported from mainland on the ferries, or in winter, on the airplane.

COMMERCIAL FISHING

Early island settlers were often fishermen as well as grape growers and some of them devoted their entire time to fishing. Commercial fishing in Lake Erie did not develop until the mid-nineteenth century. There were some feeble efforts with gill and seine nets along the shoreline and among the islands but fishing as an important industry dates from 1852 when the pound net was introduced. By 1866 there were 140 pounds nets around the islands and Sandusky area, and fifty tons of fish a day were being taken to the fish houses in Sandusky. Twenty years later there were no fewer than 700 to 800 pound nets in the lake between Cleveland, Sandusky, and Toledo. Fishing in American waters was prohibited from June 15 to September 10 but the Sandusky market was supplied from Canadian waters as Canada did not have a closed season.

The pound net was a huge twine net held up by stakes driven in the mud bottom of the lake. It was made up of three parts: the leader, 900 to 1,000 feet long; the heart, 100 to 130 feet long; and a crib thirty feet square. The pound was a kind of maze into which the fish swam but could not find a way out. The smaller fish could swim through the meshes but the larger fish were kept alive until collected by the fishermen. Pound-net fishing became the dominant method of catching fish in western Lake Erie where the waters were shallow enough to allow their use.

Another type, the gill net, formed a barrier on the bottom of the lake to catch the fish by the gills, hence the name, gill net. It could be placed anywhere, over either rock or mud bottom; but, if the fish were not removed daily or every other day, they would drown and have to be discarded.

Fresh fish were sold in the nearby markets around Sandusky; fish were also cleaned and salted for sale to more distant cities. The freezing of fish began about 1867' with West and Smith storing frozen fish in refrigerator rooms for winter consumption. In 1869 Ferdinand Geisdorf shipped twenty tons of frozen herring to Pittsburgh. The mart for Sandusky and island fish extended from Boston to St. Louis.

Many kinds of fish were caught by nineteenth-century fishermen. The herring, about a pound in weight, were the most numerous; white fish averaged two to three pounds; black bass and white bass weighed two to five pounds each. There were varieties of pickerel, the No. 1 once grew to fifteen pounds but in the 1880s only went three to five pounds. The sauger or No. 2 pickerel and the blue pickerel were smaller fish of the same species. Sturgeon were once killed and thrown away when found in the nets. They were also used for fertilizer in the vineyards. Sturgeon measured over three feet in length and weighed over seventy pounds. The meat was smoked, the bladders became isinglas, and the eggs were caviar. Twenty-five thousand sturgeon were handled in Sandusky each season. Muskelunge were once very plentiful but were scarce in the 1880s. They weighed up to seventy pounds. Yellow perch, rock bass, sun fish, mullet, and bullhead were other types of fish netted by the islanders. The sheepshead were considered to be of no commercial value. The state fish hatchery introduced the German carp into Lake Erie about 1880. These fish were gold or silver in color.

In the days before steam or gasoline engines, sailboats were used by the fishing fleets. A type of boat called the pound-net sharpie evolved over the years. The sharpie was a large, twenty-eight to thirty-six foot-long, beamy, open, flat-bottomed wooden boat. Two sails were mounted, one set well forward and the other to the stern, leaving sufficient room for the tiller man. When the nets were being raised the rudder was removed so that the nets would not catch on it.

The pound net had to be used in shallow water and over mud bottom so that the stakes holding the net could be driven into the lake bottom. The trap net was similar but did not require the stakes, being held in place by anchors and floats. William Market, Sr., in the 1890s, made the first trap net for Lay Brothers Fishery of Sandusky. Lay Brothers, Post, and the United Fisheries had fishing "rigs" operating out of Put-in-Bay as well as from mainland ports. Trap nets, varying in size, could be used over rock bottom and mud bottom. All-cotton nets were used at first, coated with tar for preservation. Synthetic fibers such as nylon are now used. They do not rot and do not require tarring.

Trap-net boats ranged in size from twenty-two feet to thirty-six feet and were open decked. The gasoline engine was housed in a small cabin forward, the exhaust running up through the roof. Heretofore, the wooden-hulled craft were "ironed-off" with metal sheathing for protection from ice, but now the boats are made of steel. A crew of three men operated the boat. About a dozen trap net boats were based among the Bass islands.

The size and kinds of fish caught varied greatly. There were "runs" of certain fish; for example, one net might yield three tons of perch and five hundred pounds of saugers. Crushed ice was spread on the catch to keep it fresh. Some fish such as mullet and carp might be put in tanks of water, taken later to Sandusky and placed in tank trucks for live shipment to New York City. Trap nets were put in the lake around March 15, if the lake was clear of ice. Once, when the lake froze again after the nets were in, the fishermen drove out to their nets in a Model T truck, chopped them out, and took them back to the island to await warmer, ice-free weather.

Gill-net fishermen were able to work from a boat that could be closed to the weather and even heated by a coal stove. The boats were from thirty to sixty feet long, with wooden, "ironed-off" hulls. The modern gill-net tug is all steel. Gill netters could handle 300 to 3,000 nets, in strings of fifty to one hundred nets each. Gill net fishing is not allowed in Ohio waters west of Huron today. The last trap-net fishing rig stationed in the Bass islands ceased operations by the mid-1960s. Gill netters quit operating about the same time or a little earlier. Sport fishermen are ever present, they can be counted by the hundreds, even by the thousands, on a clear, calm day in western Lake Erie. Only a few trap-net men go out daily to lift their nets. None are from Put-in-Bay.

6

A Room for the Night

While many islanders were farmers engaged in the production of grapes, others found an equally lucrative occupation in the resort business, especially in hotels and rooming houses. They either owned or worked in the hostelries and subsidiary enterprises such as saloons, restaurants, bowling alleys, and souvenir shops. By steamboat, Put-in-Bay was only hours away from Sandusky, Toledo, Cleveland, and Detroit.

"The steamboats brought more than commercial advantage to the lakeshore. It brought a chance for tired townsfolk to take holiday weekends on a faraway shore. It was the custom for many steamboat lines to set aside a few days of each season for an excursion. Some offered the short run to Put-in-Bay."* The Sandusky *Daily Commercial Register* exclaimed, "Excursions to Put-in-Bay are all the rage. We noticed . . . that a number of Detroit firemen intended to visit that island on the 24th [of August 1858]." Such vessels as the *Philo Parsons, Island Queen, Jay Cooke, Evening Star,* and *Reindeer* advertised excursions from Sandusky and on to Detroit. A further spur to island visitation was the Fourth of July and Battle of Lake Erie—September 10—celebrations held at Put-in-Bay in 1852, 1858, and 1859. The celebration of 10 September 1858 brought 8,000 people to the island.

The majority of the visitors coming to Put-in-Bay stayed only for just the day, returning home in the afternoon. At first there were few places to stay overnight. Tourists brought their lunch baskets with them. When the 1858 celebration was held, grocers and restaurant operators of Sandusky erected temporary lunch stands to serve the crowd.

THE FIRST HOTELS

In the early 1860s, Frederick Cooper began to add guest rooms to a grout house near the boat landing (present Parker Boat Line dock). As more guests came, more rooms were added. In 1867 Andrew Decker

---

*Randolph C. Downes, *History of Lakeshore Ohio*, 3 vols. (New York: Lewis Historical Publishing Company, 1952), 11, 686.

became a partner and the house was named The Island Home. The building was greatly enlarged, with stables, a bar, bowling alley, and beer garden. The hotel was now called the Perry House. The hostelry underwent another change of name and ownership in 1869 when it was sold to Henry Beebe and became the Beebe House.

Island contractors Gascoyne and Montgomery added a three-story front wing and an ell. Separate from the main building was the bowling alley, a billiard room, ice cream parlor, and a ballroom. The whole building was illuminated by gas manufactured on the premises. The Beebe House accommodated three hundred guests.

Mrs. Henry Beebe acted as hostess at the fancy six o'clock dinners. The hotel was the center for elaborate nineteenth-century Saturday night costume balls as well as the more informal "hops" or dances. It was customary for the black servants to give a concert for the guests once a summer. In 1910 the Beebe House was sold to W. H. Reinhart, renamed the Hotel Commodore, and sold again three years later to the Schlitz Brewing Company.

The Hotel Commodore was being operated on a lease by Mrs. Susie Sands of Toledo when it burned to the ground on 23 August 1932. There were eight guests registered, of whom only two were actually in their rooms when the fire broke out on an upper floor. They escaped without injury or loss. The island Volunteer Fire Department led by Chief Nathan H. Ladd was able to keep the blaze from spreading to other structures, but it was impossible to save the hotel. The loss was estimated at $20,000-$30,000.

Another island hotel "just grew" like the Beebe House. This was the first Put-in-Bay House. The base of this establishment was the "White House" of A. P. Edwards. Joseph W. Gray, editor of the Cleveland *Plain Dealer*, purchased the "White House" in 1861 for a rooming house. Gray's widow sold it three years later to Henry B. West and Captain Amander Moore; Dr. William R. Elder bought out Moore; Colonel Merit Sweeney (or Sweny) bought out Elder; then a Cincinnati company acquired interests in the hotel and a new firm appeared, Sweeney, West and Company.

Many improvements were made to the Put-in-Bay House. A new wing was added to the east side and the old wing moved to the west side of the road. There was a wide hall running five hundred feet through the main building on the ground floor. The hotel front, facing the bay, was five hundred feet long also, with a piazza along the whole length. In front of each wing was a fountain, the water supply coming from reservoirs in the attic of the main building. The dining room could seat nearly 1,000 diners. A dance floor, forty by one hundred feet, was in the rear of the west wing. The hotel could house eight hundred persons.

How did the vacationist of 1871 spend his time on the island? The Sandusky *Daily Register* of 8 June 1871 reported, "The Dress hop was a decided success, they all are, and the dresses of the ladies were rich, rare and elegant." Sundays in the 1870s were spent quietly. People went to church in the morning and for a row across the bay in the early evening hours after supper. Several rowboats filled with young people might collect in a group off Gibraltar Island and hold an impromtu concert as they drifted over the smooth waters. Guests could also go on a sail yacht party aboard the *Ida Mary* or the *Hummingbird*. The hotel livery provided the "surrey with the fringe on top" for a leisurely trot around the island.

Hotel patrons in the summer of 1878 planned a "grand musical entertainment and ball" at the Put-in-Bay House. A thousand tickets were expected to be sold and free transportation from Sandusky on the steamers *Jay Cooke* and *Gazelle* was arranged. The ball was to be a benefit for the yellow fever sufferers in the South. The event, scheduled for the evening of 30 August 1878, never took place. The Put-in-Bay House was totally destroyed by fire that very night.

The blaze was discovered in the cupola on top of the central main building at 6:00 P.M. and quickly spread to the wings on either side. About 250 guests escaped without injury. There were rumors of one woman losing $1,200 in clothes, another $2,000 in diamonds, and other losses in jewelry, money, and clothing. The village did not have a fire department at that time, so a bucket brigade was formed. A fashionably dressed beautiful young lady led the reluctant men to the waterfront a block away to start the line. Their efforts to save the building were futile. A few of the hotel staff looted the rooms while many other employees tried to save items of equipment. One waiter was seen saving tablecloths, jerking them off the tables, sending the silverware clattering to the floor. The fire spread, burning down a small hotel, the Bing House, the Chris Doller boot and shoe store, and a few other buildings.

Four young men who had just come to the island had gone up into the cupola for a view of the harbor and had been seen smoking when they came down. It was believed that they accidentally caused the fire. The Sandusky Fire Department sent a fire engine to the island on the steamer *B. F. Ferris*. Unfortunately it arrived one hour after the hotel had burned to the ground.

Some of the thieves who had stolen articles from the guests were caught and the items recovered. The guilty ones escaped punishment because Ottawa County was too poor to pay witness fees and mileage to the county seat at Port Clinton.

Colonel Sweeney, manager of the hotel, requested the village council to furnish special policemen to guard the hotel and guest property which had been saved. This was done and a bill of $52 was presented to the hotel owners for services rendered. The mayor and village council sent a letter to the mayor, council, and Fire Department of Sandusky thanking them for the gratis use of the fire engine. Captain William Freyensee of the *Ferris*, who furnished free transportation for the engine, was also thanked.

The destruction of the Put-in-Bay House greatly reduced the available accommodations on the island. The burned-out vacationists had to seek lodging elsewhere. Some had trouble in getting accustomed to their new surroundings. George Veily from Evansville, Indiana, for example, had a room at the Put-in-Bay House with a balcony. In the evenings he would go out and sit for a while enjoying the breeze. After the fire, he found a room at the Beebe House. Following his usual custom, he opened the window and stepped out. No balcony. It was reported that Veily suffered only a few bruises in a three-story fall.

Valentine Doller built the second Put-in-Bay House on the site of the old hotel (present Commodore Motel) in 1889. The structure was similar in style to the previous building, having a central section with wings on each side. The new hostelry was much smaller, the frontage being just two hundred feet, and it could accommodate only two hundred guests. Doller advertised for a manager. J. B. Ward, who was manager of the Ballast Island resort, accepted the position in February 1890. In 1898 Doller installed his own electric light plant which furnished power to the hotel and to the Doller store near the lake front.

The fate which destroyed the first Put-in-Bay House also overtook the second. It was burned completely on 3 September 1907. The fire had threatened, for a while, the newly-built Colonial Dance Hall, but by 1:30 A.M. the danger to the hall and other buildings was over. Island officials had called to Sandusky for help but no boat was available; anyway, it would have taken one and a half hours, at least, for such aid to arrive.

John Schmidt, a dishwasher at the hotel, confessed to setting the fire in the basement at 10:30 P.M. Schmidt escaped arrest by having someone row him to Middle Bass, a mile away, to catch the steamer *Frank E. Kirby* enroute to Detroit. Upon arrival he hid in the hold until it was safe to leave the boat. Schmidt was finally caught near Hamilton, Ohio. The hotel was owned by the Put-in-Bay Improvement Company in 1907 and John Cameron of Cincinnati was the manager.

"A SMALL HOTEL . . ."

There were a number of other hotels on the island which served the tourists. The Hunker House, located on Delaware Avenue at the eastern end of the village park, was built in 1871. The hotel had its own vineyard and fruit orchard for the home manufacture of wines, ice cream, and cobblers. There were several name changes. When J. B. Ward was manager it was the Ward Summer Resort, then the Detroit House, and finally the Crescent Hotel. Originally there were accommodations for only seventy guests, but later additions doubled that number. The Crescent Hotel has been closed since 1971.

Henry Gibbens built the Perry House about 1875, on the corner of Erie Street and Catawba Avenue. After several changes of ownership and additions it was torn down in 1939.

The Park or Deutsches Hotel is a three-story building with twenty-six rooms and had a dining room for one hundred patrons. Adjacent to the hotel is the Round House bar which actually is round, being fifty feet in diameter. This popular bar was built in Toledo, dismantled, and reassembled at Put-in-Bay in 1873. The hotel and bar are located on the corner of Delaware and Lorain avenues.

The Gill House was constructed in the early 1880s and had accommodations for forty people. This establishment went through a number of name changes, Bon Air and Smith Hotel being the more recent ones. As the Hotel Oelschlager it had a general store and a restaurant attached. The guests could purchase dry goods, groceries, and souvenirs. The restaurant boasted of having a Tuft soda fountain. No longer a hotel, the building is now an antique and souvenir store, the Country House.

John S. Gibbens built a hotel in 1870 on Bay View Avenue some distance back from the lakeshore. John J. "Jack" Day bought the property in 1906, moved the building close to the waterfront and added a third story. The Bay View House was a popular resort for people from southern Ohio. In recent years it was called the Rendezvous, then reverted to the original name. It has been closed since 1972. The hotel is adjacent to the Put-in-Bay Yacht Club.

Thomas Conlen, after gaining hotel experience by working summers at the Ward House, opened Conlen Cottage in 1896. There were eventually rooms for fifty and a dining room for three hundred people. A fire, the enemy of the wood-frame hotel, occurred in 1923 when the three-story structure partially burned. It was rebuilt as a two-story hotel and operated as such until 1940 when it was sold to Camp Wa Li Ro, an Episcopal Boys' choir. It is now privately owned.

Just two doors from the Conlen Cottage on Toledo Avenue, Julius Wurtz, Sr., built a rooming house in the 1890s. Wurtz sold out to Benjamin L. Smith, whose son, Walter Smith, operated Smith's Hotel until 1944. Briefly it was known as Morgan's Hotel, then as the Bay-shore Hotel. The kitchen and dining room areas burned on 27 May 1953. The sleeping quarters were not damaged and remained in operation for some years. The building was torn down in 1968.

A new $25,000 clubhouse for the Cincinnati Fishing Club was built on Oak Point in 1893. The club ran into financial difficulties and the property was purchased in 1898 by E. J. Dodge who operated it as a hotel. In 1917 Arthur G. Smith of Elyria, Ohio, bought it for his summer home. Smith sold it in 1938 to the Ohio Division of Wildlife. The division leased Oak Point to the Franz Theodore Stone Laboratory of Ohio State University for use as a dormitory. In December 1956 the clubhouse was razed and the grounds made into a state park with docking facilities for small boats.

The Eagle Cottage at the corner of Bay View and Victory avenues was operated for many years by the Captain F. J. Magle and A. R. Bruce families as a boarding house. Walter and Mary Laskowski purchased the Cottage in 1946 and renamed it Friendly Inn. In 1970 the Lake Erie Patrol bought the old Eagle Cottage/Friendly Inn and in 1971 converted it to the Crew's Nest, a private club for yachtsmen and islanders. The building was remodeled. The one hundred eight-year-old Crescent Hotel bar, once tended by John Brown, Jr., was installed in the new location. Besides the Eagle Cottage, the Lake Erie Patrol bought the Lawrence Slatmeyer estate adjacent to the Cottage, the Dodge coal dock nearby, the Bay View House, and several marinas. A junior size Olympic swimming pool was opened in 1972. Ladd's Marina at the foot of Catawba Avenue and Bay View Avenue was purchased in 1969 and Doller's dock at the same location was acquired in 1973.

When Henry Reibel came to Put-in-Bay in 1884 he bought ten acres of land on the south shore and built the Reibel House. He also maintained a vineyard and orchard whose products gave a "homemade" accent to the menu. The hotel is located on Langram Road about a mile from the center of the village. The Reibel House ceased operations in the mid-1950s.

HOTEL VICTORY

The lack of hotel accommodations for overnight guests had restricted the resort industry at Put-in-Bay ever since the destruction of the first Put-in-Bay House in 1878. A large hotel was very much needed. J. K. Tillotson of Toledo met with a group of islanders in December 1887 to discuss the building of a new "Put-in-Bay House." The islanders, led by Valentine Doller and Clinton Idlor, were urged to buy stock in the venture. Several locations were suggested for the new hostelry, such as the site of the old Put-in-Bay House, and on East Point facing Middle Bass. The site actually chosen was at Stone's Cove (South Bass Island State Park) and the hotel was given the name Hotel Victory. Tillotson formed a hotel company with a stock valuation of $325,000.

The site covered one hundred acres of which twenty-one were reserved for the hotel and its grounds while the remainder were divided into lots. These lots, called villa lots, were 45 by 100 feet in size. There were 475 such allotments. The sale of land was sporadic with some lots bringing as much as $400. Streets in the development were given names of naval heroes such as Perry, Jones, Farragut, Elliott, Dahlgren, Decatur, and Porter. Perry's ships, *Niagara, Lawrence,* and *Caledonia,* were also honored.

George Feick of Sandusky was awarded the contract to erect the hotel. So tremendous was the undertaking that Feick had to build his own sawmill and planing mill. He also built a dining hall and dormitories for the workmen. Many men were needed; seventy-five carpenters alone were employed at one time. The steamer *Arrow* and other boats brought men and supplies to the island. On weekends the laborers chartered the *Arrow* so that they might spend several days at home with their families on the mainland.

Elaborate ceremonies were planned for the laying of the cornerstone of Hotel Victory. The promoters picked the anniversary of the Battle of Lake Erie in September 1889 as the great day. Seven steamboats brought 8,000 people to the island. The "Lone Willow" and burial mound in the village park were decorated with flowers and flags. A banner bore the words, "We have met the enemy, and they are ours." The laying of the cornerstone took place in Victory Park on the hotel grounds accompanied by orations, band music, and the firing of salutes by the United States gunboats *Perry* and *Fessenden.* Fireworks lit up the sky while the celebrants were attending hops at the Beebe and Hunker Houses.

Hotel Victory opened its doors to the first guests on 29 June 1892, even though 275 men were still working on the building. It was not completely finished in all details until 1896. The Fourth of July celebration brought five hundred diners to the new hostelry. A formal opening banquet and ball was held on July 12. Two months later on September 12 the hotel company went into receivership.

The wood-frame structure was said to be the largest summer hotel in America. The main building was 600 feet long by 300 feet wide. A lobby which could seat a thousand persons connected the main building with the dining room, kitchen, and servants quarters. The main dining hall was 155 feet long and 85 feet wide. Counting those in private dining rooms and in children's and nurses' halls, a total of 1,200 guests could dine at one sitting. For the thirsty, sporting gentlemen there was a bar thirty feet long and a ten-table billiard room.

There were 625 guest rooms including eighty with private baths. The bedrooms were furnished in the latest 1890 style: a bed with high ornamental headboard, dresser with mirror, washstand and table, straight chairs and rockers, and light, cool mats on the floor.

The hotel grounds were landscaped in the Gay Nineties style with a rustic bridge spanning a ravine, an electric fountain, and a boardwalk leading to the lakeshore five hundred feet away. Later there was a swimming pool—100 feet long, 30 feet wide, and eight feet deep—with a roof to keep out the summer sun.

The Hotel Victory was a mile and a-half from the steamboat landings in Put-in-Bay harbor. The Put-in-Bay Water Works, Electric Light, and Railway Company was organized in 1891 and operated an electric streetcar line from the hotel to the village. Originally, the terminal at the harbor was to be at the intersection of Bay View and Hartford Avenues, but the line ended at the foot of Catawba Avenue at Bay View. The line had four motor cars and four trailer cars. Each open car could seat 96 passengers and carry a total of 150. Total carrying capacity for the eight cars was 1,200. Only four cars were put into regular use.

The first run was made on 10 July 1892 at 6:00 P.M. A Toledo firm, Arbuckle, Ryan and Company, furnished the two 250-horsepower steam engines used to generate the electricty used by the railway and the hotel. Except for stops at the caves, it was an express run between the hotel and dock.

The fare was ten cents, a charge considered exorbitant when compared to the three-cent fares for a ten-mile run in large cities. It was explained to a woman passenger who had complained about the fare that, because the railway operated only ninety days out of the year, it had to charge ten cents in order to make expenses. There was talk of extending the line around the West Shore, Squaw Harbor, back to the village, and on to the starting point—the hotel. Henry M. Strong, F. Melville Lewis, Marcellus Reid, and William Gordon petitioned the Ottawa County commissioners for a grant of right-of-way in 1913 but the line was never built.

The hotel sold a combination round-trip streetcar and noon dinner ticket for seventy-five cents. A menu card of 1904 shows the variety of foods served at the dinner:

Friday   July 8, 1904   Noon Dinner   12:30 to 2:30
Salami   Potted Ham Sandwich   Olives   Pickles
Stuffed Mangoes
Fillet of Muscalonge, Genevoise   Roast Loin of Pork,
Piquante Sauce   Breast of Lamb Fricasse with Dumplings
Potatoes Sautees   Sliced Cucumbers   French Toast   Sherry
Wine Sauce   Mashed Potatoes   Steamed New Potatoes Sugar
Corn   Boiled Rice   Stewed Tomatoes   Spinach
Cold Meats—Boiled Ham   Sardines   Beef Tongue   Bologna
Chicken Mayonnaise   Sausage   Watercress, French Dressing
Celery Salad   Pickled Beets

Apple Pie	Blueberry Pie	Ginger Snaps	Assorted Cake
Ice Cream	Bananas	Fresh Currants	Plum Preserves
	Watermelon	Bartlett Pears	
Cheese:	American Edam	Toledo Biscuits	Crackers
	Ice Tea	Milk	Coffee

The manager put on a publicity campaign to attract vacationers to Put-in-Bay and the hotel. He advertised in forty leading Southern newspapers, spread 20,000 booklets and 15,000 folders over a vast territory. By April 1897 an excursion was booked from Macon, Georgia; two from Atlanta, Georgia; and one each from Knoxville, Tennessee, and Lexington, Kentucky. The Detroit and Cleveland, Cleveland and Buffalo steamship lines and the Big Four Railroad helped to advertise the hotel.

There was a type of guest that the manager did not want to attract. He refused to offer the Hotel Victory when it was suggested as a site for an 1895 match between pugilists James J. Corbett and Bob Fitzsimmons. The manager feared the type of people that such an affair might bring to the hotel and the island.

The laying of the cornerstone and the official opening of the hotel were occasions for elaborate ceremonies. Another such event was the unveiling of the Victory Monument on the hotel grounds on 5 August 1907. The monument was a statue of a winged woman holding a staff with an eagle at the top in her right hand and a wreath in her left. Alfons Pelzer, a noted German sculptor, created the twenty-two-foot high figure.

Among the speakers of the day were Charles W. Fairbanks, Vice-President of the United States; Ohio Governor Andrew L. Harris; Oliver H. Perry, grandson of the naval hero; and Joel C. Oldt, mayor of Put-in-Bay. The Misses Marthe McCreary and Gertrude McDonnell unveiled the winged statue, which was accepted by Mrs. Charles Burt Tozler, National Vice-President of the Daughters of 1812. Unfortunately, the weather was cold and wet so the ceremonies were held indoors.

Financial troubles plagued the Hotel Victory from the beginning to the end. During construction, a half-million board feet of lumber were held up on Fox's dock (Parker Boat Line) due to court proceedings. Two months after the official opening, the hotel company went into receivership. Contractors and suppliers took stock or villa lots as a lien for money due them. The assets of the Put-in-Bay Hotel Company were the building, $400,000, and furnishings and land, $240,000—for a total of $640,000. Liabilities added up to $265,000.

In 1893 J. K. Tillotson leased the hotel from the receiver and opened for business, but bad luck pursued him. On August 9 he told the thirty to forty guests that they would have to find new lodgings as the Victory was closing for the season. (The hotel could accommodate 2,000 guests.) The manager and staff went unpaid. The United States Circuit Court sold only the building to Fallis and Company, a creditor, for $17,000. Furniture, bedding, linen, kitchen and laundry equipment were sold to the Phoenix Furniture Company, another creditor, for $7,000.

Hotel Victory was closed in 1894 and 1895, reopened in 1896, only to close again in 1909, and reopened for the last time in 1919. T. W. McCreary was one of the more successful managers in the early 1900s. The streetcar line had similar troubles and was sold to J. M. and C. W. Ryan for $16,501 in 1900. The property included the railway system, power house, all machinery, and five lots in the Victory Park Allotment.

Hotel Victory—the largest, most pretentious, and probably the most financially distressed hostelry in the history of Put-in-Bay—came to an end in a conflagration that is vivid in the memories of islanders living today. The hotel was completely destroyed by fire during the evening of 14 August 1919. The season had not been a profitable one; only a few guests were in the building, and they escaped without injury. The fire started at 7:30 P.M. in the northwest corner of the third-floor main section. The cause of the blaze was believed to be a defective light wire which had given trouble previously.

By 8:30 P.M. the structure was an inferno, the flames leaping seventy-five feet into the air and visible in Sandusky fifteen miles away. The Put-in-Bay Fire Department could only keep the fire from spreading to nearby buildings such as the Schiele residence and wine cellar. Looters, most of them strangers to the island, carried away foodstuffs, cigars and cigarettes, typewriters, and slot machines. Mayor T. B. Alexander threatened action against the thieves and some items were returned. The Hotel Victory had just been purchased by Leslie C. Thompson from the Flanders Realty Company and there was a $250,000 mortgage on the property. Little or no insurance was carried; the loss was estimated at $450,000.

THE TOURISTS

Railroads brought the tourists to such lake ports as Toledo, Cleveland, Detroit, and Sandusky from which steamboats took them to Put-in-Bay. The *Herald*, published at Put-in-Bay, listed the hotel arrivals in its very first issue—Volume 1, Number 1, 25 August 1898. A sampling of the hometowns given shows the area and distance that people traveled to reach the island: Akron, Bowling Green, Cincinnati, Columbus, Delaware, Fostoria, Glenville, Lima, Pomeroy, Toledo, and Youngstown in Ohio; Coldwater, Detroit, and Saginaw in Michigan; Erie, Middleseck, and New Castle in Pennsylvania; Utica, New York; Parkersburg, West Virginia;

Galesburg, Illinois; Fort Wayne, Indiana; St. Louis, Missouri; Macon, Georgia; Cedar Rapids, Davenport, and Des Moines, Iowa.

Lydia J. Ryall in *Sketches and Stories of the Lake Erie Islands*, 1898 edition, describes the "tourist types": Cleveland and Detroit crowds bear with them an atmosphere redolent of teeming streets and busy marts . . . Blank, blasé individuals; women with inartistic touches of powder on their cheeks . . . merchants, office clerks . . . mechanics and artisans . . ." Of the farmer she commented, "Bronzed hands and a countenance ruddy and honest are his . . . A lingering suspicion of hayseed upon his collar . . . At his side, in fluffy lawn and bright ribboned hat, appears the rustic belle . . ." and the Canadians, "While not exactly foreign in appearance, their manners and speech are somewhat Frenchified, and they are generally distinguishable from citizens of Uncle Sam's territorial limits."

Put-in-Bay became a popular site for conventions of social, fraternal, and military organizations. The Ohio State Teachers Association, The Ohio State Bar Association, and the State Prosecutors Association were just a few of the many groups to meet on the island.

Among more unusual meetings were those of the Fat Men's Convention held in 1872, 1873, and 1874. John Templeton, Swanton, Ohio, was elected permanent chairman because he carried the most weight— 437 pounds. There were several members from the islands: C. Brick, 215 pounds; S. F. Atwood, 235; George M. High, 211; and John Stone, 233, a member of the executive committee.

They met again in 1873, and the Put-in-Bay House prepared for the event by ordering, among other delicacies, one hundred bushels of clams. For the 1874 convention the members planned the usual events: foot, sack, wheelbarrow, and tag races; wrestling, baseball, croquet, and pole climbing. An island specialty was a sailboat race and a rowboat race around Gibraltar Island. When the convention convened on 11 September 1874, John Templeton was still chairman, although he had lost nine pounds. John Stone, too, had lost three pounds.

Another event was the celebration of Emancipation Day by the black population of Sandusky. Usually an excursion was planned to Put-in-Bay or Middle Bass with orators, music by military bands followed by a picnic, and a baseball game. Emancipation Day was not held on the actual anniversary of the proclamation, September 22, but on August 1.

THE OLD CAMPGROUND

Camping on an island appealed to both civilian and military men. Various militia units from Ohio and other states, sometimes accompanied by the wives and children of the men, came to Put-in-Bay for martial exercises as well as relaxation. East Point was a popular campground. The Seventh Ohio Volunteer Infantry Regiment set up sixty tents there in 1890. It was the custom to name the site after a member of the unit who had served bravely in wartime. The East Point location was called "Camp Lauterwasser" after a sergeant killed in action.

The units brought their bands with them and there were drills and alerts; it was not all play. Artillery regiments fired their blackpowder, muzzle-loading cannon and occasionally there was an accident. A soldier might lose fingers, a hand, or an arm when an unextinguished spark caused a premature explosion. The navy often visited Perry's old base of operations, Put-in-Bay harbor. When the USS *Michigan* dropped anchor in the bay soldier and sailor visited each other's station.

As time passed, the older men, soldiers of the Mexican and Civil wars, faded away and the lines of a popular wartime song were paraphrased, "Dying tonight, dying tonight, dying on the old camp ground."

Civilian camps were more numerous, and the tents were festooned with flags and decorations. Today the state maintains South Bass State Park for campers and boaters and Oak Point State Park for boaters.

Besides the various hotels with their dining facilities, there were numerous restaurants and taverns. The Doller store was built in 1872. It is now Ted's Tackle Shop and the Corner Store. John Weigand leased the basement for a restaurant and stocked it with "the choicest liquors." For those who desired milder potables there was an "elegant ten-syrup Tuft's soda fountain." Stacey's Saloon sought customers from both sexes in an advertisement placed in the 8 June 1871 *Daily Register*. "A saloon for ladies and gentlemen—serves ice cream, lemonade and native wines—also has a billard room and bowling alley—patronized by ladies as well as gentlemen."

After dining and wining himself and family, the tourist could explore other island attractions. The Put-in-Bay Museum, established by A. B. Richmond, claimed to have 10,000 curiosities on display: collections of animals, birds, reptiles, relics of Indians, and of Perry's victory. The museum was later operated by Louis and Chris Engel. In two adjacent structures the men could play billiards or bagatelle. The women could wait for their menfolk in the "Ladies' Ice Cream and tea and coffee parlor."

Men, women, and children flocked to the two public bathing beaches. Louis Deisler, who came to the island in 1884, built a two-story bathhouse with 350 dressing rooms, he had 4,000 bathing suits for rent. The beach had a toboggan, rubber slides, a merry-go-round, floats, and rafts. A lifesaving crew kept their eyes on the swimmers. The *Herald* described the 1898 swim suit for young ladies:

The swimming dress is this year no longer than ever, and quite a number of young ladies have abbreviated their costume somewhat to give a freer action to the limbs. This is as it should be but fashion says no with a big N. Fashion says that short skirts are not good form today. The skirt must come below the knee . . . The stockings—opera length—are not to be the color of the dress but of the trimmings and should be of good silk. Water boots may be worn or not. . . .

Naphtha launches, sail, and rowboats and fishing tackle were rented at two boathouses. W. H. Ladd operated the Banner Boathouse at the dock near the Beebe House and the Haas Brothers and Jones were the proprietors on the other one at the foot of Catawba and Bay View avenues. The museum, bathhouse, and boathouses are no longer in existence.

EPIDEMIC!

The summer season of 1898 ended with a flurry of excitement—a smallpox epidemic scare at the end of August. Five mild cases and one serious case of smallpox were discovered among the black help at the Hotel Victory. Many hotel guests and summer cottage residents fled from the island on any boat that they could get, but the authorities at Port Clinton and Catawba would not let the boats from Put-in-Bay land. The Victory had two hundred guests and 250 employees, mostly black, at the time. A quarantine was declared, a pest house near the Victory established, and Dr. John Bohlander commanded a quarantine patrol.

The city of Detroit also placed Put-in-Bay under restriction, and the Detroit boat, the *Frank E. Kirby*, did not stop at the island. The spread of the disease was halted after only twenty-seven persons came down with smallpox. A health officer who came from Detroit and another from Sandusky found no cause for a quarantine because those who had become ill were isolated, and the boats were running the next day.

Since Hotel Victory was in the township, not the village section of the island, the township trustees hired and paid the health marshals who patrolled the grounds twenty-four hours a day—Ray Standish, Otis Haller, Smith Harrington, Robert Schiele, Hugo Engle, Jobe Parker, Ed Miller, William La Rue, Elmer Benning, Louis Foye, Frank Schiele, De Orr Webster, F. W. Burggraf, C. P. Engle, Walter Ladd, John Murray, W. H. King, Joseph Phillips, Andrew Schiele, and John Hollway. George E. Gasoyne furnished a horse and buggy for the doctor and the Put-in-Bay *Herald* printed ribbon badges for the health marshals. The opening of the school term was delayed until September 26 because of the epidemic.

THE COLONIAL

The Sandusky *Daily Register* in October 1905 reported the organization of an island company to promote the construction and maintenance of better facilities for the visitor. The Put-in-Bay Improvement Company bought the second Put-in-Bay House and its electric light plant and planned the construction of a dance hall—the Colonial. Officers and directors of the new company were: T. B. Alexander, president and general manager; Henry Fox, vice-president; S. M. Johannsen, secretary-treasurer; John Hollway and Gustav Heineman, directors.

The Put-in-Bay House burned down in 1907, but the dance hall is still serving tourists and islanders. An 18,000-square foot dance floor occupies most of the second floor. The roof is self-supporting and does not need any additional columns which might interfere with the dancers. Live orchestras furnished the music in the afternoons and evenings. On the first floor was an eight-lane bowling alley and a restaurant and bar. The Improvement Company published a booklet in 1906, *Put-in-Bay, Ohio,—The Saratoga of the West,* describing the Colonial and other island attractions.

The Colonial changed ownership several times. George Lonz of Lonz Winery owned it for many years. The South Bass Island Company purchased the building from Lonz in 1965. The old bowling alleys with their manual pinsetters were replaced by four automatic alleys. The new alleys are air-conditioned and heated for year-round use. The old wine room was redecorated in the style of a nineteenth-century saloon and named the "Bay '90s." In 1968 the island grocery store was moved from the old Rittman Market to the Colonial.

An older store, Schnoor's, which had served the island for over fifty years burned down 12 March 1964. It was located next to the Colonial on Catawba Avenue and just across the street from the town hall which houses the fire engines. It had been known in the past as Johannsen and Schnoor and as Schnoor and Fuchs. Lynn Schnoor built a smaller building—a bakery and hardware store—to the rear of the ruins of the old store.

MOTELS AND COTTAGES

Put-in-Bay in the nineteenth century met the needs of the steamboat tourist by building a number of wood-frame hotels which, for their day, were quite modern. At the turn of the century, thirteen hostelries were serving the public, ranging from the huge Hotel Victory to smaller units like the Eagle Cottage or Oak Point Cottage. The Park Hotel is the only one in business today. Some like the Hotel Victory, Beebe House, the first and second Put-in-Bay House were destroyed by fire. Others like the Perry Hotel were torn down. A few were converted to other uses: Hotel Oelschlager is a souvenir store; Eagle Cottage is a private club. The Crescent Hotel, Reibel, and Bay View House stand idle—outmoded relics of an earlier century.

Replacement for the hotel on the island as well as on mainland has been the motel—that type of accommodation that allows the traveler to drive right up to the door of his room to unload luggage. The first modern motel on Put-in-Bay, the Baytel, was built by Richard Powers. Construction began in 1954 and the first units were opened in 1957. A swimming pool, sixty-eight feet by forty feet and nine feet deep, was added in 1959. Other units were erected and individual cottages were built in 1965. The Baytel complex, located on Toledo Avenue, ceased operation at the close of the 1973 season.

Other motels followed—the Fox Motel adjacent to the post office in 1959, the Commodore Motel next to the Colonial, the Airport Motel, and the Victory Park Motel on Meechen Avenue opposite the South Bass State Park. The last three have swimming pools of various sizes.

Somewhat similar to the motels are the rental cottages. These are larger units than the motel accommodations. The cottages are composed of one, two, or three bedrooms, a living room, bath, and kitchen. A few of them have swimming pools and tennis, shuffleboard, or badminton courts.

Saunders Cottages on the lake and across the road from the state park has a nine-hole golf course. The Chamber of Commerce 1974 directory lists Borman's, Gump's, Mae-Tone Kostal, East Point, Saunders, and Victory Park cottages as being available.

Another type of tourist facility is the tourist home. Twenty years ago the directory listed over twenty homes available to the public; today only three homes are listed.

7

On, Under, and Over the Ice

Theresa Thorndale [Lydia J. Ryall], in the 1898 edition of *Sketches and Stories of the Lake Erie Islands,* describes the nineteenth-century wintertime at Put-in-Bay:

> The pretty summer cottages and club resorts are all vacant . . . At the bay dancing pavilions, bowling alleys, boathouses, bathing houses, groves and gardens are empty . . . The observer may walk from end to end on the main village street without meeting a person. The inhabitant . . . after a busy summer, rests contentedly, and if the ice closes in early and remains solid until spring, his happiness is complete . . . The provident islander always lays in ample supplies . . . while the lake is unfrozen. His less wise neighbor . . . sometimes runs short of comforts and necessities of life when they are most difficult to procure. The most calamitous thing that can happen . . . is when the beer supply runs dry, with no way to obtain a fresh supply.

The passenger steamboats ceased operation about September tenth. Some boats hauled the grape crop to market in the fall. Other vessels, such as the *American Eagle, Lakeside,* or *Tourist,* tried to run as late as possible or until the ice became too thick to break through. Travel over the ice was usually difficult, sometimes hazardous, but only infrequently fatal.

The twentieth-century islander is still isolated, but not to the same degree as was his father or grandfather. The Parker Boat Line makes three round trips between Port Clinton and Put-in-Bay in September. This is reduced to two in October and then to just one trip a day or two or three weekly until early December when there is ice in the lake. Miller Boat Line to Catawba cuts down to five and then four trips daily from a summertime twelve, and the last trip is made just before Thanksgiving. The Island Airlines' flights from Port Clinton are reduced to five and then four daily runs and continue through the fall, winter, and spring. Fog, snow, or high winds occasionally delay or even cancel flights.

Weekday tourist traffic is almost nil after Labor Day, especially after the city schools begin the fall semester. A pleasant late-summer or early-fall weekend can bring a fair number of visitors to the island. Summer cottage owners linger on until the ferries stop running, and even then a few hardy ones commute by airplane. Fishermen and hunters come in search of their finny or feathered quarry. Winter fishing through the ice around the islands brings to the angler a new thrill, a different type of fishing that is a challenge to his skill. Most of the motels, rental cottages, tourist homes, and restaurants close by mid-September. Accommodations for visitors are quite limited in the wintertime.

After the lake freezes over, around the first of the year or sometimes earlier, skating and iceboating are popular sports. A bonfire to warm up chilled toes and fingers can be built on the ice; the heat will not melt the ice when it is thick enough to skate on. Iceboating was very popular in the late nineteenth and early twentieth-centuries.

ICEBOATING

The Put-in-Bay Ice Yacht Club was formally organized in February 1889. H. G. Foye was named commodore and George T. Hollway, vice-commodore. Of the twenty-five islanders who belonged to the club, fourteen of them owned iceboats. The boats varied in length from fifteen to twenty-four feet. Sail area went from the 144 square feet of the *Gypsy* to the 392 square feet of the *Cyclone*. Picturesque and appropriate names were given to the swift craft: *Icicle, White Wings, North Wind, Snow Bird, Arctic, Winter King,* and *Jack Frost.* All were sloop-rigged except for the *Gypsy* which had a lateen sail. Regattas and races were conducted according to a detailed set of regulations.

Iceboats were used to take islanders to mainland. The Sandusky *Register* reported such an excursion 3 March 1914: "A fleet of ice boats brought a number of islanders, including women and children, to Sandusky . . . Seven boats composed the fleet which will make daily trips to and from Sandusky unless weather conditions are too bad. Several boats made the trip in less than an hour."

A tragic accident took the life of an iceboater the next day. George Morrison was thrown from his boat when it ran into a crack in the ice while traveling about forty miles an hour. He landed on a pile of frozen snow and slush, suffering broken ribs and a fractured right arm. Another iceboater rushed Morrison to Sandusky, where he died of his injuries that night. Islanders did little iceboating for years afterward.

A few of the older, large iceboats were used until recent years when they were replaced with small, one-man boats. The new boats are of the DN class, a type developed by the International DN Ice Yacht racing Association. A DN boat is twelve feet long and has a beam [runner plank length] of eight feet, measurements which are just half that of the 1889 *Cyclone!* DN sail area is sixty square feet. Speeds up to seventy miles per hour can be attained by the tiny craft. There are now ten such iceboats in the island area.

THE ICEBREAKERS

The steamboats on the Sandusky-islands route tried to operate as late in the winter and as early in the spring as lake conditions would allow. The *Island Queen* in 1866 tried to make a trip in early April but got only as far as Kelleys Island. There was too much ice in the lake for the boat to continue on to Put-in-Bay. John Brown, Jr., reported to the Sandusky *Daily Register* the difficulties encountered by the *American Eagle* in trying to run the six-mile distance between Carpenter's point on Kelleys Island and Wehrle's dock at Middle Bass on 18 February 1886.

An icebreaking steamboat could plow right through thin ice, but heavier ice required a different technique. When no further forward progress could be made, the boat would back up in the open channel, then speed ahead. When the bow hit the ice, the boat would be forced up on it, usually for about half the boat's length, and the weight of the boat would break the ice. The ice was sometimes too thick to be broken in this manner, and assistance was needed.

George E. Gascoyne and a crew of men came out to assist the *Eagle*. With ice plows drawn by horses they cut six-inch grooves in the ice, not enough to cut through but sufficient to weaken it so that the boat would break it. A groove was cut on each side of the boat, and holes were cut every eighty to one hundred feet. Captain F. J. Magle backed the boat up, sped ahead, and, when the boat ran up on the ice, it broke easily. The *Eagle* finally reached the Middle Bass dock at 4:00 P.M.; the ship had started the icebreaking operation at 7:00 A.M.

A voyage made in February 1895 was not as difficult. The *American Eagle* cut through ten to fifteen inches of clear ice without much trouble until the boat reached the middle of Sandusky bay where the vessel ran into very thick ice. Two passengers, perhaps irked by the slow progress, got off the boat and walked over the ice to Sandusky.

A similar incident took place aboard the steamer *Lakeside* in 1904. Kelleys Island mail carrier Alfred Erne had put his small boat on the *Lakeside* for the journey to Sandusky. When the boat got stuck off Cedar Point, Erne lowered his boat to the ice and with George Dwelle and Ed Ward pulled it to town.

An uneventful first trip was made by Captain E. J. Dodge in the *Tourist* in 1915. The steamer cut through ice ten and eleven inches thick between Put-in-Bay and Middle Bass. Ice was also encountered near Kelleys Island and near the Cedar Point jetty. The trip took three hours and the *Tourist* debarked forty passengers and considerable freight when the boat arrived at Sandusky at 10:45 A.M. The *Tourist* was still breaking ice forty-two years later when, under the ownership of John Gilbert and converted to an oil-burner, the vessel transported gasoline and other freight to Kelleys Island from Sandusky in December 1937.

ICE FISHING

Early island settlers had comparatively little to do in midwinter. The summer tourist had long since left the island for mainland; wine makers and grape growers occupied themselves with routine chores; there was ample time for fishing through the ice. Enough fiish could be caught before breakfast to feed the family and give a few to a neighbor. Herring, averaging nine or ten pounds, were the main catch. When it was learned that fish not needed for domestic use could be sold to mainland fish buyers, an avocation became a vocation.

The early fishing was done near the shore through holes cut in the ice. Fishing for profit meant that the angler had to fish all day long and had to move farther from shore. The islanders disliked sitting out in the cold, exposed to the elements for the entire day, so they developed the fish shanty about 1890. At first this was a small hut made of wood with a hole in the floor; it accommodated a number of men. Some huts were so large as to require a team of horses to pull them out to the desired fishing area.

Over the years, the shanty evolved into a lightweight, wood-frame, canvas-covered shelter mounted on runners. A small, one-man shanty is five feet long, forty-two inches wide, and fifty-eight inches high and is mounted on seven-foot-long oak, iron-bound runners. The canvas is painted to make it wind and watertight and in varying color schemes for identification. In one corner is a small coal stove. Oil and gasoline heaters also have been used in recent years. A burlap bag is hung in the other corner for the expected catch. A bench spans the width of the other end. In the middle is a hole in the floor which is centered over a similar-sized hole in the ice. The fishing equipment differs from that used by the angler in unfrozen waters. A heavy twine is used and two hooks are attached to a dipsey, a semicircle of wire with a lead weight in the center. Two such lines are suspended from the roof. On exceptional days a fisherman cannot pull up his catch—double catches sometimes— fast enough to remove the fish, rebait the hooks, and send the dipsey sailing to the depths before the other line has caught another fish or two.

The shanty is light enough to be pulled by hand or towed by iceboat or stripped-down ice car.

Because a fisherman pulling his shanty from the shore or walking back to land needed something to prevent slipping on the ice, the ice-creeper was devised. It can best be described as a large leather sandal, worn over the boot or shoe, with sharp metal cleats on the heel and sole. The "crunch-crunch" sound of creepers can be heard for a considerable distance over the ice.

Another item of specialized equipment is the spud, the tool used to chop a hole in the ice. The spud is essentially a heavy iron bar with one end flattened and sharpened to form a blade. A typical spud might measure fifty-two inches long with a three-inch wide blade and weigh about fourteen pounds.

The ice-fishing season usually begins in the early part of January and lasts until the middle of March. In 1912, when the winter was bitterly cold, the ice attained a thickness of thirty-eight inches in places, and the season lasted from the first week in January to April tenth. Fishing was good, and there were sixty-four days of safe hauling of the catch over the ice to Port Clinton. The principal ice-fishing area is between Middle Bass, North Bass, Rattlesnake, and Green islands and the west side of South Bass where the ice is locked in between those islands and South Bass. When the ice is especially heavy, some fishing is done on the east side of South Bass.

There is always the possibility that the ice may break away from the shore and be blown out into the open lake—shanties, fishermen, and all. This has happened a number of times. In 1898, a gale wind blew about one hundred shanties and seventy-five fishermen, including some women, out into the lake. Rowboats were brought out, all were rescued but some shanties were lost. Eighty unoccupied shanties were lost in 1939; fifty-two shanties were saved in 1948. Such incidents are commonplace. If the islanders think that there is a possibility of an ice floe breaking away, they pull their shanties to shore for the night. Many times they can rush to safety before the floe has drifted too far, jumping across the crack in the ice and pulling their shanties after them.

Winter ice fishing provided a welcome extra income for islanders during the nonproductive cold weather season. The angler pulled his shanty out to a selected fishing spot at dawn, chopped a hole in the ice, pulled the shanty over it, lighted a fire in the stove, baited the hooks with minnows, and settled down to the task of filling one, two, or more grain sacks with fish—pickerel and perch in recent times. If the fish were biting he stayed in the same place; if not, a move was made to another location. The shanty was frequently left overnight. It was "anchored" by placing a stick crosswise in the hole and tying it securely to the shanty floor.

The day's catch was hauled to shore in a hand sled, iceboat or, in more modern times, in a stripped-down automobile. There were usually several fish buyers on the island. Fred Schiele, Kenneth Morrison, Robert Parker, Lee Miller, Gordon Dodge, Ethan Fox, Richard Fox, Ramon Rittman, Edwin Smith, Edward Traverso, and John Nissen were some islanders who brought fish over the years. A small shed or a large room equipped with a sorting table and a scale was all that was needed. No. 1 and No. 2 pickerel had to be at least thirteen inches long, and perch eight and one-half inches to be salable. The undersized fish were returned to the fishermen.

John Nissen bought fish for twenty years, from 1949 to 1969. Prices varied from fifteen cents a pound to thirty-two cents for No. 1s, twelve to twenty-eight cents for No. 2s, and four to twenty-five cents for perch. In paying for the catch, pennies were eliminated from the change; for example, a fisherman whose catch brought $8.61 or $8.62 received $8.60; if it counted out at $8.63 or $8.64, he got $8.65.

The fish, packed in ice in boxes weighing 125 pounds, were hauled over the ice to Port Clinton. When Island Airlines began serving the islands, the fish were flown to mainland, and the boxes were reduced to sixty pounds for easier handling in the Ford trimotors. At peak periods Nissen bought three tons of fish a day, and he was not the only buyer on the island. Signs listing the high catch of the day and of the season were posted in the fish houses. John Nissen had a high catch of $68.50 in 1947, many islanders made $35.00-$40.00 per day. Some days the fisherman returned home empty-handed.

Commercial hook-and-line ice fishing declined drastically after World War II. Nissen bought only $75 worth of fish during the 1968 season, in which only six islanders fished commercially. Many of them had become ice-fishing guides and rented shanties to sport fishermen.

Ice fishing appealed to the sport fisherman as well as to the islander who fished for extra income. Ice fishing was also engaged in around the Catawba peninsula and Sandusky Bay area. Fish-shanty rental began on a limited scale in the late 1930s. Gordon Dodge, Walter Smith, and Nathan Ladd were among the first islanders to offer this service. After World War II the shanty rental business became the wintertime occupation for many islanders.

When the ice froze to a depth of four inches, it was safe to go ice fishing. The average thickness was ten to twelve inches and occasionally twenty-four inches. The one-man shanty was used at first; two persons could fish, but not comfortably in the shelter. Larger two-man shanties were developed for the rental trade.

Ice-fishing guides usually worked in pairs; one would get the shanties ready for the fishermen, clear the hole of overnight frozen ice, light a fire in the stove, provide the bait, or move the shanty to a new location if necessary. Transportation to Put-in-Bay in the winter is by airplane. Special early-morning flights are made from the Port Clinton airport to the island. Island Airlines has used Ford trimotors, a twin-engined Boeing 247, and numerous single-engine Cessna airplanes to bring the angler to South Bass.

The other guide would meet the planes, load the fisherman into his ice car, and speed over the ice to a warm shanty for a day's fishing. The sport fisherman averaged twenty-five to thirty pounds of fish per day while the islander, an expert in this field, might hook over two hundred pounds on a good day. Weekends bring up to one thousand people to the island. With the summertime motels and tourist homes closed, accommodations are limited. The 1956 Chamber of Commerce Directory listed two hotels and ten tourist homes in operation during the winter. Some of the ice-fishing guides provided room and board for their guests. Twenty-nine ice-fishing guides were named in the 1956 directory.

Fishermen start coming to the island Friday, continue through Saturday, and even a few come Sunday morning. On Sunday afternoon there is a big rush to the airport where scores of fishermen await the flight back to mainland. Planes land, load up quickly with the anglers, their gear, and the weekend catch, and take off for mainshore eight minutes away. Once in a while an unexpected heavy snow, fog, or high wind will prevent the planes from flying for a period, or, very infrequently, may cause cancellation of flights for the day. Then there is a frantic scramble to find overnight accommodations for the stranded fishermen.

WINTER MAIL CARRIERS

When the lake froze over and the ice became too thick for the ice-breaking steamboats to operate, the ice itself became a "bridge" between the islands and mainland. The ice on the lake is not skating-rink smooth. Sections may be like glass, but most of the ice is rough—where cakes have frozen together, where wind and currents have piled the ice into furrows, where cracks open and close as the wind shifts, and where there is dangerously thin ice or open water. The shortest distance between Put-in-Bay and the mainland is not always the safest. The route is often a circuitous one as the islander makes his way among piled ice, cracks, open holes, and thin ice. In the depths of winter, when the ice is thick, the passage to mainshore is relatively safe.

During the navigation season, the mail and other supplies were brought to the island by steamboat. Once the lake was frozen, the mail contract was given to several men who agreed to haul the mail from December 1 through March 31. Fish, wine, and other island products were also transported and various supplies brought back. The method of transportation depended on the condition of the ice.

In December 1898 Captain Amos Hitchcock was carrying the mail between North Bass and Middle Bass when he encountered thin ice. He strapped the sack of mail to his back, lay face down on the ice so as to distribute his weight evenly, and crawled over a mile to Middle Bass. Before the days of the automobile, a horse and sleigh were used when the ice was strong enough to support them. Once, Hitchcock was coming from Port Clinton with horse and sleigh when he came upon a crack too wide to cross. He had two or three passengers and several hundred pounds of mail. The resourceful carrier chopped out a large cake of ice—big enough to support horse, sleigh, passengers, and freight—ferried everything across the crack and continued his journey. Hitchcock's father had been a mail carrier and his two sons became carriers also.

Because the horse and sleigh would occasionally break through the ice, ropes, poles, and hoisting apparatus were carried so that the helpless animal could be pulled out. Islanders found out that when the horse became numbed by the icy water the only way to force it to struggle to get out was to put a rope around its neck and choke it. As the horse kicked, the men pulled on the ropes; if they were lucky the horse was able to get on firm ice. Sometimes the men brought along a bottle of brandy or whiskey to stimulate the chilled animal. Any remaining liquor was disposed of by the men—internally.

When the ice was not strong enough to support a horse and sleigh or when there were areas of open water to cross, the mail carrier used a rowboat called an ironclad. The ironclad was developed over the years from the ordinary flat-bottomed rowboat. It was sheathed in metal to protect the wooden hull from the ice and had a pair of runners mounted on the bottom so that it could be easily pulled over solid ice. The boat was about fourteen feet long. Oars were used when in open water. A sail, and later, an outboard motor provided propulsion. When the boat was on firm ice the two carriers, ropes over their shoulders, pulled the craft along.

The ironclad could be pulled over smooth, thick ice without much effort, or rowed or sailed on open water, but when the ice was broken up or thin it became much more difficult. Lynden and Ernest Hitchcock in the 1890s found the ice breaking into cakes on one trip between Middle Bass and Put-in-Bay. They had one passenger, Blanche Vroman, in the boat. They could not use the oars because of ice cakes and had to pull the boat from one cake to another, often sinking waist deep in the water before leaping to the next cake.

George Morrison and Carl Rotert were hauling freight between the Catawba peninsula and Put-in-Bay in January 1903 when they ran onto weak ice shortly after leaving Catawba. Rotert fell through and disappeared beneath the water before Morrison could free himself and come to his aid. The body was recovered in the spring.

An article in the *Cleveland Press* in January 1923 described a journey between the island and the mainland. Reporter Fennel Smith told of how the ice "bowed" or bent but did not break when they walked on it. The carriers, Arnold Burggraf and Maurice Arndt, wore hip boots and creepers and every once in a while they would break through and have to jump into the boat. The party passed an "iceberg" twenty-five feet high, two hundred feet wide, and three hundred feet long. The carriers, Smith, and a photographer rowed quickly through open water. Loose ice slowed progress, but, with oars and pikes, they made headway. When they hit thin ice, they had to break their way through at the rate of about a foot a minute. The last part of the trip was made through rough ice. Everyone helped to push, pull, and lift the ironclad over the piled ice. When finally, they reached Put-in-Bay, the three-mile voyage had taken two hours. Fare for the passengers was one dollar, one way. Put-in-Bay residents sometimes think that the news media overly dramatize normal, everyday, island events.

Most of the passages between the island and mainland were made in about an hour. The carriers left Put-in-Bay around 9:15 A.M. and arrived at Catawba about 10:30 A.M. They left on the return trip at 12:30 P.M. and arrived at Put-in-Bay about 1:30 P.M. Weather and ice conditions could lengthen the time required to make the crossing, delay, or even, cancel the trip. The carriers kept a log, noting such things as "weather—freezing, thawing, clear, foggy. Ice—good, getting bad, fair sea, heavy northwest gale." Also such comments as "Feb. 6, 1920, autos cross channel; Feb. 23, 1920, two Fords in the lake, one gotten out. Dec. 27, 1920, lay at Catawba all night." The number of passengers was recorded, from the minimum of one to a maximum of eighteen. Arndt and Burggraf carried the mail for four seasons—December 1919/March 1920 through December 1922/March 1923 period—averaging 340 passengers for each four-month term.

In December 1929 an ironclad and its contents were destroyed by fire off Mouse Island, an islet near the Catawba ferry dock. The carriers Lee Miller and Cletus March, Maurice Arndt, and Robert Parker had just started for Put-in-Bay when the blaze was discovered. They were unable to extinguish it. The boat was salvaged and later rebuilt.

The automobile is used today to transport the sport fishermen to and from their shanties and the island. The early cars were either of the open type or touring cars with a cloth folding top. If an open car or a touring car with the top down broke through the ice, a hasty exit could be made to safety. Closed cars were sometimes used when the ice was quite thick. The favorite island vehicle for many years was the Model T Ford and, later, the Model A. The top would be cut off a closed car exposing the occupants to a chilly but safer ride. Some Model A's had the back panel removed; benches replaced the rear seat and some measure of protection from the elements was afforded the passengers, yet a quick exit still could be made. All cars were equipped with tire chains to provide better traction.

The mail carriers used cars or trucks when the ice was heavy enough. Miller and March were driving from Catawba to Put-in-Bay in January 1930 when they came upon thin ice. The lighthouse keeper noticed their plight and notified Postmaster William Schnoor. Schnoor and William M. Miller brought out planks, which were laid on the ice, and the truck was pulled over them to thicker ice.

Some islanders who carried the mail over the ice were the Hitchcocks: Amos M. Sr., Charles, Amos, Lynden, and Ernest R. Others were Jake Merkley, Captain A. J. Fox, George A. Runkel, Mike Seitz, George Axtell, George and Charles Morrison, Carl Rotert, Fred Schiele, Clifford Morrison, Arnold Burggraf, Maurice Arndt, Lee Miller, and Cletus March.

ICE ADVENTURES

Automobiles provided the islanders with a reliable means of transportation on the ice. The wind could die out and leave an iceboat stranded far from shore. Bass Island residents drove among the islands to pay each other friendly visits, play cards, and attend dances. Trips were made to Port Clinton for supplies and evening jaunts brought islanders to see a "movie." New cars and trucks purchased after the boats stopped running were often driven over the ice to Put-in-Bay. This was usually done in midwinter when the ice was very thick. One story tells of a well-known boatman, experienced in the ways of ice travel, who bought a new Model T Ford but was so unfortunate as to have it break through and plunge to the bottom of Lake Erie. Too embarassed to tell what happened, he went back to mainland, bought another Model T and returned without incident to Put-in-Bay.

Clyde Foye and Val Traverso were returning to the island from Port Clinton in a Model T truck in February 1925 when they broke through the ice halfway between Green Island and Put-in-Bay. Traverso was able to get out before the truck went down but Foye, the driver, rode the Ford to the bottom. He kicked the windshield out and swam to the surface, fortunately coming up in the open hole the truck had made when it went in the lake. The truck was recovered the next day. A scaffold was erected over the hole on good, solid ice, and with ropes and hoists the vehicle was pulled out. A number of island ice cars still in operation have been to the bottom of Lake Erie at least once, or even twice. Many times the cars cannot be recovered; the ice may have shifted and they cannot be found, or the ice is just too poor to risk an attempt to raise them. A number of islanders can cite similar experiences.

ICE TRAGEDIES

There have been fatalities when a car and riders plunge through the ice. The island doctor, Theodore C. Greist, and his nurse, Sylvia Schultz, were drowned in February 1923 when their car ran into an open hole, fifty foot in diameter, west of Green Island. The doctor had planned a trip to mainland the next day and he went out to scout around the area the night before. Evidence indicated that he tried to stop but could not. A search party of forty islanders found an oil slick in the open hole and recovered the body of the nurse. The car was pulled up from a depth of thirty feet. The body of Dr. Greist was found the next day, the head and hands frozen to the ice.

Another island physician, Dr. George J. Edam with his wife and two children were drowned in February 1940 when their car broke through thin ice near Middle Bass. The doctor had come to the island the previous November and was taking his family for a ride before visiting patients on Middle Bass. Islanders had warned him that the route he took was unsafe. Mrs. Mildred McCann, the postmistress, saw the car break through and summoned her son, William McCann, who—with Fred Young, Gaius Hallock, Alfred Parker, Maurice Arndt, Edmond Miller, Ethan Fox, and Arnold Burggraf—pulled the doctor and his wife from the lake. Efforts to resuscitate them failed. The children's bodies were also recovered.

In 1955 Charles Schneider and John Klacik lost their lives when their car broke through the ice one hundred feet from the shore at Middle Bass. The water was ten feet deep at that point. The wives, Thelma Schneider and Jean Klacik, escaped through the open rear end of the car. Charles Schneider, Jr., and Richard Bretz following in another car rescued the women. They dove into the chilling waters in a vain attempt to save the men. The party had been returning to Middle Bass from the Firemen's Dance at Put-in-Bay.

THE ICE INDUSTRY

With the growth of the resort industry in the 1870s, a need arose for ice refrigeration at the various hotels. The Beebe House, Park Hotel,

Crescent Hotel, Put-in-Bay House, Herbster's Hotel, Hotel Victory, and other establishments all had their own icehouses. Valentine Doller, George E. Gascoyne, and Andrew Wehlre, Sr., bought part of Peach Point in 1878 and erected a series of icehouses with a total storage capacity of 13,000 tons. The ice was shipped to Cleveland. The Forest City Ice Company of Cleveland purchased the property from the islanders about 1883 and increased the capacity to 15,000 tons.

A crew of seventy men could harvest seventy-five to one hundred tons of ice an hour. Ice-cutting fields were laid out both inside and outside the harbor. Work began when the ice froze to a thickness of twelve to fourteen inches, the field being cut into cakes twenty-two inches square. The ice was first grooved to a depth of seven inches by an ice plow and the final cut made by a handsaw. Channels were cut from the field to the icehouse; men with pikes pushed the cakes to shore, where a two-chain elevator pulled the ice into the storage house where it was packed in sawdust.

Island ice trade was handled by Frank Rittman, who had an icehouse on Doller's dock. William M. Miller and Henry Jones also supplied islanders with ice. Their icehouse was on the present Miller Boat Line downtown dock. Frank Miller, a pound-net fisherman, had a large icehouse in which he froze the herring he caught. He sold out to Miller and Jones.

Two crews—one hired by Miller and the other by S. M. Johannsen, T. B. Alexander, and Lucas Meyer—were employed to fill the local icehouses. Mechanical refrigeration and health standards requiring sterile, artificial ice led to the demise of the lake ice business. Frank Miller installed an ammonia plant in his fish house in 1895. The Forest City Ice Company ceased operations at the turn of the century. William M. Miller was still putting ice from the bay into his own icehouse and those of the Crescent and Park hotels in the 1930s. He eventually tore down the big, old icehouse and built a much smaller one which he filled with manufactured ice brought from the mainland. The old icehouses on Peach Point were razed and the land offered for sale as cottage lots by Louis Schiele and John Hollway after 1905.

WINTER LIFE

Life in winter at a summer resort proceeded at a slow pace but there was activity. Skating parties and iceboat trips were made when the ice was safe enough for such sports. There was the traditional New Year's Eve Dance. Finsel's orchestra, which had played at the island during the summer, came down from Detroit, crossing over the ice from Port Clinton, to furnish music for some of the dances. The Odd Fellows Lodge gave masquerade balls at which prizes were awarded for the best costume. The prize for the 1909 Lincoln Day Ball was, appropriately, a book on the life of Lincoln. Dances for the young people were held in the Round House; the girls brought box lunches for the boys. The event was chaperoned, of course. The high school presented plays, musicals, and operettas.

Even with radio and television there is still considerable activity at Put-in-Bay during the cold-weather months. The Volunteer Fire Company still sponsors the New Year's Eve Dance; the orchestra comes from mainland by airplane today. There are men's and women's bowling leagues, a Wednesday afternoon ladies' card party, and the American Legion and its Auxiliary give a Pot Luck dinner on Veterans' Day. The Yacht Club has a change of watch meeting—installation of new officers—in January. Lent is ushered in with a Fasnacht and Bingo party by the Mother of Sorrows Church. There is the inevitable school Christmas play and other productions put on by the school or adult drama group. Some organizations find it difficult to secure an open date in which to give a party or dance because so many events have been scheduled. But there are many quiet days and nights when the islander can relax, remembering past summers or planning for the next busy three months of June, July, and August.

THE COMING OF THE AIRPLANE

During the navigation season the steamboats provided excellent mail, passenger, and freight service to the islands. Wintertime transportation varied from uneventful, routine trips on an iceboat, ironclad or ice car to hazardous, cold, and time-consuming voyages, battling the elements every inch and minute of the way.

Interest in the establishment of an air service to the islands was stimulated when a Parker Brothers airplane from Sandusky landed on the ice off Gibraltar and taxied into the bay. The pilot was Milton Hershberger and the passenger the Reverend Joseph E. Maerder, pastor of the Catholic churches on Put-in-Bay and Kelleys Island. School was dismissed that winter day in February 1929 so that the students could watch the plane land. Mayor T. B. Alexander and other islanders met with Hershberger and Maerder in the town hall to discuss the possibility of building a landing field on South Bass. Other flights were made and on 25 December 1929 pilot Joe Esch brought Father Maerder to Put-in-Bay to conduct Christmas services. This time the landing was made in a field. The pastor of the Catholic churches still commutes between Put-in-Bay and Kelleys Island by plane but the aircraft is a modern monoplane with an enclosed cabin, not an open-cockpit biplane as in 1929.

Milton Hershberger left Parker Brothers Airline and organized the Erie Isle Airways. Islanders volunteered their services to help clear the landing field of grape vines, rock, and other debris. The first flight of the line was made on 11 November 1930 with Hershberger flying a three-place Waco biplane. His first passenger was Roy Webster, a local vintner who was flown to Port Clinton. The next day Mayor Alexander, Ramon Rittman, Alfred Parker, William Kiinzler, and Mrs. Roy Evans made flights.

Lieutenant Walter Hinton, U.S. Navy, retired, was the guest speaker at the airfield dedication ceremonies held in late November 1930. One morning and one afternoon flight was scheduled, but the planes made a dozen trips to Sandusky, one to Toledo, one to Camp Perry (west of Port Clinton), and one to Catawba. Because of the weather conditions the *Erie Isle* and *Mascot* did not make the lake journey to Put-in-Bay that day.

The fare was $4 one way and $7 round trip in 1930 with the plane stopping at Put-in-Bay, Middle Bass, and North Bass. The plane flew to Kelleys Island on a different schedule. Although the airline did not have the mail contract in 1930, Hershberger helped the Kelleys Island mail carrier and flew the mail to mainland when running ice prevented the regular carrier from making the trip in an ironclad.

AIR MAIL AT REGULAR RATES

Lee Miller, who had carried the mail via the ironclad or ice car, John Parker, and the Erie Isle Airways bid on the mail contract with the Erie Isle Airways eventually securing the contract. The route flown was from Sandusky to Kelleys Island, Put-in-Bay, Middle Bass, and North Bass. Mail sent to the latter island has to be addressed to Isle St. George, the official post office designation for North Bass. The mail route is known as a star route and the regular first-class rate is charged for a letter, not the air mail rate, although all mail, first class through parcel post, is carried by airplane.

The mail was carried by air only from December 1 through March 31 in the years 1931 and 1932. In summer the mail came by boat. An exception was made in the case of North Bass which has no regularly scheduled boat service. Year-round mail service by air began on 16 July 1931 to North Bass. Hershberger started flying passengers from the Port Clinton airport in 1931 also although the mail contract called for flights from Sandusky because the mail went through the Sandusky post office. The postal contract was switched to Port Clinton in 1932 and after that year mail to all the islands went by airplane twelve months of the year.

THE FORD TRIMOTOR

Various types of airplanes were used: open cockpit Wacos, Travelairs, Monocoupes, and the enclosed cabin Cabinaires. The favorite plane in the early days was the Standard biplane seating four passengers in the front cockpit. The helmeted and begoggled pilot flew the craft from a cockpit to the rear. Needless to say, it was a cold ride in the wintertime. Larger and enclosed planes were needed; and Hershberger tried a number of aircraft, including some small trimotors. The airplane that became the mainstay of the Erie Isle Airways was, and is, the famous Ford trimotor—the Tin Goose—an all-metal, high-wing monoplane that had been the pride of the commercial airlines until replaced by faster, low-wing aircraft such as the Boeing 247 and Douglas DC-1. In 1935 Hershberger acquired five trimotors and changed the name of the line to Island Airways.

The first 4-AT Ford trimotor series appeared in July 1926. The three engines inspired confidence; the Ford could fly on two engines as well as on three. Level flight could be maintained with only one engine operating. The aircraft was all metal in an era of cloth, veneer, and wood airplanes. Gone were struts and wires; the wing was thick, of internally-braced cantilever construction, with a span of seventy-four feet. The fuselage was forty-nine feet ten inches long Three air-cooled radial engines, 235-horsepower Wright J-6s—one in the nose and one each on the side beneath the wing—gave the trimotor a cruising speed of approximately one hundred miles an hour.

Twelve passengers sat in comfortable seats, six on each side. Because of the high wing, the view out of the big windows was unobstructed except for those seated next to the outboard engines. The two pilots sat up front in a compact, enclosed cockpit. Henry Ford would sell you one of these 1926 marvels of the air, fully equipped, gas tanks filled, and on the ramp for $42,000, F.O.B. Detroit.

The lone remaining Ford trimotor of the Island Airlines is painted white with red and blue trimming. Gone is the polished plywood paneling, replaced by a spartan interior: no murals, no curtains at the windows. In the place of the easy chairs are small, straight-backed metal seats, safety belts dangling on each side. Fifteen passengers—plus luggage, mail, and freight—make up the island-hopping load. The plane is still drafty and cold, but even a midwinter flight seldom lasts more than eight minutes. Engine noise makes conversation almost impossible, but there is still the unhindered view out of the big windows: the "doll" houses and "miniature" autos, the boats or ice-fishing shanties out in the lake, and, as you approach the Put-in-Bay airport, Perry's Victory and International Peace Memorial jutting into the sky—a guidepost for all to see.

The airline has, at various times, owned a larger version of the Ford trimotor, the 5-AT, which could carry seventeen passengers. An even rarer aircraft, the Boeing 247D, was in the fleet for some years. Only seventy-five 247s were built, whereas Henry Ford constructed 198 trimotors in the period 1926-1933. The Boeing was an all-metal, low-wing, twin engine airplane faster than the Ford. It and the Douglas DC-1 had replaced the trimotor on the national airlines in the 1930s. The larger Ford and the 247 served the islands for a while but were eventually sold—The reliable old 4-AT, in a sense, replacing its more modern successors.

During the time he operated the airline Hershberger acquired seven Ford trimotors including two of the larger 5-ATs. When there was good winter ice fishing, he often used four trimotors at one time to transport the fishermen to and from the islands. Fridays, Saturdays, and Sundays were peak periods of air travel to the ice-bound archipelago. Many of the islanders fished through the ice commercially and the fish were flown to mainland. Hershberger hauled from 100 to 150 boxes of fish a day when the catches were good.

The Island Airlines has a remarkable safety record, carrying hundreds of thousands of people since it went into operation in November 1930. There have been a few accidents over the years. Milton Hershberger was flying alone in a Standard biplane in May 1934 when the engine flew apart and he landed in the water near Lakeside. He and seven sacks of mail were rescued by a commercial fish boat. Air mail service resumed on schedule that afternoon. Once, while in flight, the center engine of a Ford trimotor lost power. The pilot returned safely to the field on the two remaining engines.

A FATAL CRASH

The only fatalities on the Bass Island/Port Clinton route occurred on 29 December 1937 when a Standard biplane crashed in the water near Starve Island in a dense fog. The pilot had picked up three passengers at North Bass, had landed and taken off from Middle Bass, and was headed for Put-in-Bay when a heavy fog settled rapidly over the area. The plane had no radio, and efforts to reach the pilot by phone at North Bass and Middle Bass airports failed. He had just taken off when the order to remain on the ground came. Seeing an open space in the fog, the pilot tried to land on what he thought was ice, but the plane plunged into the lake. Three passengers—one woman and two men—were drowned. Islanders who heard the plane crash hurried out to the site and rescued the pilot.

On 31 July 1954 a Ford trimotor crashed at Kelleys Island with the pilot sustaining serious injuries, and on 21 August 1972 another Ford crashed on takeoff at the Port Clinton airport when an engine failed. There were no fatalities but some injuries, most of them slight.

SHORTEST AIRLINE IN THE WORLD

In August 1953 Milton Hershberger sold the airline to Ralph I. Dietrick of Sandusky. The name was changed to Island Airlines, although the corporate title is Sky Tours, Incorporated. Dietrick operated out of Sandusky and Port Clinton until 1962, when he moved the main office to Port Clinton and concentrated on service to the Bass islands. He sold his interest in the Sandusky/Kelleys Island/Pelee Island route.

Passengers for the Ford flight to the islands gather at the mainland terminal just off the Route 2 bypass near Port Clinton and purchase their tickets. The stub may be retained as a souvenir and has a photo of a Ford trimotor and the slogan "The Shortest Airline in the World" printed on it. Put-in-Bay is only twelve miles away. Tickets are exchanged for colored metal tags—a kind of priority system—when several planeloads of people are awaiting a flight. For example, the first planeload may have blue tags; the second, red; the third, yellow, and so on. The proper number of tags to fill one plane is distributed, thus speeding the loading and departure of each flight.

The passenger enters the Ford through the wide oval door. His luggage, fishing gear, and groceries are placed in the freight compartment; he sits down in the metal seat, fastens his seat belt and is ready for the takeoff. Empty seats may be loaded with luggage and freight, while the aisle may be filled with mail sacks, supplies for the islanders and island store, fresh-caught fish, lumber, appliances, a sick dog or cat on the way to the veterinarian, and hunting dogs. Ill or injured persons on a stretcher can also be accommodated. Even the dead can be flown to or from the island for burial.

Upon arrival at Put-in-Bay, the vacationer can rent a bicycle, golf cart, or car at the airport and tour the island. Island Airlines also operates a five-unit motel, a restaurant, and a swimming pool. Amateur pilots who buy cottage lots near the lake or main road can fly to the island, land at the airport, park their planes next to their cottage, get out the boat, and go fishing or sailing within minutes of their arrival.

As mentioned in the chapter on island education, schoolchildren from Middle and North Bass and Rattlesnake islands commute to school at Put-in-Bay. The pastors of the Catholic churches on Put-in-Bay and Kelleys Island still commute back and forth. The Reverend Lee Lindenberger, rector of St. Paul's Episcopal Church, flew his own plane, a Cessna 140, to Middle and North Bass islands and held services for his isolated parishioners. He also flew to Port Clinton, Sandusky, and Toledo to visit church members who were in the hospital. Mr. Lindenberger served St. Paul's from 1955 to 1961.

Dr. Heinz Boker came to Put-in-Bay in 1956 and served as island physician for six years. He moved to Lakeside but commuted by plane and boat to the islands. He now flies his own Cessna to Put-in-Bay, Kelleys Island, and the other islands two or three times a week. A registered nurse lives the year round at Put-in-Bay.

In 1973 Island Airlines acquired a new large plane, a Britten Norman Islander—a high-wing, all-metal, ten-place aircraft (it was sold in late 1974). It was powered by two Lycoming engines rated at 260 horsepower each. Other planes include single-engine Cessnas—high-wing, all-metal craft carrying four, six, and seven persons.

The oldest pilot in terms of service is Harold Hauck, who has flown trimotors for twenty-two years. Island Airlines carries more than sixty thousand people to and from the Lake Erie islands annually.

During the summer months ten round trips are made daily between Port Clinton and Put-in-Bay. Three round trips are made to Middle and North Bass. The number of flights is reduced in the fall and winter, although additional flights are made when required on weekends, holidays, and during the ice-fishing season. Weather conditions—fog, snow, or high winds—sometimes delay or even cancel flights. Island Airlines was sold to a group of four men from Mansfield, Ohio, in 1973.

Since the coming of the airplane in 1930 the islanders have not had to rely on the ice bridge as the only link to mainland. But the ice bridge can still be used. Ice cars are still used to carry islanders and sport fishermen to their shanties, and there is traffic between the three Bass islands and occasionally Canadians from Pelee Island drive to Put-in-Bay. Young islanders vie for the honor of being the first to drive over the ice to mainland although such trips are no longer a necessity but a sport.

Dehumidifying equipment was to be installed in Perry's Victory Memorial in the winter of 1960-1961 but the lake froze before the machinery could be hauled by boat to the island. Theodore McCann, Bernard "Mac" McCann, Charles "Sonny" Schneider, and William Market III hauled two 3,000-gallon fuel oil tanks and various pieces of machinery—some weighing two to three tons each—across the ice to the island. The equipment was put into operation in March 1961.

8

The Monument

One of the tourist attractions on Put-in-Bay is Perry's Victory and International Peace Memorial. A series of celebrations were held in the 1850s to raise money to build a monument to Perry's victory in the War of 1812, but these efforts met with failure. As the centennial of the Battle of Lake Erie approached, plans again were made to erect a monument to the 1813 victory and the century of peace that followed. Plans became reality when the 352-foot high shaft was opened to the public in 1915. Over 100,000 persons visited the Greek Doric column during the 1974 season.

The three American and three British officers killed in the Battle of Lake Erie were buried in a common grave near the lakeshore of Put-in-Bay harbor. For almost a century their monument was the "Lone Willow." Serious efforts to erect a more imposing memorial did not take place until thirty-nine years later when five companies of the Ohio Volunteer Militia met in a three-day encampment at Put-in-Bay in 1852.

A. P. Edwards, owner of the island, placed Put-in-Bay under the control of the military commander Captain R. R. McMeens. Probably to the soldiers' disappointment no intoxicating liquors were allowed. It was the first military camp on the island since William Henry Harrison had brought his army there after Perry's victory in 1813. Four steamers were needed to bring the estimated 2,500 persons to the celebration. As July Fourth 1852 was a Sunday, the ceremonies were held on Monday, July 5.

On the way over from Sandusky, interested parties held a meeting on the [first] steamer Arrow and appointed a committee to plan the formation of an organization to erect a monument on "Gibraltar Rock" commemorating Perry's defeat of the British. The work of the committee was presented to the assemblage, which gave their approval, and "The Battle of Lake Erie Monument Association" was created. The constitution listed the various officers to be elected. There was the usual president, and Lewis Cass was chosen for this position. There was the unusual requirement that there be twenty-five vice-presidents! Captain Stephen Champlin, one of Perry's veterans, was a vice-president.

A Provisional Executive Committee was appointed, and A. P. Edwards and Eleutheros Cooke were named to the committee. Unfortunately, nothing further was done toward the building of a monument to the American victory. Public attention was diverted by a serious outbreak of cholera in the lake region, and a presidential election campaign; moreover, the local character of the celebration caused the public to lose interest in the association.

The movement was revived in 1858 under the leadership of Eleutheros Cooke, father of Jay Cooke. He appealed to the people of Buffalo, Erie, Cleveland, Toledo, Detroit, and Sandusky to participate in the celebration of the forty-fifth anniversary of the Battle of Lake Erie on September tenth. More than 8,000 people came to Put-in-Bay for the event. Eight steamers and twenty-four sailing vessels provided the transportation. The USS *Michigan* and USS Revenue Cutter *A. B. Brown* were anchored in the bay.

The day began with a dampening rain falling on the crowds, but by the time the ceremonies were scheduled to start the sun came out. The ships in the bay fired salutes and were answered by several artillery companies on shore. Bands from Sandusky, Cleveland, Toledo, and Detroit furnished the music. Various orators made comments appropriate to the occasion.

Governor Salmon P. Chase of Ohio made the introductory address, stressing the peaceful relations that then existed between the United States and Great Britain:

> . . . we have met today to indulge in no feelings of exultation over a conquered foe . . . Why should we exult over that nation which was then our foe? Instead of meeting on the fields of battle we are now peacefully engaged in commerce. Instead of answering cannon, and exchanging salutes on the field of battle, our shouts of welcoming fly across the ocean and are re-echoed from thence across our mountains . . . [The first trans-Atlantic cable was then in use] . . . and lighting now speeds our words of cheer and welcome to our Anglo-Saxon brethren . . . "God bless them."

Eleutheros Cooke then spoke and introduced the surviving members of Perry's fleet who were in attendance. First was Captain Stephen Champlin, commander of the *Scorpion*, who fired the first and last shot of the battle; then came William Blair, a soldier of Harrison's army who had served aboard one of the ships; next to be presented was Lieutenant

Thomas Brownell, second in command of the *Ariel;* and lastly, Dr. Usher Parsons, surgeon aboard the *Lawrence.* Parsons gave a detailed and lengthy account of the naval engagement. Mayor Samuel Starkweather of Cleveland followed Parsons as speaker and, was in turn, followed by Joshua R. Giddings, who had been a soldier in the War of 1812.

Permanent officers for the Battle of Lake Erie Monument Association were named. Lewis Cass of Michigan was again chosen president. Many prominent or soon-to-be prominent men received vice-presidential appointments. Veterans of the battle—Usher Parsons, Thomas Brownell, and Stephen Champlin were so honored. Others were: Edward Everett, William H. Seward, Millard Fillmore, Salmon P. Chase, Samuel Starkweather, Eleutheros Cooke, August Belmont, and Lieutenant-General Winfield Scott. Among those named to the Committee of Management were Eleutheros Cooke, Pitt Cooke, J. B. Steedman, Morrison R. Waite, Stephen Champlin, Sardis Burchard, W. W. Dobbins, and Joseph de Rivera St. Jurgo had written to the organization offering land on Gibraltar Island in perpetuity as a site for the monument.

The next year, 1859, the association again met at Put-in-Bay on September tenth to lay the cornerstone for Perry's victory monument. De Rivera St. Jurgo was willing to donate as much as one-half of Gibraltar to the association. The board of management commissioned T. D. Jones, a Cincinnati sculptor, to design a column. Jones produced plans for a shaft 160 feet high and twenty-seven feet wide at the base. An eighteen-foot statue of Oliver Hazard Perry standing on a capstan was to surmount the edifice and a spiral staircase would lead to the observation platform.

Fourteen steamers—from Buffalo, Cleveland, Detroit, Toledo, and Sandusky—two tugs, and many sailing craft brought an estimated 15,000 persons to Put-in-Bay for the cornerstone laying ceremonies. The USS *Michigan* and two revenue cutters joined the fleet.

The orations began at 2:00 P.M. with Dr. S. A. Bronson offering prayer. He praised the men who had fought the battle and said that both the United States and Great Britain should promote the "good of mankind and the glory of God." The speaker of the day was Rufus P. Spalding who expounded on the causes of the War of 1812 and the Battle of Lake Erie.

Militia companies from Sandusky, Cleveland, Toledo, and Detroit put on a martial display. Four veterans of the battle were then presented: Dr. W. J. Taliaferro who served on the *Somers;* William Blair, a soldier who was on the *Niagara;* Benjamin Fleming, also on the *Niagara;* and John Tucker on the *Caledonia.* William Coleman, a veteran of the War of 1812 but who had not served in the battle, was also introduced to the audience.

The Masonic Order officials who were to lay the cornerstone then went from Put-in-Bay to Gibraltar for the ceremony. The following articles were placed in an airtight copper box to be enclosed within the stone: the Declaration of Independence; constitutions of the United States, the state of Ohio, and of the Battle of Lake Erie Monument Association; names of officials in the federal and state governments, officers of the association, United States coins, and papers of the day. The Masons added the Holy Bible, the Masonic constitution, bylaws, and newspapers.

Despite the great amounts of oratory expended at the 1858 and 1859 celebrations, the Battle of Lake Erie Monument Association was never destined to erect a monument to the victory that Perry won in 1813. Jay Cooke, the Sandusky-born Philadelphia financier, purchased Gibraltar from Joseph de Rivera St. Jurgo, in January 1864, for the sum of $3,001. The deed contained a qualifying clause, ". . . subject to rights, if any, of . . . the Battle of Lake Erie Monument Association started in Sandusky on or about the year 1859."

Shortly after the purchase, Cooke built a small monument—a pedestal with an urn on top—on the old cornerstone with the inscription, "Erected by Jay Cooke—Patriotic Financier of the Civil War—to Mark the Corner Stone of a Proposed Monument Commemorating Commodore Perry's Victory at the Battle of Lake Erie—Sept 10, 1813 "We have met the enemy and they are ours.' " Local legend has it that Cooke put up his monument to prevent the association from claiming one-half of Gibraltar. He could point to his modest monument and state that there already was a memorial to Perry's victory on the island.

Yet the idea of a monument would not die. In 1868 another celebration was held at Put-in-Bay on the fifty-fifth anniversary of the battle. Three survivors of that action were present, photographs of whom were sold to raise funds for the memorial. It was proposed to build the monument on Put-in-Bay and not on Gibraltar. A year later, another ceremony took place on 11 September 1869. The location of the monument was to be near the "Lone Willow." Two survivors of the battle, Dr. W. J. Taliaferro and John Norris, were special guests. The various lake cities sent 4,000 people to Put-in-Bay. There were some fund raising activities carried on but they were not sufficient for the purpose intended. A further effort was made in 1891 when the Maumee Valley Monumental Association, headed by former President Rutherford B. Hayes, met at Put-in-Bay on September 10. The Perry's-victory-monument question was raised and a Congressional appropriation was sought but without success. September tenth continued to be celebrated as a holiday in the nineteenth century and the various steamboats brought excursionists to the island to participate in ceremonies honoring Perry and his men.

A MODEST MEMORIAL

Captain J. J. Hunker, USN, who had a summer home on the island, wrote to C. West that the federal government would give obsolete Civil War cannon to "Memorial societies" for decoration purposes. West formed a "memorial society" to receive the gift together with Richard Waite and Judge William Lockwood. Eight cannon and eighty-eight cannon balls were shipped from the Brooklyn Navy Yard to Sandusky on the Baltimore and Ohio Railroad. The freight bill was $126.11. It was estimated that it would cost $60.00 to haul them from Sandusky to Put-in-Bay. The Fox brothers brought the guns to the island on the *A. H. Burch* for only $36.00. The cannon and cannon balls lay on the beach for over a year. They were to be erected in the village park.

The problem of paying the bills and mounting the cannon fell upon the mayor and council of Put-in-Bay village. Joel C. Oldt, the school superintendent, was mayor in 1898. There was $7.31 in the village treasury along with a host of unpaid bills. Oldt and council member T. B. Alexander were members of the local dramatic club which had put on plays for the benefit of the church and school. The group produced *Reddy— the Mail Girl* in January 1899 and Treasurer William Kiinzler turned over $62.03 to the cannon fund. Another play, *The Hidden Crime*, netted the fund $52.26 in February. The village council called a citizens' meeting to discuss the cannon question and $19.50 was raised in a general collection. A letter from Alexander to Jay Cooke brought a return of $15.00. The fund lacked $1.50 to complete payment of the freight bill. The council members dug into their own pockets for the necessary amount.

The Park Committee—Daniel P. Vroman, George E. Gascoyne, and S. M. Johannsen—began to mount the cannon. Vroman and Gascoyne hauled the guns from the beach to the park in 1899 and put them in stone foundations. They are mounted on the lakeshore side of the park along Bay View Avenue. The "Lone Willow" over the 1813 burial site had fallen because of decay, so a fitting marker was needed for the grave. The cannon, but not the cannon balls, were emplaced. Park Chairman Vroman suggested that a pyramid of the cannon balls be built over the grave and offered to build the cement base. Oldt asked the operators of the Hotel Victory for a donation, and they responded with a gift of five dollars. Vroman paid $4.25 for labor in emplacing the cannon balls. This left a balance of $1.56 in the treasury which was used to put an iron chain fence around the pyramid. A modest, homemade monument now honored the fallen heroes of the United States and Great Britain.

CENTENNIAL SUCCESS

Although great celebrations were held at Put-in-Bay at the forty-fifth and fifty-fifth anniversaries of the Battle of Lake Erie, nothing concrete was accomplished toward erecting a permanent memorial to Perry's victory. As the one hundredth anniversary drew near, a movement developed which succeeded where the others had failed—a monument to the victory and the century of peace that followed was finally built. The initial movement began when Rodney J. Diegle, director of publicity, Put-in-Bay Board of Trade (Chamber of Commerce) proposed at a board meeting 28 December 1907 that "a great centennial celebration on land and water be held at Put-in-Bay from June to September, 1913" and invited "the National and State governments and the American people . . . to participate . . . in such ceremonies . . ." The suggestion was supported by leading island citizens and board members: S. M. Johannsen, Henry Fox, T. B. Alexander, Lucas Meyer, George E. Gascoyne, J. J. Day, H. A. Herbster, M. Ingold, Emil Schraidt, William Kiinzler, John Esselbach, Gustav Heineman, S. Traverso, John Hollway, William Schnoor, and Dr. P. B. Robinson.

The next move was to seek aid on the state level. Ohio Governor Andrew L. Harris responded by appointing in June 1908 a commission composed of George H. Worthington, Cleveland; Webster P. Huntington, Columbus; S. M. Johannsen, Put-in-Bay; William R. Reinhart, Sandusky; and Mayor Brand Whitlock, Toledo. Nicholas Longworth, appointed in 1911, served until he was elected Speaker of the House of Representatives in 1925. He was then appointed an honorary member for life.

The state of Ohio appropriated for all purposes in connection with the celebration and memorial a total of $182,550. The project began as a proposal to hold a centennial celebration in 1913, but a report of the Ohio Commission in December 1908 recommended that any memorial honoring Perry's victory should be in the form of a permanent structure on Put-in-Bay.

The commission suggested that a marble memorial chapel be built in the village park. Ohio and the other seven lake states whose destinies had been decided by the American victory in 1813 were to install memorial windows "historically significant and artistically executed." In January 1909 Webster P. Huntington met with John Eisenman, a prominent Cleveland architect and engineer, to discuss the chapel which was to cost no more than $150,000. Since Oliver Hazard Perry was a native of Rhode Island, Emilius O. Randall, secretary of the Ohio Archaelogical and Historical Society, suggested that Rhode Island be asked to participate. Since soldiers from Kentucky served aboard the American fleet and made up the bulk of William Henry Harrison's Army that state was also invited at the suggestion of J. Howard Galbraith, a leading newsman of the day. The project, begun as a local affair, had now moved beyond the state level. The commissioners met at Put-in-Bay on 10 September 1910 to organize the "Inter-State Board of the Perry's Victory Commissioners" for the purpose of "promoting the . . . celebration and the erection of the . . . Perry Memorial . . ." The board had two functions, to plan the 1913 centennial celebration and to build a monument to Perry's victory.

The officers of the organization as of July 1913 were: President-General George H. Worthington, Cleveland; First Vice-President-General Henry Watterson, Louisville, Kentucky; Secretary-General Webster P. Huntington, Cleveland; Treasurer-General A. E. Sisson, Erie, Pennsylvania; and Auditor-General Harry Cutler, Providence, Rhode Island.

Although the various states were now involved in the celebration, one further step was taken. The prestige and financial assistance of the federal government was very much needed. After a struggle in Congress, where so many previous pleas for aid had gone unheeded, a bill appropriating $250,000 was passed in March 1911. In May, President William Howard Taft appointed the United States commissioners: Lieutenant-General Nelson A. Miles, USA, Retired; Rear Admiral Charles H. Davis, USN, Retired; and Major-General J. Warren Keiffer.

The Inter-State Board was composed of commissioners from the federal government and the states of Ohio, Pennsylvania, Michigan, Illinois, Wisconsin, New York, Kentucky, and Rhode Island. The board went before the state legislatures seeking support and, especially, financial aid. The Ohio Commission in July 1910 adopted a design of a monument drafted by John Eisenman which was used for publicity purposes when the Inter-State Board appeared before the lawmakers. The board had not approved any design at that time.

The Eisenman monument was to be a four hundred-foot high, steel-framed concrete structure. Ten participating states would each have a floor dedicated for their use. Eight states made up the Inter-State Board; the remaining lake states, Indiana and Minnesota, did not join the others in the centennial. There were also to be such utilitarian features as radio and lifesaving stations, an aquarium, and a convention hall. Elevators would take the visitors to the top.

Eisenman had worked for the U.S. Lake Survey and was familiar with the topography of South Bass Island. The site he selected for the column was the narrow isthmus between the smaller East Point section and the larger main part of South Bass. (He proposed a lagoon through the isthmus on which the monument was to be built.) Despite the swampy appearance of the isthmus, solid rock lay not very far below the surface. On 10 September 1910 the Inter-State Board declared the site acceptable.

A NATIONAL CONTEST

The Eisenman design, an early twentieth-century style, used to create interest among the states was not built. A design thousands of years old— a timeless design, that of a Greek Doric column—stands today at Put-in-Bay. President Taft suggested that the newly-created National Fine Arts Commission conduct a contest for the best design for the monument. A total of 147 architects and firms applied for admission to the contest. Eighty-two were admitted, and fifty-four exhibits were presented at the National Museum in Washington, D.C., by the end of January 1912. The architects of the various designs were unknown to the judges; the exhibits were identified only by a number. When the winning design was chosen, Colonel Spencer Cosby, secretary of the National Fine Arts Commission, presented sealed envelopes containing the names of the winners to officers of the Inter-State Board. President-General Worthington announced the awards. The winners of the first prize—architects of the memorial—were Joseph H. Freedlander and Alexander D. Seymour, Jr., of New York City.

Freedlander described his design:

> Three elements in the composition immediately suggested themselves: the shaft, the Museum and a statue flanked by a colonnade, typifying peace by arbitration.
>
> The composition was born in an instant—the shaft took the form of a great Doric column, with the Museum on the left and the Colonnade on the right. All were placed on a broad plaza elevated only slightly above the ground so that the entire Memorial would appear to rise from the sea and be further enhanced by its reflection in the rippling waters.
>
> The Column stands alone so that it may be seen over the water from all points of the compass . . . The Museum and Colonnade are distant from it some three hundred feet. . . .

The proposed museum would contain a collection of books and artifacts connected with Perry, the Battle of Lake Erie, and the War of 1812. The building was to be eighty-five feet long, sixty-four feet wide, and forty-two feet high above the level of the terrace. The interior would be divided into a large exhibition hall, lighted from above by means of a large skylight and with offices in the rear for the curator and board members. On the opposite side of the shaft from the museum was the colonnade, its height the same as that of the museum. The central feature

The Bay View House. (Top) RJD.   The Hotel Victory had 625 rooms.
(Bottom) OGH-KKJ.

The Hotel Victory fire 14 August 1919. *(Top)* OGH-KKJ.   The Str. *Tourist* encountering heavy ice, 9 February 1911. *(Bottom)*.

The O. T. Sears was owned by Walter Ladd, 1889. (Top) OGH-KKJ.
Ramps provide easy access to the ice. (Bottom) RJD.

Robert Ladd drives ice fishermen to their shanties, 1956. *(Top)* RJD.
Gordon A. Dodge displays a double catch, 1948. *(Bottom)* RJD.

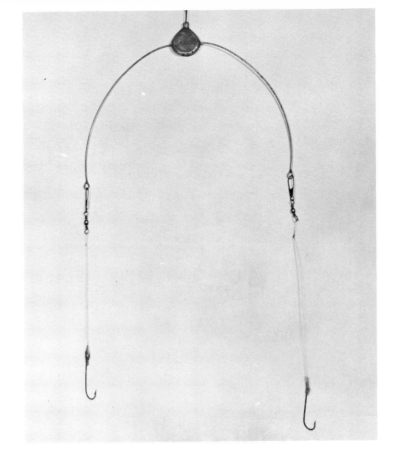

The dipsey is standard ice fishing tackle. *(Top)* RJD.　H. A. "Alex" Herbster uses a spud to chop a hole. *(Bottom)* RJD.

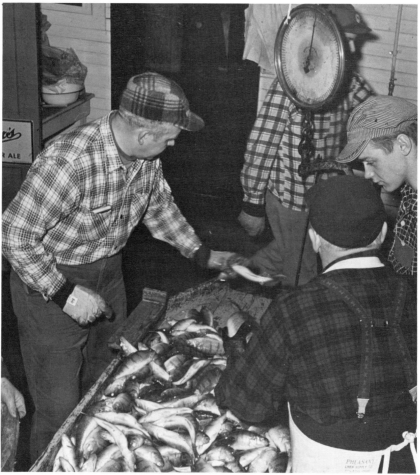

Hundreds of shanties dot the ice around Put-in-Bay; here are a few, 1954. (Top) RJD. Islanders selling their ice-caught fish to local buyers, 1954. (Bottom) RJD.

Lake ice was once cut and stored for summer use. (Top) OGH-KKJ.   Put-in-Bay at Christmas time, sometime in the 1950s. (Bottom) RJD.

Milton Hershberger and the Reverend J. E. Maerder meeting with T. B. Alexander to discuss air service to Put-in-Bay, 1929. *(Top)* OGH-KKJ.   Mainland is only minutes away in the Ford trimotor. *(Bottom)* RJD.

Engines roaring, the *Tin Goose* swiftly hops off the ground. (*Top*) RJD.
The Boeing 247D was faster than the Ford. (*Bottom*) RJD.

Put-in-Bay airport, 1954. *(Top)* RJD.   Perry's Victory Memorial—laying
the first course of stone, 1913. *(Bottom)* OGH-KKJ.

Just above the rotunda dome is the elevator landing. *(Top)* OGH-KKJ.
Constructing the gallery was a difficult task. *(Bottom)* OGH-KKJ.

Perry's Victory and International Peace Memorial, 1974. *(Top)* RJD. The monument was cleaned and repointed in 1952 and again in 1963. *(Bottom)* RJD.

U.S. Secretary of the Interior Douglas McKay speaking at the joint Canadian-American Legion Peace Ceremonies in 1953. *(Top)* RJD.   Old Glory and the Maple Leaf fly side-by-side at the monument. *(Bottom)* RJD.

Put-in-Bay Harbor from the monument, 1950. *(Top)* RJD.   Put-in-Bay harbor from the monument, 1974. *(Bottom)* RJD.

Put-in-Bay Town Hall. (Top) RJD.   Parker's Garage, 1974. (Bottom) RJD.

The post office was built in 1961. *(Top)* RJD.
by J. B. Monroe. *(Bottom)* RJD.

Inselruhe was built in 1875

was a seated figure, about fifteen feet high, signifying "Peace by Arbitration." Neither the museum nor colonnade were ever built.

The Inter-State Board met on 10 September 1912 and decided that not enough money was available to construct a three-part unit. Hence, the Doric column and plaza alone would constitute Perry's Victory Memorial.

Two years later, the Inter-State Board appealed to all the states, patriotic organizations, and individuals for financial aid in constructing the Temple of Peace as they now called the museum. Estimated cost was $300,000. It would be more than a museum; it would be an institution for the promotion of peace, to be used by contending nations seeking to negotiate their differences. (World War I had just broken out in Europe.) The funds were not forthcoming and the Temple of Peace was not built.

CONSTRUCTION BEGINS

J. C. Robinson and Son, New York and Chicago, was awarded the contract for the construction of the column. The amount was $357,588. The plaza at the base of the shaft was built by the Stewart Engineering Corporation, New York, for $102,000. An informational brochure about the monument states that the total cost was nearly one million dollars. The federal government and the several states gave the following funds for construction purposes: The federal government, $240,000; Ohio, $126,000; Pennsylvania, $50,000; Michigan, $25,000; Illinois, $30,000; Wisconsin, $25,000; New York, $30,000; Rhode Island, $25,000 Kentucky, $25,000; and Massachusetts, $15,000. (The stone used in the construction came from Massachusetts.) Other moneys were used in the 1913 celebration, which was separate from the construction phase of the centennial program. The total of the above amounts is $591,000; however, there were additional expenses such as the purchase of the site, the costs of the architectural competition, engineering fees, and the funds necessary for a retaining wall.

The state of Ohio condemned the land where the monument was built. The cost, $15,227, was shared by the Ohio Commission which donated $8,825 and the Put-in-Bay Board of Trade which paid the balance. Ohio ceded the fourteen acres to the United States in May 1913. The federal government accepted the gift 3 March 1919, but did not accept any responsibility for the operation or maintenance of the memorial.

The site had to be cleared before the actual construction began. John H. Feick of Sandusky undertook the task. The work began 24 June 1912 and took an unexpected three months to complete. Excavation for the foundation was begun on 4 December 1912 and finished twenty days later. Work was then halted for the winter. The first pourings of concrete were made in the late spring of 1913, and the first course of granite set in June. The shaft is essentially a hollow concrete cylinder with a facing of granite blocks. At the base, it is forty-five feet in diameter and the walls are nine feet six inches thick. At the neck, just below the observation gallery, it is thirty-five feet six inches in diameter and the walls are five feet thick. The interior diameter is twenty-six feet six inches throughout.

The facing stone used on the exterior is pink Milford, Massachusetts, granite. The delicate pink color was chosen to counteract the tendency of pure white stone to take on a bluish cast under an open sky. The monument appears to be pure white when viewed from a distance. Fine vertical lines were channeled into each of the blocks to give them a sparkle and brilliance similar to that which a diamond cutter imparts to a gem. The column was built in the following manner: beginning at the plaza level, twelve feet above the ground, a row or two of blocks was laid; concrete was poured behind them, another row laid, more concrete poured, until the seventy-eighth and last course of the shaft itself was reached. Thirty blocks in three basic patterns make up each row or course. There are twenty flutes or grooves in the column. Some of the granite blocks in the lower section weigh as much as five tons; others in the shaft, two to two and one-half tons; and some in the cap or top weigh four to four and one-half tons.

The concrete was mixed in a large mixer on the outside of the column, then poured down a chute through the foundation walls to the center, where it was raised in a bucket to the level needed. Consequently, neither the floor or the dome of the rotunda on the first floor could be completed nor the permanent elevator shaft installed until the need for concrete was ended. A scaffold was built inside the column to hold the equipment needed to raise the concrete bucket and to haul up the stone blocks. A boom extended over and beyond the work and the blocks were pulled up from the outside. The scaffold was continually moved upward as the work progressed.

CENTENNIAL CEREMONIES

The building of the monument was but one part of the centennial. A series of ceremonies were planned not only for Put-in-Bay but for other lake ports also. The "Put-in-Bay Celebration," as the Inter-State Board called it, had its beginning with the Fourth of July laying of the cornerstone and ended with the reinterment of the officers in the crypt in the monument on 11 September 1913.

Construction work was slowed by the various observances. Thousands of people journeyed to Put-in-Bay. So many, in fact, that private homes had to be opened to take care of them. Many patriotic societies, educational, military, and industrial organizations held their annual meetings on the island. The Fourth of July ceremonies began at 10:00 A.M. with local school children decorating the gravesite of the officers killed in the 1813 battle. Rev. J. M. Forbes, pastor of St. Paul's Episcopal Church, conducted a brief religious service.

The cornerstone-laying rite began at 1:00 P.M. under the auspices of the Ohio Masons with the Most Worshipful Grand Master Edwin S. Griffiths conducting the service. Others in attendance were: members of the Inter-State Board and various state boards, Lieutenant-Governor Hugh L. Nichols of Ohio and members of the Ohio Assembly. Several thousand Knights Templar, militia, and naval units were in the parade from the gravesite in the village park to the construction site.

A steel box was placed in the cornerstone containing documents relating to the memorial and the celebration. President Woodrow Wilson and former President William Howard Taft wrote tributes, which were included. The Daughters of the War of 1812 contributed a silk American flag of the 1812 period. The Masons donated a gold cup, a silver cup, and a golden rule—symbolic of their order. Since the construction site was not suitable for the other ceremonies, they were held elsewhere.

The Inter-Lake Yachting Association—an organization of twenty yacht clubs in Ohio, Michigan, Pennsylvania, New York, and Ontario—sponsored a six-week regatta at Put-in-Bay. Commodore of the I-L.Y.A. in 1913 was George H. Worthington who was also President-General of Perry's Victory Centennial Commission. (He had been Commodore in 1896, 1905, and 1908.) The regatta began with sail yacht races on 22 July. Ten classes of boat competed for prizes varying from $20 to $400. Powerboat races were held at the end of July and the first of August. The boats varied in length from under twenty feet to over sixty feet. Awards were made either in cash or trophies. An aviation week was scheduled for August 18 through the twenty-third. Races and other exhibitions were held and daily passenger-carrying flights were made. Under the heading "Other Sports Program," canoes competed over courses from 110 yards to one mile, and there was a rowing regatta. Swimming and diving events ended the I-L.Y.A. celebration.

The theme of the September observance was the reinterment of the remains of the six officers killed in the Battle of Lake Erie in a crypt beneath the rotunda floor of the monument. The officers buried at Put-in-Bay in 1813 were: on the American side—Marine Lieutenant John Brooks and Midshipman Henry Laub of the *Lawrence*, and Midshipman John Clark of the *Scorpion*; on the British side—Captain Robert Finnis of the *Queen Charlotte*, Lieutenant John Garland of the *Detroit*, and

Lieutenant James Garden of the Royal Newfoundland Regiment (Soldiers served aboard the British fleet as well as the American).

The pyramid was dismantled, a plank wall around the gravesite kept out the curious, and the excavation began. Charles E. Sudler, superintendent of construction at the monument, supervised the operation. He reported September 5, "We have found a few bones scattered all round . . . without question the bones are those of these officers." The remains were sealed in a casket and the fence torn down. Sudler rebuilt the pyramid over the now vacant burial mound in the summer of 1914.

A large number of invited guests stayed at the Hotel Breakers at Cedar Point the night of September 9. A fleet of boats brought them to Put-in-Bay the next morning. The ceremonies were scheduled to start at 11:45 A.M., the time the Battle of Lake Erie had begun exactly one hundred years before. A program of commemorative speeches was conducted at the Coliseum (Colonial Dance Hall). President-General George H. Worthington opened the program by commenting on the twofold nature of the celebration:

> We are assembled upon an occasion of more than national significance—one not only commemorating the history of one hundred years ago . . . but one also typifying the fraternal relationship that has existed among the English speaking peoples for a century and point to the coming era of permanent peace, by means of arbitration, among all the enlightened nations of the world.

Worthington, a Cleveland businessman born in Toronto, then introduced the master of ceremonies, James M. Cox, governor of Ohio. Cox presented former President William Howard Taft, who gave the featured address. He was followed by James A. MacDonald, managing editor of the *Toronto Globe*, representing Canada; Rhode Island Lieutenant Governor R. B. Burchard; and the Reverend A. J. Carey, a black minister from Chicago (a reminder of the fact that one-fourth of Perry's crew had been black).

The solemnity of the occasion was preserved on South Bass Island by the prohibition of all sales of alcoholic beverages between the hours of 10:00 A.M. and 4:00 P.M. on both September tenth and eleventh. No music or entertainment not sanctioned by the Inter-State Board was allowed on either day or evening.

The ceremonies of 11 September 1913 began at noon. Harry Cutler, a Rhode Island commissioner, was Grand Marshal and led the parade. A battalion of United States infantry, assorted Rhode Island infantry, artillery, and naval units, officers and men of the USS *Wolverine* [Ex-*Michigan*], *Essex*, *Dorothea*, *Don Juan de Austria*, and *Hawk* escorted the clergy, guests of honor, state governors, state commissioners, and members of the Inter-State Board from the old gravesite to the monument.

The procession stopped at the old burial ground, where Secretary-General Webster P. Huntington and Financial Secretary MacKenzie R. Todd placed a silk American and a silk British flag on the sealed casket. The flag-draped casket was then put in the catafalque for the journey to the final resting place. Minute guns resounded from the ships in the harbor, island church bells tolled, and the strains of the Chopin "Funeral March" were heard—the only sounds that broke the hushed stillness of the thousands honoring the dead of two nations.

The funeral cortege proceeded to the monument, where religious services were conducted by the Right Reverend James de Wolf Perry, Jr., Bishop of Rhode Island, and the Venerable Arch-Deacon H. J. Cody, rector of St. Paul's Church, Toronto, Ontario. Hymns were sung by the choirs of the Episcopal churches of Sandusky. When the catafalque reached the crypt, the box containing the remains was removed and lowered into the open space. The ceremony ended with a solitary bugler blowing "Taps" over the last resting place of the six officers who had lain, united in death, for one day less than a century.

After the War of 1812, the *Niagara*, Perry's second flagship, and the other ships had been sunk in Misery Bay, Erie, Pennsylvania, for preservation. The *Niagara* was raised from the waters and rebuilt in 1913 by the Pennsylvania Commission. The old brig was towed by the *Wolverine* to many of the lake ports where the vessel attracted large crowds. The *Niagara* visited her 1813 base of operations, Put-in-Bay harbor, several times during the summer of 1913. Today, twice more rebuilt, the brig rests, out of water, at the foot of State Street in Erie, Pennsylvania.

CONSTRUCTION CONTINUES

Once the July and September ceremonies were over, construction proceeded uninterrupted. Course after course of stone rose slowly until, sometime in July 1914 (the exact date is unknown), the seventy-eighth and last course on the main column was set. The seventy-ninth course began the assembly of the echinus or molding under the abacus or observation gallery of the Doric column. Construction of the gallery presented special problems because there is an overhang of fifteen feet measured on the diagonal. To hold the granite in place on the soffit or underside of the gallery, supporting forms were built. The stones, after being cut with keys on the upper surface, were laid on the forms and reinforced concrete poured until the whole became a homogeneous mass. The supporting forms were then removed. The observation gallery is forty-eight feet square.

On the top of the penthouse is a bronze urn twenty-three feet high, eighteen feet wide, and weighing eleven tons. The urn (it has been called a tripod and a lantern) was designed by Freedlander and was cast by the Architectural Bronze Division of the Gorham Company. The eight-footed urn was made at the company's Rhode Island foundry, assembled for inspection there, disassembled for shipment to Put-in-Bay and final reassembly on the top of the monument. There is a glass dome with a row of electric lights beneath which produce a soft glow at night. The urn cost $14,000.

Construction of the upper plaza began in the fall of 1914. The plaza is twelve feet above the ground level and the foundations and supporting pillars extend down to bedrock as do the foundations of the column itself. Not all of the planned work on the plaza was completed at the initial stage. The Stewart Engineering Corporation contract of $122,000 was reduced by $20,000 because of lack of funds. This primarily affected the landscaping of the grounds. Moreover the paving of the upper plaza was not done until 1924-1925 when a federal appropriation was obtained. The lower plaza facing the bay front road was finally paved in 1926.

Because concrete used in building the shaft was hauled up through the center of the column, certain work, such as the completion of the rotunda dome, could not be finished until the last concrete was poured. That day came in October 1914 when the scaffold and equipment were dismantled. Meanwhile stone carvers were able to work on the historical tablets on the rotunda walls. The engraving proceeded intermittently from October 1913 through the winter of 1914-1915. Indiana limestone was used in the walls, while the floor is composed of pink Tennessee marble with a central star made of marble from Italy, France, and Greece. The crypt was not identified until 1918 when a marble slab with bronze letters stating, "Beneath this stone lie the remains of three American and three British officers killed in the Battle of Lake Erie . . ." was set into the floor near the front doorway.

On the rotunda walls are carved the names of the American ships engaged in the battle and those crewmen who were either killed or wounded—a total of 123 casualties. At the rear of the rotunda is a stairway leading up two flights to the elevator landing. Bronze plaques on this floor list the remaining crew members who served with Perry—444 names —for a grand total of 567 men who drew prize money.

A stairway of 467 steps leads to the observation gallery. It is now used only for maintenance and emergency purposes. An elevator whisks the visitor to the top in less than one minute. From the gallery one can see where the Battle of Lake Erie took place, as well as many American and Canadian islands, and the Ohio mainland. On an exceptionally clear day, visibility is extended for forty miles, to the Michigan and Ontario mainland.

The column was opened to the public on 13 June 1915. There were no elaborate ceremonies such as those held in 1913. When the season closed on September 16, 22,000 visitors had paid a total of $470.95 to ride the elevator to the top. It was also possible to climb the stairway to the observation gallery. Employees hired for the initial season were: Adam Heidle as guide on the gallery; Herman Wagner as elevator operator; William E. Marks as engineer; and Dorothea Miller as ticket seller.

Islanders have been employed at the monument since 1915. Salaries paid for the year 1928, for example, were: William Schnoor, custodian, $750 per year; Horace Norton, superintendent of grounds, $150 per month; Fred Ingold and Fred Foye, guides, $105 per month; Henry Fuchs, Jr., elevator operator, $150 per month; Grace Williamson, cashier, $65 per month; and Isobel Brown, clerk at the souvenir stand, $40 per month. The custodian was employed the year round; the others worked approximately three and one-half months. During the depression period of the 1930s only two men were employed as guide and elevator operator. Anthony J. Kindt and William Market Jr., worked on the grounds in the morning, ate lunch, changed into uniforms, and opened the column to the public at noon when a woman cashier came in to sell tickets.

The commissioners had hoped that the revenue from the elevator-ticket and souvenir-booklet sales would meet operating costs. In general, this was true until the coming of the depression and several poor seasons due to weather conditions. There were other expenses such as the filling in of land and landscaping of the grounds. Unforeseen events caused expenses too. Unprecedented high lake levels and severe storms in the spring and early summer of 1929 inundated the memorial grounds four times washing out shrubbery. Damage to the north sea wall was extensive. Lightning struck the northwest corner of the observation gallery on 6 July 1920 knocking a two foot by eight inch piece of granite loose. The stone fell 312 feet through the upper plaza and buried itself in the ground beneath. An adequate lightning protection system was eventually installed.

The federal government had appropriated $250,000 for use in building the memorial and the centennial celebration in 1911. In 1924 a further $99,185 was granted to complete the plazas, landscape the grounds, and build a new south sea wall. Federal money in 1928 provided for floodlighting the shaft and the construction of a utility building. The cost was $14,374. Island-produced electric power was expensive. A mainland company, the Ohio Public Service Company, laid an underwater cable from the mainshore to Put-in-Bay and the rates were considerably reduced.

The monument was self-sustaining ever since it opened in 1915 but the seasons of 1928 and 1929 were unprofitable. Cold weather caused a decrease in the number of visitors and thus the receipts were less. The commissioners decided that, if economies of administration were practiced the memorial could be kept open at a cost of slightly more than $5,000 per year.

THE FORMAL DEDICATION

There had been no gala celebration when the monument began operation in 1915. The grounds needed landscaping and the plazas were unpaved. By 1931 many improvements were made. The Perry's Victory Memorial Commission decided that a formal dedication of the memorial should be held. The date set was 31 July 1931. Commission President Webster P. Huntington saw to it that the news media received news and feature articles about the event. The highlight of the dedication was the unveiling of four bronze tablets placed in the two side doorways of the rotunda.

One tablet contained the 150-word Rush-Bagot Agreement of 1818 which had reduced naval armaments on the Great Lakes. The state of Ohio donated this tablet. John H. Clarke and Newton D. Baker gave the Woodrow Wilson tablet—his 1913 statement which was enclosed in the cornerstone. Robert A. Taft presented the William Howard Taft plaque— also a 1913 declaration made by the former president and put in the cornerstone. The Henry Watterson tablet was a gift of his daughter, Mrs. Bainbridge Richardson. His observation appeared in a 1917 history of the memorial. Expenses of the dedication were defrayed by contributions from the commissioners and from Put-in-Bay citizens: Gustav Heineman, Henry Fox, B. F. McCann, William Kiinzler, T. B. Alexander, C. E. Seibert, Gordon A. Dodge, William M. Miller, R. L. Todd, and James A. Poulos.

The ceremonies were held under the joint auspices of the state of Ohio, the Perry's Victory Memorial Commission, and the Canadian Club of New York—the latter organization representing the equal interest of Canada and all English-speaking peoples in the occasion. The memorial which commemorated the American victory in 1813 and the century of peace that followed the war was formally dedicated to the principle of international peace by proportional disarmament. Former Associate Justice of the United States Supreme Court John H. Clarke was the chairman of the dedicatory exercises. The official party was composed of Ohio Governor George White; state officials and legislators; Louis L. Emerson, governor of Illinois; Commission President Webster P. Huntington; federal and state commissioners; Edwin A. Scott, A. W. J. Flack, and Case R. Howard, officers of the Canadian Club of New York.

Detachments of sailors and marines from the USS *Wilmington, Hawk,* and *Paducah,* military bands, and others escorted the official party to the memorial. The Reverend Angus E. Clephan, St. Paul's Episcopal Church, Put-in-Bay, gave the invocation. The officials assembled in the rotunda and proceeded to unveil the tablets. Justice Clarke read the text of the Rush-Bagot tablet which was unveiled by Case R. Howard, who removed a British flag, and by Mrs. Webster P. Huntington, who withdrew the American flag. The texts of the Wilson, Taft, and Watterson plaques were then read and the tablets unveiled.

The remainder of the ceremonies took place on the upper plaza. The Ohio National Guard band played "America," which the Canadians could properly interpret as being "God Save the King." Huntington then introduced Chairman Clarke. Clarke presented Governor White, Governor Emerson, and Case R. Howard, each of whom gave brief addresses. The general theme was the peace which had existed between the United States and Canada since the War of 1812 and the disarmed boundary between the two nations.

A public address system carried the orations to the audience on the lower plaza and to the yachts in the harbor. The National Broadcasting Company aired the program nationwide. Expenses were more than met. A balance of $133.88 in the tablet fund was used to publish an illustrated souvenir program of the dedication. Copies were sold at the memorial for fifteen cents each.

FINANCIAL TROUBLES

By the time the commission met on 22 August 1932, the effects of the national depression had been felt in the operation of the monument. For the first time, receipts had failed to meet the actual costs involved in operating the memorial. The commission shortened the hours of employment of the guides and cashier, dismissed the superintendent of grounds, and cut down the hours of floodlighting. The commission, although negotiating a lower rate for electric power, was still in debt to the Ohio Public Service Company in the amount of $4,500. Receipts had averaged $8,321 a year from 1919 (when the federal government accepted ownership of the monument) through 1928. Revenues began to drop in 1928—$7,829 to $2,527 in 1933. Operating costs were reduced to $2,422 in 1933.

The only financial resources of the memorial were the elevator fees —twenty-five cents adults and ten cents for children—and souvenir stand sales. The season was short, only three and one-half months. Seventy-five percent of the patronage occurred on Saturdays and holidays, the majority of visitors coming to the column between 11:00 A.M. and 5:00 P.M., the time of arrival and departure of the large passenger steamboats. It was estimated that between 200,000 and 300,000 persons visited the monument, but only 50,000 went to the observation gallery per season. Visitors could choose to pay the elevator fee or walk up the 467 steps at no charge. A breakdown in elevator service would lower receipts to almost nothing.

More financial problems faced the commission in 1933: a new north sea wall was needed, the south sea wall was in disrepair, the elevator cables were due for replacement, and better lightning protection was urged. The fiscal year 1932 ended with a cash balance of $37.37. Fortunately, the state of Ohio had taken over the maintenance of the road in front of the monument, which had cost the commission $2,000 in the past. The next year, 1934, the federal government appropriated $25,025 as an emergency measure to meet the cost of the most urgent repairs. In an effort to economize, minor repairs were neglected and the shaft and the grounds could no longer be kept as clean and orderly as they had been in the past. Floodlighting of the column was curtailed.

THE MEMORIAL BECOMES A NATIONAL MONUMENT

The commission and the United States Department of the Interior decided that the memorial should be put completely under federal control. To that end, legislation was introduced at the first session of the Seventy-fourth Congress to "assign control, administration, protection and development of the Memorial . . . to the National Park Service under the direction of the United States Secretary of the Interior . . ." The legislation was favorably received. The Federal Register reported on 9 July 1936 that the "74th Congress . . . authorizes the President of the United States . . . to proclaim and establish the Perry's Victory and International Peace Memorial National Monument." The monument was placed under the administration of the National Park Service, United States Department of the Interior, by the Act of 2 June 1936.

The Perry's Victory Memorial Commission became a board of directors for the secretary of the interior. Those persons employed by the commission continued to be employed, at the discretion of the secretary, by the National Park Service. Commissioner S. M. Johannsen, Put-in-Bay, had been appointed custodian of the memorial when it was opened in 1915 and served in that capacity until his death in 1925. He was succeeded by his former business partner, William Schnoor. When the National Park Service took over the administration in 1936, Schnoor was retained as custodian. The first Park Service-trained superintendent was Joseph R. Prentice who began his tour of duty on 28 August 1947. Under Park Service management, additional rangers were hired during the busy summer season and the hours and season of visitation extended.

The change of commands from Perry's Victory Memorial Commission to the National Park Service called for another ceremony. Leading speaker on this occasion was Secretary of the Interior Harold L. Ickes. Other guests were: Arthur E. Demaray, associate director of the National Park Service; Wallace McClure, head of the treaty division of the Department of State; Colonel T. E. Codlin, commander of the Kent Regiment, Ontario, Canada; and Mrs. W. S. Haley, president of the Daughters of the War of 1812. In the 11 September 1938 celebration, the speakers again stressed the peaceful relations which existed between the United States and Canada. At the conclusion of Ickes's speech, 125 pigeons were released from the top of the monument to symbolize the century and a quarter of peace between the United States and Canada.

A FATALITY

Hundreds of thousands of people have visited the monument since the first tourist went to the top in June 1915. The only fatality among the visitors occurred on 27 July 1945 when an eighteen-year-old girl jumped or fell to her death from the observation gallery. She came to the island on the boat from Detroit with a sister and a friend on an excursion to Cedar Point, but got off at Put-in-Bay while the others continued to Cedar Point. It was learned later that she had a terminal illness and was despondent over the fact that she had been unable to be graduated with her high school class that spring. The wall at the gallery is four feet high and two and one-half feet wide.

REPOINTING

No major repairs were required on the shaft itself until 1952. The lightning damage of 1920 was repaired and lightning protection installed; the elevator cables were replaced and other similar projects completed without major expense except for a new elevator in 1939.

By 1952, the shaft needed repointing; that is, the mortar between the granite blocks was cut out to a certain depth and replaced with a waterproofing compound and mortar. An estimated twenty tons of masonry sand was used in the repointing. The column and plaza walls were also cleaned by sandblasting with sixty tons of the coarsest and hardest sand available. All the work on the shaft was done from a scaffold hung on cables from the top of the monument. The project cost $40,000. The monument was closed during the repair operations.

THE "INLAND SEAS" CEREMONY

In 1959 the St. Lawrence Seaway was opened for operation. Many of the larger oceangoing ships could now sail to Great Lakes ports. "Operation Inland Seas" was the title given to the many celebrations held that summer. The United States Navy sent a small fleet of warships into the Great Lakes to participate in the observances but not before special diplomatic consultations were held between the United States and Canada, because such a fleet "violated" the Rush-Bagot Agreement of 1818. Approval was given and the American fleet passed through the Welland Canal on its way to Lake Erie and the upper lakes.

The U.S. Navy and the National Park Service planned a ceremony at Perry's Victory and International Peace Memorial to honor Oliver Hazard Perry and the peace that followed his victory. On 21 July 1959 the destroyer *Willis A. Lee* dropped anchor between Middle Bass and Rattlesnake islands. On board were Rear Admiral Edmund B. Taylor, commander of the Atlantic Destroyer Fleet, and Eivind T. Scoyen, associate director of the National Park Service. Other guests were: Admiral Joseph Kerrins, United States Coast Guard; Colonel Glenn E. Nida, Erie Ordnance Depot; Lee Bracken, commodore of the Inter-Lake Yachting Association; Aubrey F. Houston, superintendent of Perry's Victory; and Mayor Earl Parker of Put-in-Bay. After brief speeches, Admiral Taylor and Director Scoyen placed a wreath over the crypt in the rotunda. An honor guard fired three volleys, a bugler blew "Taps," and the band played the national anthems of the United States and Canada to close the ceremony.

The *Willis A. Lee* one of the newest of the DL-2 class of frigates, displaced 4,750 tons and was 493 feet long—four times the length of Perry's flagship *Lawrence*.

FURTHER REPAIRS

Despite the repointing and waterproofing done in 1952, moisture remained a problem in the preservation of the shaft. Storm-driven rainwater found its way into the interior of the column. The monument is a huge mass of concrete and granite. Winter weather reduces the temperature in the shaft and, when the warm spring and early summer winds blow through the column, moisture condenses on the walls and floors. Dehumidifying equipment was installed in 1961. Some of the equipment was hauled over the ice in the winter of 1960-1961 after the regular navigation season closed.

The monument was repointed and waterproofed a second time in 1963. This time steel scaffolding was built from the upper plaza to just underneath the observation gallery—a height of three hundred feet. A liquid solution under high pressure was used to clean the stone rather than sandblasting, and the column was kept open to the public during the work. The project was completed in the first week of August.

THE SESQUICENTENNIAL CELEBRATION

New celebrations were held on the sesquicentennial of the battle in 1963. The initial observance was a small-scale peace ceremony sponsored by the local American Legion Post, Scheible-Downing No. 542, and the First District American Legion units on May 26. This was followed by the local Fourth of July ceremony, the parade featuring tableaus depicting American and Canadian frontier scenes, Perry crossing from the *Lawrence* to the *Niagara*, and American soldiers and Indians. Reigning queen of the celebration was Mary Wulkowicz [Sabo], a 1963 graduate of Put-in-Bay High School. Kathy Crowe [Patton] and Susan Powers [Morrow] were her attendants.

The Inter-Lake Yachting Association also held a sesquicentennial ceremony on August 8. Lee Bracken, past commodore and I-L.Y.A. sesquicentennial chairman, presented the main speakers. Representing the United States was Rear Admiral R. W. Cavenagh, USN, Fourth District, Philadelphia, and Commander G. H. Davidson, HMCS *Patriot*, Royal Canadian Navy, representing Canada, from Hamilton, Ontario. In port were the USS *Whitehall* and *Amherst*. The ships were open for inspection to the public.

The federal government sponsored the largest and final celebration of the year. Congress established the Battle of Lake Erie Sesquicentennial Commission on 24 October 1962. Named as chairman by President John F. Kennedy was Mrs. Prudence Lamb, Maumee, Ohio. Other members of the commission were: Albert S. Close, Sandusky; Lawrence Litchfield, Jr., Pittsburgh; George J. Mead, Erie, Pennsylvania; Senators Frank J. Lausche and Stephen Young, Ohio; Senators Kenneth B. Keating, New York, and Hugh L. Scott, Pennsylvania; Representatives Thomas L. Ashley, Delbert L. Latta, and Charles A. Mosher, Ohio; and Thaddeus J. Dulski, New York. Senator Young was vice-chairman and Conrad L. With, director of the National Park Service, was executive officer.

Approximately 3,000 people gathered in front of the monument to witness the ceremonies on a warm, sunny 8 September 1963. A parade highlighted by the United States Marine Corps School Band, Quantico, Virginia; the Stategic Air Command Drill Team, Omaha, Nebraska; the Canadian Legion Kilt Band, Leamington, Ontario; the Legion Post, Pelee Island, Ontario; the Port Clinton and Sandusky High School bands, Moose marching units and Eaglettes; units from the USS *Whitehall,*

Amherst, and *Holidaysburg;* and various floats from Put-in-Bay, Port Clinton, and Fremont escorted the dignitaries to the monument.

Chairman Prudence H. Lamb introduced the master of ceremonies, Lieutenant-Governor John Brown of Ohio. Principal speakers were I. V. Macdonald, consul for Canada in Detroit, and Victor M. Longstreet, assistant secretary of the United States Navy. Two of Perry's relatives were presented to the assemblage: Ensign Matthew C. Perry, a great-great-grandnephew, and Daniel Wooley, a great-great-great-grandson. The two had not met previously. Ralph W. Findlay, director of Public Health and Welfare, Cleveland, commented on the role of black men in the Battle of Lake Erie. Mrs. Garold C. Jenison, president of the Ohio chapter of the Daughters of the War of 1812, presented a replica War of 1812 flag to George A. Palmer, assistant regional director of the National Park Service.

One of the more interested guests was Roy H. Robinson who, fifty years before as a young man of thirty, had been the contractor's (J. C. Robinson and Son) representative at the construction site. Standing as tall and straight as the column he built, he told of how the engineers of the time said that the monument could not be built. "But," he proudly stated, "there it stands—fifty years later."

State Representative Earl Wiseman, Port Clinton, placed a wreath on the crypt in the rotunda. Then came the unveiling of the peace plaques mounted in the rear entranceway. The American plaque was uncovered by the United States Peace Queen, Sue Tanner, Toledo, and the Canadian plaque by the Canadian Peace Queen, Sue Allen, Windsor, Ontario. The tablets read as follows:

UNITED STATES PLAQUE

This single column commemorates the end of a battle and the heralding of a lasting era of peace between Canada and the United States—two neighbors dedicated to brotherhood and progress within the family of free nations throughout the world. It provides lasting testimony that our common values of freedom and diversity can be attained and strengthened through mutual respect and regard.

JOHN F. KENNEDY, White House
1963

CANADIAN PLAQUE

This plaque is dedicated to the 150 years of peace which followed the War of 1812, in which so many lost their lives, and to the hope that this harmony between two neighbors may be a symbol of international cooperation in a world striving toward the goal of lasting peace.

LESTER B. PEARSON
Ottawa, Canada
1963

The ceremony closed with a short concert by the Marine Band and a drill exhibition by the Strategic Air Command team.

ANOTHER CEREMONY

A temporary Visitor Information Center was erected at the foot of the lower plaza facing Bay View Avenue in 1971. Rangers stationed in the small building answer questions relating to the monument, the Battle of Lake Erie, and the islands. A model of Perry's flagship, the brig Lawrence, is on display as is a small cannon and historical illustrations. Books, color slides, postcards, and other souvenirs are on sale.

The year 1972 marked the one hundredth anniversary of the National Parks, and Perry's Victory Memorial took part in the centennial observance on July 6. Keynote speaker was R. Allen Kilpatrick, Canadian consul in Cleveland. Rear Admiral Albert A. Heckman, Commander, Ninth Coast Guard District (Great Lakes area), Cleveland, presented American, British, and Canadian flags which are now on permanent display in the rotunda. Master of ceremonies was Ben Butterfield, assistant director of the Northeast Region of the National Park Service. Musical interludes were played by Ranger Michael Bianchi.

OLD GLORY AND THE MAPLE LEAF

The National flag of Canada was presented to Perry's Victory and International Peace Memorial in another colorful outdoor ceremony held 30 June 1974. Superintendent Harry J. Bosveld, Fort Malden National Historic Park, Amherstburg, Ontario, raised the Maple Leaf flag to the Lake Erie breeze. The two banners, Old Glory and the Canadian emblem, symbolize the peace which has existed between the United States and Canada.

Representative Delbert L. Latta, Fifth District, Ohio; and Douglas P. Wheeler, deputy assistant secretary, U.S. Department of the Interior spoke briefly. Merrill D. Beal, acting regional director, Midwest Region, National Park Service, was master of ceremonies.

9

Conclusion

Put-in-Bay has been a summer resort for over one hundred years. Fourth of July and Battle of Lake Erie celebrations were held on the island as long ago as 1852. More than twenty-one million people now live within a radius of 250 miles of the Lake Erie islands. Enclosed within this area are portions of the states of Michigan, Indiana, Illinois, Kentucky, West Virginia, Pennsylvania, New York, and the province of Ontario, Canada, as well as the entire state of Ohio. Visitors to Put-in-Bay can drive on excellent turnpikes and freeways to the ferry lines at Port Clinton and Catawba and to the Port Clinton airport. Owners of yachts and aircraft can find facilities for vacations on the island.

Permanent settlement on Put-in-Bay dates from the middle of the nineteenth century. With the development of steamboat lines, it became possible for the mainland tourist to visit the island for a few hours, a few days, or a few weeks.

Put-in-Bay is well known in history as the base of operations from which Oliver Hazard Perry sailed to defeat the British in the Battle of Lake Erie in 1813. The Bass Island area also became known for its fine grapes and excellent wines which were, and are, enjoyed by both visitor and resident alike. Other attractions were the natural caves and the federal and state fish hatcheries. The early years of the twentieth century saw the construction of the Perry's Victory and International Peace Memorial, now administered by the National Park Service, United States Department of the Interior. South Bass and Oak Point state parks are maintained by the state of Ohio.

The resort industry continues to be the main industry of the island. The period of visitation begins slowly in April, continues through the peak months of July and August, and tapers off after Labor Day. Hunters come to Put-in-Bay during the pheasant and rabbit season, and the airline which operates the year round brings in numbers of sport ice-fishermen in January and February.

The grape and wine industry experienced a boom after the Civil War and up to World War I. Prohibition, depression, and competition from other wine-producing areas caused many grape growers to abandon their vineyards and pursue other professions. There is one winery operating on Put-in-Bay today and several other vineyards are maintained. Much of the old vineyard land, especially that along the lakeshore, has been sold for summer cottage lots. Other vineyards have become overgrown with weeds, brush, and trees. The "good old days" of the family-owned vineyard and winery will probably not return, but, with the increased American interest in wine, the present facilities will survive and perhaps expand.

Grape growing was the predominant agricultural pursuit on the island, although some islanders had small orchards or grew a few vegetables for the produce market. Several small dairies were also in operation. Put-in-Bay residents now get all but a minuscule portion of their food supply from the mainland.

Commercial fishing on Lake Erie has been declining for a number of years, and no fish boats sail from Put-in-Bay. Sport fishing continues to increase. The sport fiisherman can launch his small boat at numerous marinas on mainland and head for a day's fishing among the Bass islands. Others bring their boats on trailers to Put-in-Bay and thus have a shorter trip to the fishing reefs. Some islanders who otherwise might have been commercial fishermen cater to the yachtsmen and fishermen by operating marinas and bait and tackle shops.

Only one of the hotels in existence at the turn of the century is now in operation. In their place are motels, tourist homes, and rental cottages. Many summer visitors have built their own cottages on the island, and there is a migration of wives and children to Put-in-Bay after school lets out in June. Husbands commute on weekends from the city, and all return to mainland after Labor Day and the start of school. Some cottage owners come back to the island during the hunting and ice-fishing season or for the holidays.

In the development of service facilities for the visitor, the developer must take into account the total possible number of people who can be transported to Put-in-Bay, by both public and private means, and not overbuild. For example, a 100,000-seat stadium on the island would be an absurdity. The old Hotel Victory, which suffered many financial reverses, was too large for the island to support.

Vacation resorts depend on good weather for maximum use. Cool, rainy, and stormy weekends can cause great economic loss to owners of motels, restaurants, and marinas. Winter ice fishing depends on the lake freezing over in early January and remaining frozen until early March. Warm spells or weekend snowstorms that prevent flying can mean disaster for the ice-fishing guide.

The energy crisis of the 1970s could have a detrimental effect on all resort areas. On the other hand, Put-in-Bay can draw tourists from a 100-mile radius—an area which would include populations from Cleveland, Warren, Canton, Akron, Columbus, Lima, Toledo, and Detroit, Michigan, and Windsor, Ontario. Vacations to distant places like the Grand Canyon or Washington, D.C., might be replaced by gasoline-saving jaunts to Put-in-Bay by the people living within this hundred-mile radius.

Islanders earn most, if not all, of their yearly income during the summer months. There are few year-round jobs. The ferryboat crews work only from April to late November, and those employed at the restaurants and bars have an even shorter period of full-time employment. In prosperous times this short period of work provides sufficient income for the entire year.

Just as outsiders come to Put-in-Bay to staff the restaurants, motels, marinas, and other island attractions in the summer, many islanders leave and find employment on the mainland. Some pursue careers not found on the island; others cannot find work and must leave Put-in-Bay although they may not desire to do so.

The island government—the village mayor and council, and the township trustees—faces problems common to both small towns and large cities: pollution and the necessity of providing pure water and sanitary sewage disposal and of maintaining adequate police and fire protection. The lake storms during the high-water period of 1972-1974 caused concern about erosion and flooding not only at Put-in-Bay but along the entire shoreline of western Lake Erie. The cost of governmental services has increased while the tax base has remained static, levied on the property of only 350 islanders. Federal and state aid is a necessity for such small communities as Put-in-Bay.

The isolated position of Put-in-Bay has created unique problems for the tiny community, but such isolation is also its asset and appeal. Tourists enjoy the ferryboat or plane ride to the island. Cottage owners look forward to summer weekends when the stress and strain of the job and the city can be forgotten until the following Monday morning. Some islanders travel to mainland only under the pressure of business or a doctor's appointment. Even those who left Put-in-Bay decades ago consider themselves islanders still. To many residents life on an island is isolated splendor.

Appendix A:
The Battle of Lake Erie

An excerpt from "The Struggle For Control of Lake Erie" (Part II) by Robert J. Dodge in the Northwest Ohio Quarterly, Vol. XXXVI, No. 2, Spring, 1964, pp. 70-97.

The British fleet was first sighted at 5:00 A.M. by a lookout in the masthead of Perry's flagship, the *Lawrence*. Another lookout in the masthead of a British ship, the *Queen Charlotte*, reported seeing the American fleet among the Bass islands at daybreak. By 7:00 A.M. the entire enemy fleet was visible in the northwest at a distance of approximately ten miles. There were two ships, two brigs, one schooner, and one sloop. The northwest wind gave the British commander, Barclay, the choice of position and distance at which to fight. Oliver Hazard Perry would have to wait and accept battle.

Fortunately for the American fleet, the wind changed at 10:00 A.M. to the southeast, giving Perry the advantage. He could now choose the position and distance at which to engage the six enemy vessels. The American flotilla numbered nine war craft.

When the battle seemed imminent, all hands were piped to their stations and Perry had his battle flag hoisted to the topmast. It was a large, blue banner on which were crudely inscribed the dying words of Captain James Lawrence: "Don't Give Up the Ship."

With the wind against him Robert H. Barclay waited the attack. The two fleets were about a mile apart when the British opened fire with long guns. At that range, no gun on the *Lawrence* could reach the enemy. An entry in the log book recorded the time—11:45 A.M., 10 September 1813.

Perry ordered two of the smaller boats, the *Scorpion* and the *Ariel*, to assist him in the fight as he struggled to bring the *Lawrence* into action. The battle had just begun when the British ship, *Queen Charlotte*, lost her captain, Robert Finnis, and Lt. James Garden, second ranking officer. The *Caledonia* caused most of the damage aboard the *Queen Charlotte*, Barclay stated later. The *Niagara*, Jesse D. Elliott, commander, had been assigned to engage the *Charlotte* but for some reason failed to do so.

Perry had to take the long-range cannonading of much of the British fleet until he could get within canister range (330 yards) with the thirty-two pound carronades of the *Lawrence*. It took about thirty minutes to get within effective range. The action between the *Lawrence* and the *Detroit*, the British flagship, continued at a furious pace. Captain Barclay was wounded in the thigh about an hour and a half after the start of the conflict. He returned to the deck but was wounded again an hour or so later. John Garland, the first lieutenant of the *Detroit*, was mortally wounded. The American captain seemed to lead a charmed life as he directed the contest from the battered deck of the *Lawrence*. Marine Lieutenant John Brooks was mortally wounded as he stood talking to his commander.

The deck of the *Lawrence* presented a grim sight to the surviving crew members. Blood, brains, hair, and bone fragments mingled with the debris of dismounted guns, broken rigging, and the bodies of the dead. The heavy discharges from the British fleet ripped the sails of the *Lawrence* to rags, making it impossible for the brig to be controlled by the sailing master. The log book notes that the time was 1:30 P.M.

By 2:30 P.M. not a gun was left in action. The American flagship was defenseless. A wind had sprung up and the *Niagara* came into close action. Perry saw a great opportunity to snatch victory from apparent defeat. He boarded a small rowboat with four men, passed through enemy fire, and reached the *Niagara*. At 2:45 P.M. Perry gave the signal for close action. All possible sail was made on the *Niagara*. Casualties on her were light, only one man killed and three wounded at the time Perry came on board. (The *Lawrence* had twenty-two killed and sixty-one wounded.)

It was the American commander's intention to sail through the British line and this was accomplished in fifteen minutes. Perry was able to rake the *Detroit* and *Queen Charlotte*, i.e., shoot down the length of the vessels, a position from which the enemy could not effectively reply. British maneuvers to avoid being raked failed when the *Queen Charlottle* ran afoul of the *Detroit*, locking the two ships together. A few minutes past 3:00 P.M. the cannonading ceased. The entire enemy fleet had been captured. Control of Lake Erie, lost since the war began, returned to American hands.

AMERICAN FLEET	BRITISH FLEET
Lawrence	Detroit
Niagara	Queen Charlotte
Caledonia	Lady Prevost
Somers	Hunter

Ariel	*Chippewa*
Trippe	*Little Belt*
Scorpion	
Porcupine	
Tigress	
Killed—27	Killed—41
Wounded—96	Wounded—92

Appendix B:
Mayors and Postmasters of Put-in-Bay

Andrew Hunker	1877-1878*	
Dr. C. H. J. Linskey	1878-1880	
Valentine Doller	1880-1889	
Andrew Hunker	1889-1890	
F. W. Burggraf	1890-1891	(Acting Mayor)
J. B. Ward	1891-1892	
F. W. Burggraf	1892-1894	
Henry Fox	1894-1898	
J. C. Oldt	1898-1908	
J. J. Day	1908-1910	
T. B. Alexander	1910-1913	
Dr. P. B. Robinson	1913-1914	
Thomas Conlen	1914-1918	
Walter S. Ladd	1918-1919	
T. B. Alexander	1919-1936	
Lucas Meyer	1936-1938	
Henry Fox	1938-1949	
William B. McCann	1949-1956	
Earl Parker	1956-1963	
James A. Poulos	1963-1971	
Richard Fox	1971-	

---

*Andrew Hunker, 1877-1878, was appointed by the court; Dr. Linskey was the first elected mayor.

Postmaster	Appointed	Postmaster	Appointed
Valentine Doller	1860	Gerhart Rotert	1899
LeRoy Webster	1876	Walter S. Ladd	1910
Charles W. Salter	1881	Carl B. Johannsen	1916
Henry G. Foye	1882	William Schnoor	1921
George E. Gascoyne	1885	Bernard McCann	1934*
Leslie G. Bruce	1892	Nathan H. Ladd	1940
Clinton Idlor	1892	Nello F. Bianchi	1966
Mathias Ingold	1895		

---

*Bernard McCann died in office, his widow, Mildred McCann, served the remainder of the appointment.

Bibliography

PUBLIC DOCUMENTS

Board of Education, Put-in-Bay Township, Ottawa County. *Report for year ending 31 August 1868.*

Board of Education, Put-in-Bay Special District. *Report for year ending 31 August 1880.*

Board of Education. *Manual of the Put-in-Bay Public Schools embracing the course of study and names of pupils and rules and regulations and statistics, etc., 1895.*

Board of Education. *Report of the Public Schools at Put-in-Bay, Ohio, by the Superintendent, 1896.*

Board of Education. *Minute Books.* 4 vols. 1898-1948.

Chamber of Commerce. *Minute Books.* 2 vols. 1948-1973.

    The Chamber of Commerce was called the Board of Trade, 1902-1927.

Ottawa County Commissioner's Journal. Vol. 1, 1840-1862; Vol. III, 1874-1881; Vols. IX, X, 1910-1915.

Ottawa County Recorder's Office, Deed Records.

Perry's Victory Memorial Commission. *Annual Report, 1909-1936.*

Perry's Victory and International Peace Memorial. *Temple of Peace, 1914.*

Perry's Victory Memorial Commission. *Annual Report to the Secretary of the Interior, 1919-1936.*

Perry's Victory Memorial Commission. *Report of the Special Committee on Historical Tablets and Dedication of the Memorial, 1932.*

Perry's Victory Memorial Commission. *Communication from the President of the United States Transmitting a Special Report of the Perry's Victory Memorial Commission, 1932.*

Perry's Victory and International Peace Memorial National Monument Commission. *First Meeting of the Commission, 26-27 February 1937.*

_____. *First Report to the Secretary of the Interior of the United States, 17 March 1937.*

Put-in-Bay Auxiliary of the American Red Cross. *Minute Book—World War I and World War II.*

Put-in-Bay Township Trustees. *Record of the Proceedings of the Trustees, 1895-1929.*

U.S. Army Corps of Engineers, North Central Division. *Great Lakes Shoreline Damage, Causes and Protective Measures, October 1971.*

U.S. Bureau of the Census. *Ottawa County, Put-in-Bay Township,* 1880. A microfilm in the main library, Toledo, Ohio.

U.S. Department of Commerce, NOAA-National Ocean Survery, Lake Survey Center, Detroit, Michigan. *Monthly Bulletin of Lake Levels for July 1973-June 1974.*

Village of Put-in-Bay. Ordinance Record Book No. 1, 1876-1892.

_____. *Ordinance Record Book No. 2,* 1893-1924.

_____. *Minute Book No. 3,* 1878-1881.

_____. *Minute Book No. 4,* 1881-1895.

Women's Civic Improvement Association. *Minute Book,* 1912-1939.

World War II. *Roster of Men from Put-in-Bay Township Who Served Their Country.* Wooden plaques originally mounted outside the town hall.

BOOKS

An Account of the Organization and Proceedings of the Battle of Lake Erie Monument Association and the Celebration of the 45th Anniversary of the Battle of Lake Erie, at Put-in-Bay Island, on September Tenth, 1858. Sandusky, Ohio: Henry D. Cooke and Company, 1858.

Baker, Howard W. *National Park Officials, Centennial Edition.* Washington, D.C.: U.S. Government Printing Office, 1972.

Brown, Samuel R. *Views of the Campaigns of the Northwestern Army, Comprising Sketches of the Campaigns of Gens. Hull & Harrison and a Minute and Interesting Account of the Naval Conflict on Lake Erie.* Philadelphia: William G. Murphy, 1815.

Brown, Ted W., Ohio Secretary of State, compiler. *Ohio Population Report—Nineteenth Federal Census,* 1970.

The Cardinal. Put-in-Bay High School Yearbook, 1922; Vol. II, 1924.

Chapelle, Howard I. *The National Watercraft Collection.* Washington, D.C.: Smithsonian Institute, 1960.

Coles, Harry L. *The War of 1812.* Chicago: University of Chicago Press, 1965.

Commemorative Biographical Record of the Counties of Sandusky and Ottawa, Ohio. Chicago: J. H. Beers and Company, 1896.

Constitution and By-Laws of the Put-in-Bay Ice Yacht Club, Put-in-Bay, Ohio. Cleveland: J. B. Savage, Printer, 1889.

Dobbins, Captain W. W. *History of the Battle of Lake Erie (September 10, 1813) and Reminiscences of the Flagships "Lawrence" and "Niagara."* 2nd ed. Erie, Pennsylvania: Ashby Printing Company, 1913.

Downes, Randolph C. *History of Lakeshore Ohio.* 3 vols. New York: Lewis Historical Publishing Company, 1952.

Frohman, Charles E. *Put-in-Bay—Its History.* Columbus: The Ohio Historical Society, 1971.

_____. *Rebels on Lake Erie.* Columbus: The Ohio Historical Society, 1965.

Hardesty, L. Q. *Illustrated Historical Atlas of Ottawa County, Ohio, from recent and actual surveys and records, under the superintendence of L. Q. Hardesty, C. E.* Chicago: H. H. Hardesty, 1874.

Hines, Philip R. *The Wines and Wineries of Ohio.* Franklin, Ohio: The Catawba Press, 1973.

Historical Hand-Atlas Illustrated—Complete Reference Map of the World—History of the United States—History of Ottawa County, Ohio. Chicago and Toledo: Godfrey Jaeger and Company, 1881.

Huntington, Webster P. *The Story of the Memorial—The Perry's Victory Memorial.* Akron, Ohio: Commercial Printing and Lithographing Company, 1917.

Ingells, Douglas J. *Tin Goose—The Fabulous Ford Trimotor.* Fallbrook, California: Aero Publishers, 1968.

Inter-Lake Yachting Association Yearbooks, 1963, 1964, 1966, 1969, 1972, 1973.

International DN Ice Yacht Racing Association Yearbook, 1972-1973.

The Islander. Put-in-Bay High School Yearbooks, 1972, 1973, 1974.

Islands of America. Bureau of Outdoor Recreation, Department of the Interior. Washington, D.C.: U.S. Government Printing Office, 1970.

Jordan, Philip D. *Ohio Comes of Age, 1873-1900.* Vol. V of *The History of the State of Ohio.* Edited by Carl Wittke (6 vols). Columbus: Ohio State Archaelogical and Historical Society, 1943.

Krammes, B. B. *Illustrated Port Clinton and Environs, Catawba Island and Put-in-Bay.* Norwalk, Ohio: B. B. Krammes, 1898.

Langlois, Thomas H. *The Biological Station of the Ohio State University.* Columbus: The Ohio State University, 1949.

Langlois, Thomas Huxley and Langlois, Marina Holmes, *South Bass Island and Islanders.* Columbus: The Ohio State Univesity, 1948.

McCreary, T. W. *Ain't That Funny.* Toledo: by the author, 1901. (McCreary was the manager of the Hotel Victory.)

Mahan, Captain A. T. *Sea Power in Its Relations to the War of 1812.* 2 vols. Vol. II, 1905. New York: Greenwood Press, 1968—a reprint.

Marchman, Watt P. *The Hayes Memorial.* Columbus: Ohio State Archaeological and Historical Society, 1950.

Mongin, Alfred. *A Construction History of Perry's Victory and International Peace Memorial.* National Park Service, United States Department of the Interior, 1961.

    A typed manuscript in the library at Perry's Victory Memorial.

Nichols, G. G. *Nichols' Handy Guide to Put-in-Bay, Middle Bass and Kelley's Island.* Sandusky, Ohio: I. F. Mack and Brother, 1888.

_____. *Sandusky of Today.* Sandusky, Ohio: I. F. Mack and Brother, 1888.

Oration of Hon. Rufus P. Spalding with an Account of the Celebration of the Anniversary of the Battle of Lake Erie and Laying the Cornerstone of the Monument, September 10th, 1859. Sandusky, Ohio: H. D. Cooke and Company, 1859.

The Perry's Victory Memorial, Put-in-Bay, Ohio—Official Souvenir. A paperback published 1926-1932(?)

The Perry's Victory Memorial, Put-in-Bay, South Bass Island, Lake Erie, Ohio—Dedication Souvenir. Published by the state of Ohio, 1932.

Pollard, James E. The Journal of Jay Cooke or the Gibraltar Records, 1865-1905. Columbus: The Ohio State University Press, 1935.

Put-in-Bay High School Guide to Courses and General Information, 1973.

Put-in-Bay Yacht Club Yearbook—Lee Miller Memorial Issue, 1973.

Reynolds, James C., compiler. Official Illustrated Guide and Souvenir of the Islands and Sandusky. Sandusky, Ohio: Register Press, 1901.

Roseboom, Eugene H. and Weisenberger, Francis P. History of Ohio. Columbus: Ohio State Archaeological and Historical Society, 1958.

Ryall, Lydia J. Sketches and Stories of the Lake Erie Islands—Perry Centennial Edition 1813-1913. Norwalk, Ohio: The American Publishers Company, 1913.

The Saratoga of the West. Battle Creek, Michigan: Put-in-Bay Improvement Company, 1906.

Thorndale, Theresa [Lydia J. Ryall]. Sketches and Stories of the Lake Erie Islands—Souvenir Volume. Sandusky, Ohio: I. F. Mack and Brother, 1898.

Tummonds, Harry A. A History of the Put-in-Bay-Yacht Club. A mimeographed history of the club, no pagination but the paragraphs are numbered, completed in sections in 1959, 1961, 1962.

Van Sickle, H. B., compiler. Put-in-Bay Island—Illustrated. Toledo, Ohio: The Toledo and Island Steamboat Company, 1892.

Van Tassel, Charles S. The Story of the Maumee Valley, Toledo and the Sandusky Region. Chicago: S. J. Clarke Publishing Company, II, 1929.

Williams, W. W. History of the Firelands, comprising Huron and Erie Counties, Ohio, with illustrations and biographical sketches of some of the prominent men and pioneers. Cleveland: Leader Printing Company, 1879.

(The Put-in-Bay account was written by Dr. C. D. K. Townsend, pp. 519-24.)

Willoughby, Malcolm F. Rum War at Sea. Washington, D.C.: U.S. Government Printing Office, 1964.

Winter, Nevin O. A History of Northwest Ohio—a narrative account of its historical progress and development from the first European exploration of the Maumee and Sandusky valleys and the adjacent

shore of Lake Erie, down to the present time. 3 vols. Chicago and
New York: The Lewis Publishing Company, 1917.

NEWSPAPERS

The Columbus Star.
The Detroit Free Press.
The Ohio Legion News, a monthly.
The Ottawa County Exponent [Oak Harbor, Ohio].
The Ottawa County Republican [Port Clinton, Ohio].
The Peninsular News [Lakeside, Ohio—weekly].
The Port Clinton Daily News.
The Port Clinton Herald and Republican.
The Put-in-Bay Gazette [weekly, summers only].
The Put-in-Bay Herald.
The Sandusky Clarion.
    This paper began publishing in 1822 and is known as the Reg-
    ister today. Other names used were: Daily Commercial, Daily
    Register, Daily Commercial Register, and Register-Star-News.
The Star-Journal. Also known as the Star.
The Toledo Blade.
The Toledo News-Bee.

PERIODICALS

Dodge, Robert J. "The Struggle for the Control of Lake Erie" (Part
    One). Northwest Ohio Quarterly XXXVI (Winter, 1964), 10-30.
————. "The Struggle for the Control of Lake Erie" (Part Two).
    Northwest Ohio Quarterly XXXVI (Spring, 1964), 79-97.
————. "First Plans for a Monument." Northwest Ohio Quarterly
    XXXVII (Summer, 1965), 100-103.
Federal Register Vol. I, Number 84, 9 July 1936, p. 877.
Ferris, Theodore N. Jr. "Islands Ho! The Story of a Boat Line." Inland
    Seas XXIX (Spring, 1973), 27-32.
Hudgins, Bert. "South Bass Island Community." Economic Geography
    XIX (April, 1943), 16-36.
Karol, Robert. "Put-in-Bay 1959." Road and Track XI (October, 1959),
    58-59.
Keyes, C. M. "The Fishing Industry of Lake Erie, Past and Present."
    Bulletin of the United States Fish Commission XII, 1893, 349-52.
Kirn, Thomas G. "Flights to Nostalgia." Air Classics III (July, 1966),
    16-20.
Langlois, Thomas H. "The Caves on South Bass Island." Inland Seas
    VII (Summer, 1951), 113-17.

————. "The Ice Industry at Put-in-Bay." *Inland Seas* IV (Spring, 1948), 41-43.

"Miller Boat Livery." *Bulk Station News of Standard Oil of Ohio* VII (August, 1949), N.P.

"America's Most Intriguing Island." *The Ohio Edisonian* (July, 1951), 3-9.

> Article gives information on submarine electric cable to South Bass but its discussion of the Battle of Lake Erie is inaccurate.

Rideout, Mrs. Grant Ann. "Grandee of the Erie Isles." *Inland Seas* II (July, 1946), 165-76.

> The Grandee is Joseph de Rivera St. Jurgo.

————. "Origin of Put-in-Bay." *Inland Seas* III (July, 1947), 195-96.

Wolcott, Merlin D. "Boatbuilding Near Lakeside, Ohio." *Inland Seas* XXVII (Summer, 1971), 131-35.

PROGRAMS, PAMPHLETS, MAPS

Airplane schedules—Island Airline schedules for the spring, summer, fall, and winter for 1973.

American Legion—Original charter, Scheible-Downing Post No. 542, 1922.

Ardnt, Maurice—Wintertime Mail Carrier—1919-1923—Log Book.

Boat Schedules, assorted—Steamboats and ferryboats dating from 1898 to present.

Canadian-American Legion International Peace Memorial Service, 20-21 June 1953, original program.

Cave, Perry, and Cave, Crystal. Brochures given out to tourists describing the respective caves, 1973.

Directory and Map—Put-in-Bay Chamber of Commerce, 1950, 1963, 1973, 1974.

Destroyer USS *Willis A. Lee*, 1959. A brochure describing the ship and its history.

Episcopal church. Original brochure telling of the return of the parish to the Protestant Episcopal church, 1913.

Grape vine price list—Dr. H. Schroeder, Bloomington, Illinois, 1887.

Grape Festival—Second Annual, 1949; Seventh Annual, 1954. Programs.

Hartman, Mary Vroman—An account of life at Put-in-Bay in the early days, written on wallpaper, undated.

Hotel Victory—Menu card for 8 July 1904; Victory Monument program, 1907.

Kiinzler, William—original blacksmith shop statements, 1906-1913.

Langlois, Thomas H.—Langlois Papers—a collection of 4x6 file cards at the Rutherford B. Hayes Memorial Library, Fremont, Ohio.

Many dates and some material are incorrect, many items are not documented.

Mother of Sorrows Catholic Church—Fund Drive brochure, 1956; brochure, 1966 telling about the faceted glass windows and including a brief history of the church.

Ohio State University—Program—Dedication of the Franz Theodore Stone Laboratory, Put-in-Bay, Ohio.

Ohio State University—1972 Summer Quarter Bulletin of the Franz Theodore Stone Laboratory, Put-in-Bay, Ohio.

Ohio State University, School of Music, Music Camp at Put-in-Bay, Ohio. Programs, 1959-1973.

Perry's Victory Memorial—Official Souvenir Program of the Perry's Victory Centennial, 1813-1913, and Celebration of One Hundred Years of Peace, 1913.

Perry's Victory Memorial National Monument—Battle of Lake Erie Sesquicentennial, 8 September 1963—Souvenir Program.

Perry's Victory and International Peace Memorial National Monument. Assorted programs of slide talks, open house, lectures.

Preview: Put-in-Bay Road Races, 1963, original program.

Prohibition Era—original brochure given out by wineries to purchasers of grape juice telling them what to do if their juice started to ferment and become wine.

Put-in-Bay High School Commencement programs, 1895, 1942, 1973, 1974.

Put-in-Bay High School programs, *College Days*, a musical comedy and *Patricia*, an operetta, 1924.

Steamer *Tourist*, original American Shipbuilding Co. contract, 1908.

INTERVIEWS—JULY 1972—JUNE 1974

Maurice Arndt; George Borman; Arthur F. Boyles, assistant manager, South Bass State Park; Ruth Burggraf; Gerta Cooper; Gustav Cooper; Gerda Crowe; Wilbur F. Dodge; Katherine Duff; Kelly E. Faris, superintendent, Put-in-Bay School; Ethan O. Fox; Marie J. Fox; Verner I. Fox; Hilda Fuchs; Louise Fuchs; Ruth Hallock; Milton Hershberger; Anthony J. Kindt; Nathan H. Ladd; Robert N. Ladd; Theodore McCann; Mame March; William Market III, fire chief; Ernest Miller; John Nissen; Elizabeth Parker; Richard Powers; Loren S. Putnam, director, Franz Theodore Stone Laboratory, O.S.U.; Ada May Schiele; Franz Schillumeit, police chief and township constable; Robert A. Schmidt; Russell E. Smith, George Stoecker, Joe Zura.